MELISSA

C000220946

Do Not
Awaken Love

Do Not Awaken Love
Copyright © 2020 by Melissa Addey. All rights reserved.

First Paperback Print Edition: 2020 in United Kingdom
Published by Letterpress Publishing

The moral right of the author has been asserted.

Cover and Formatting by Streetlight Graphics
Map of the Almoravid empire illustrated by Maria Gandolfo
Map of Spain illustrated by Veronika Wunderer
Illustration of Tuareg jewellery by Ruxandra Serbanoiu

eBook: 978-1-910940-26-6
Paperback: 978-1-910940-27-3

No part of this book may be reproduced, scanned, or distributed in any printed or electronic form without permission. Please do not participate in or encourage piracy of copyrighted materials in violation of the author's rights. Thank you for respecting the hard work of this author.

For my daughter Isabelle, who is so full of love.

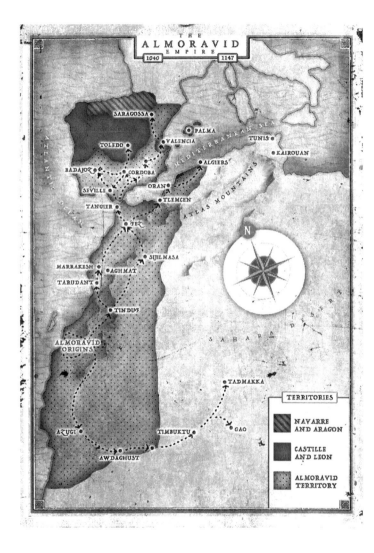

THE
ALMORAVID
EMPIRE
1040 — 1147

SARAGOSSA

PALMA
VALENCIA
TOLEDO
TUNIS
KAIROUAN
BADAJOZ
CORDOBA
ALGIERS
SEVILLE
ORAN
TANGIER
TLEMCEN
FEZ

MEDITERRANEAN SEA

ATLAS MOUNTAINS

SIJILMASA
MARRAKESH
AGHMAT
TARUDANT

TINDUF

ALMORAVID
ORIGINS

SAHARA DESERT

N

TADMAKKA

AZUGI
TIMBUKTU
GAO

AWDAGHUST

ATLANTIC OCEAN

TERRITORIES

NAVARRE
AND ARAGON

CASTILLE
AND LEON

ALMORAVID
TERRITORY

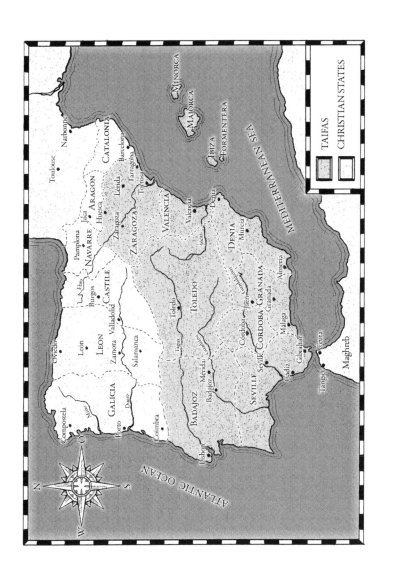

The Almoravids would have been what we call Berbers (preferred contemporary name, Amazigh). They belonged to many tribes and had various names for themselves, including Tuareg. They were known for their blue indigo-dyed robes and beautiful silver jewellery.

Amongst these people it was traditionally the men, not women, who veiled their faces.

Yusuf left his Muslim empire of North Africa
and Spain to Ali, the son of a Christian slave
girl nicknamed 'Perfection of Beauty.'

al-Bayān al-Mughrib
by Ibn Idhāri of Marrakech, approx. 1312
(Book of the Amazing Story of the History of
the Kings of al-Andalus and Maghreb)

And now I will tell you of the news that came from beyond
the sea, of Yusuf, that king, who was in Morocco. The King
of Morocco was vexed with My Cid Don Rodrigo. "He
has made himself strong in my lands," he said, "and he
thanks no one for it but Jesus Christ!" The King of Morocco
gathered up all his forces, fifty thousand men, all armed.
He is going to Valencia to seek out My Cid Don Rodrigo!

The Poem of The Cid
(translated by Lesley Byrd Simpson)

I adjure you, O daughters of Jerusalem,
do not stir up or awaken love...

Song of Solomon, 8:4

Galicia

(Northern Spain)

The Door, 1106

Who is this that cometh out of the wilderness?

Song of Solomon, 3:6

W*E PASS BY THE APPLE orchard, still there after all this time. I rein in my horse for a moment. On the breeze, the faint scent of the pink and white blossom comes to me. I wonder if Alberte's body was ever found amongst these trees. I make the sign of the cross, blessing him in his gentle goodness, his affinity with all God's creatures. I think that if it were harvest time I would dismount and pluck a fruit, bite into its sweetness, the taste that set me out on a journey I never asked for. But it is a different season now.*

Imari watches me for a few moments. "Do you wish to stop here?" he asks at last when I do not move on.

I shake my head. "No, thank you. I was only thinking."

He does not enquire further. Imari was never a man to question the thoughts of others.

We ride slowly, staying each night in a convent or monastery where we receive warm welcomes. They believe us pilgrims, returning home. I am not in a hurry. I know that once I enter the convent again, I will never leave and so this is the last time

I will see the world. And the world is a beautiful place. I am glad to have seen it, to have known what it is to walk its ways before bidding it a final farewell.

It is mid-morning when I see, far away, the tall cream walls of the Convent of the Sacred Way. I glance at Imari, riding by my side. He catches the movement and nods to me, confirming that we are almost at our destination. I find my conversation has died away, preparing me for the silent life to which I am about to return. The fields and woods pass us by as the hours move on and when a farmer bids us a good day, I cannot find my tongue, only nod and smile.

The great door towers over me and I pause for a long moment. I think it must be time for the mid-afternoon prayer, None. *By the time* Vespers *comes, I will kneel among my sisters again after two decades of absence.*

"Do you wish me to knock?" asks Imari behind me.

I shake my head. I lift my wrinkled hand, take the great knocker, then let it fall. The deep sound reverberates around us. I look back over my shoulder. In the bright light of spring, I see Imari on horseback, a dark shadow in the sun's rays, fulfilling his last duty to a master who is now dead and gone.

When this door opens, we shall both be set free, returned to our former lives.

Before I was taken.

The Sacred Way, 1048

A garden inclosed is my sister.

Song of Solomon, 4:12

"SHE CAN WRITE A GOOD script," my mother says, trying not to sound boastful, aware of the sin of pride. But I know that in truth she is proud that I can write, it is a rare skill in a girl my age, from my background. "And I have taught her such healing herbs as I know, from my garden," she continues.

The Mother Superior nods. "What is your name, child?"

"Isabella, Reverend Mother," I say clearly, mindful of my mother's instructions on the way here to speak up and not whisper or shrink back.

"And how old are you?"

"Twelve," I say.

"And is it your wish to enter the Convent of the Sacred Way? To be a nun here, when you are older?"

"Yes," I say. "I have been promised here since I was born," I add, with a touch of the storyteller to my pronouncement. "My birth was a gift from Saint James himself."

The Mother Superior raises her eyebrows and my mother hurries to explain.

My mother was barren. There was not a saint on whose name she did not call in desperation for a child. The carvings on the beads of her rosary were worn away with her whispered prayers. At last, in despair, already past her fortieth year, she made the pilgrimage to Santiago de Compostela, walking barefoot for twenty days. She would have felt dread at being so far from her home and husband, for she was a meek woman, driven only by quiet desperation, not any bold sense of adventure.

There in the holy place she knelt, feet bleeding from her journey, and swore that should she have a child she would dedicate them to God, to be a nun or monk. Then she returned home, weary and having used up her last hope, for what else could she do, where else could she turn to beg for a child? When after three months she did not bleed, rather than laugh with joy she wept, for she believed her last chance had gone, and that old age was coming to claim her. Instead, it was a child that was coming, and true to her word, my mother promised me to this convent.

"The saint heard my prayers," says my mother. "And after his great gift to us, my husband agreed to move close to his shrine. We live by the road that the pilgrims take, we offer them water and food from our table daily. Isabella has helped me since she was a small child."

"What work does your husband do?"

"He is a bookseller and scribe," says my mother. "He

writes letters for those who cannot write, he sells such books as his customers request. Books of learning, to scholars. Many are holy books," she adds, anxious to make a good impression. "He is a good Christian."

The Mother Superior is nodding, though I know that my mother could be charged with lying by omission. She is not mentioning that some of those holy books are sold to people of other faiths. My father has customers who are Jews and even, occasionally, Muslim scholars, although they are rarer, since the Muslim kingdoms, the *taifas*, are all to the South. The Mother Superior would not like to hear about these customers, just as my mother does not like them coming to my father.

"They are heathens," I hear her chastising my father. "Let them go elsewhere for their sacrilegious texts."

"They are scholars and men of learning," my father always replies, and she will huff and mutter to herself and insist that they visit discretely, she does not want people gossiping about us. When she has gone, my father will smile at me and say, "Books are a precious gift, Isabella. They teach us to see the world with new eyes."

"But what if they contain blasphemy?" I ask, a righteous child who has been raised knowing I will be a nun one day.

My father shakes his head when I say this. "It is men who speak blasphemy when they presume to speak for God," he says gently. "It is not blasphemy to seek to understand our fellow men, even if they speak of their God with a different name. For God is always God, no matter what name we poor mortals may give Him in our ignorance."

"*He should not be called by any other name,*" I say, certain of the Church and my mother's teachings. "*He is God. And it is blasphemy to call Him by any other name.*"

My father smiles at my certainty. "*Not so very long ago, far south of Galicia, away in Al-Andalus, was a city called Cordoba, where men of learning lived side by side and spoke with one another of what they knew. They shared their understanding of God and they made great discoveries in medicine, in mathematics, in astronomy and other studies. And the women of that city were calligraphers and poets, teachers and lawyers and doctors. There were more than twenty schools, open to all so that any who wished to learn might enjoy the knowledge shared. There was a library with more than four hundred thousand books. It was a community of great scholars.*"

"*And were they all Christians?*" I ask, suspiciously.

"*They were Christians and Jews and Muslims,*" says my father. "*And they made a land of knowledge and culture the like of which has never been seen before. Or since,*" he adds, sadly. "*Wars led to Al-Andalus being split into many small kingdoms. And now they bicker endlessly with each other, and so the great strides forward that were made are left to fade away.*"

"*Well, I am glad we live in a Christian kingdom away from the heathen Moors,*" I say. "*And I hope our king will one day conquer Al-Andalus, for the glory of God.*"

My father only nods, having heard my words coming from my mother's lips for many years. "*Let us practice your calligraphy,*" he says. "*It will stand you in good stead when you join the convent, for an educated woman will rise higher than one who has no learning.*"

"I seek only to serve God," I say. "It is not seemly to seek glory." But I bend my head to my studies anyway, for there is a little part of me that would like to be praised, who sometimes gives way to the sin of pride and imagines becoming a great Mother Superior or an Abbess, with a convent at my command, known for both my holy demeanour and brilliant mind.

The Mother Superior asks me to copy a verse from the Bible and nods at what I produce.

"Sister Rosa runs our infirmary and she is advancing in years now, she has need of an apprentice. The herbs and other ingredients she uses require a fair hand to label and as you say, Isabella has been taught the beginnings of the uses of herbs. If you do well, child, one day you will run the infirmary yourself, and there can be no greater service to God than to heal the sick that come to us. We care mostly for pilgrims," she explains to my mother, "as we are placed here, on the last part of the road to Santiago. I am sure she will do well with us. Say goodbye to your mother, Isabella."

My mother's eyes shine with tears. In part, of course, she is sorry to lose her only child, to bid me farewell, but at the same time she is fulfilling her promise to Saint James, she is seeing her long-ago pilgrimage come to its sacred conclusion. She is filled with a joyful pride that she, a woman from a lowly estate, has given a daughter to the Church who may one day run the infirmary of a large and important convent. "Thank you, Reverend Mother," she all but whispers. Her farewell to me is brisk and full of reminders of my sacred duty to obey the nuns in all things and to fulfil her promise to Saint James with reverence. I nod to everything she says, and then Sister Rosa comes to take me into the garden.

Sister Rosa is old, her skin is wrinkled and burnt brown by the sun as though she were a peasant, after all her years tending the garden to fill the still room and infirmary with remedies.

"We pray when we gather the herbs and we pray when we administer them," she wheezes, "for it is through our prayers that God acts to heal the sick. It is neither our own skills nor the roots and leaves we use, that heal. Both are only conduits for His powers."

"Yes, Sister," I murmur.

"You will learn from me all the properties and righteous uses of plants, including trees, as well as all those other things on which we can draw in our work. The elements and humours, of course, metals and stones, and also all those creatures whom God created for man's use: animals, fish, reptiles and birds. Naturally, you and I will focus on those that heal, but remember that healing comes also through everyday food, work and prayer, not just through the treating of an illness. It is part of our work to ensure that our sisters and visitors eat a health-giving diet. Meat, for example, should not be eaten too frequently, for it may inspire lust and that is incompatible with being a bride of Christ."

"Yes, Sister."

"Saint Benedict himself, when writing the Rule by which we live, said that caring for the sick was one of the instruments of good works. And so, you and I are blessed, Isabella, in that each and every day, we will be able to do good works through our humble tasks."

Sister Rosa, I will discover, talks a great deal, but she has kind eyes and a warm smile. The heady smell of sunwarmed lavender is all around me as we walk through the garden, the peaceful stillroom and the infirmary.

For nearly twenty years, this is my home.

The Apple Orchard

Let my beloved come into his garden,
and eat his pleasant fruits.

Song of Solomon, 4:16

"ONCE AGAIN, YOU HAVE SHOWN yourself a true bride of Christ, Sister Juliana," says the Mother Superior as the pilgrim leaves us, bowing and promising that he will praise my name at every footstep from here to Santiago de Compostela, for without my knowledge of herbs he might well have died before ever reaching his holy destination.

I bow my head over the mortar and pestle. "I was only doing my duty," I say. "It is God's hand that cured him."

Mother Superior nods. "Indeed. But I have had to speak with some of the youngest sisters for their... *unnecessary* attention to that young man. I am afraid that in their youth and inexperience, they have been swayed by his name and fortune. As well as his looks," she adds, getting to the real cause for her concern. She sighs. "Temptation is everywhere, Sister."

"Yes, Reverend Mother," I say, carefully pouring the ground cinnamon into its container, its sweet smell scenting the air around us. The bark of the tree is very hot in nature and is good for banishing ill humours, therefore despite its expense I use it frequently to dose my sisters, that their humours may be good.

"And yet you were not led astray," says the Mother Superior with satisfaction. "It shows both your maturity and devotion to God and does you credit."

"Thank you, Reverend Mother," I say.

She looks around my stillroom, at all my remedies. The careful script marking each little bottle and jar, the cleanliness and order. "You are a credit to the name you took when you joined us," she adds.

I think of Saint Juliana, patron of the sick, a devoted Christian who refused to marry a pagan husband and was scarred for her disobedience. "I have not had to face her tribulations," I say. "I have been well treated here, Reverend Mother."

She pats my shoulder. "You have worked hard ever since you were a child and your skill with the sick is your reward, by which you serve God," she says. She stands for a moment but does not leave, gazing out of the window at my neat beds of herbs in the garden, as though turning something over in her mind. "I have a task for you," she says at last. "You are to leave the convent and travel beyond Santiago de Compostela, to the coast at A Lanzada, to collect a novice, a girl named Catalina. Her father is ill, and she cannot travel alone. You will be accompanied by Alberte."

"The stablehand? He does not have his full wits about him, Reverend Mother."

"He is obedient and strong," says the Mother Superior a little reproachfully. "We all have different gifts, given to us by God. You will also be accompanied by Sister Maria, so that there can be no impropriety in your travelling with a man."

"Yes, Reverend Mother," I say obediently, although privately I think that Sister Maria is a poor choice for a companion on a journey away from the convent. She is altogether too worldly for my liking, speaking often of life in the outside world as though it is something to be longed for, not grateful to be set apart from.

"I am entrusting you with this task because of your dedication to our convent," says the Mother Superior. "I know that you will not be swayed in your faith by seeing the world outside our walls, that you will provide an example to our novice as she journeys here, to view entering our convent as a homecoming, rather than a loss of her childhood freedom."

I stand a little straighter. "Yes, Reverend Mother," I say.

"It is so exciting to be out in the world!" says Sister Maria on the morning when we set out.

I watch Alberte hoist her up into the saddle. Being both short and plump she is unable to mount alone. Her horse is skittish and once she is seated, Alberte bows his head to the mare's muzzle and whispers to her, stroking her neck to calm the beast.

"It is an honour to bring home a young soul who is destined for the spiritual life," I say.

Sister Maria beams at me as Alberte adjusts her stirrups. "I am sure our Reverend Mother has seen great qualities of devotion in you," she says without jealousy. "Perhaps she sees a future for you as a Mother Superior yourself and this journey is a mark of her favour."

I put a foot in my stirrup and lift myself into the saddle in one move. "You should not say such things, for I have no expectations," I say. "The service I give in the infirmary is all that I desire." I know that this is not quite true and note that I will need to do penance for the little burst of pride her words gave me, the thought that this journey, if well carried out, might lead to possible future elevation within our community.

Sister Maria is not in the least abashed. She readjusts her habit so that it falls more gracefully from her high seat. "Bless you, Alberte," she says, looking down at the stablehand with an undiminished smile. "You have an affinity with horses, they listen to you. The Lord has given you a gift." She is always free and easy with her compliments to those about her. I suppose she means well, although she may not realise that such comments can lead to the sin of pride in others.

"We must make a start," I say to them both. "We cannot waste time."

I feel a little anxious as we make our way through the gates of the convent and out into the open farmland that surrounds us. I have not left these walls except for brief walks to forage for plants since I came here as a child, excepting very occasionally to tend to a local noblewoman. To look back and see the convent recede into the distance is unnerving. Alberte's expression is mostly blank, although he murmurs to his horse from time to time and I note that he watches the birds as they fly past. He is a good-natured lad, I suppose, it is not his fault that he was born with a simple mind. He works hard and is obedient enough. Sister Maria, of course, cannot be relied upon to maintain an appropriate silence.

"The crops are doing well this year," she announces to no-one in particular. "I believe we will be able to give thanks for a generous harvest."

As I recall Sister Maria came to us from farming stock, so it is no wonder she interests herself in such matters. I do not reply, hoping that she will recollect in due course that we should obey the rule of silence, since there is no need to speak. My hopes are not met.

"Good morning!" she cries when we pass a farmer and his children in a wagon, on their way to work in the fields.

"Good morning, Sisters," he returns politely. "I wish you a pleasant journey."

I bow my head but do not answer, while Sister Maria beams down at his children. "May the Lord bless you," she says as they trundle slowly by. She twists her head to watch them. "Ah, Sister Juliana," she says. "I know we are blessed to live a holy life, but I do sometimes think that it would have been a great joy to bear children."

"There is no greater joy than to serve God," I remind her a little sharply, but she does not look in the least humbled.

"There is joy in all walks of life," she says. "For God is in our hearts, whatever work we turn our hands to."

"Perhaps we may think on that blessing in silence," I say and at last Sister Maria stills her tongue for a little while.

With Alberte's orders to stick to a brisk but dignified pace, we reach the outskirts of Santiago de Compostela itself in three days, riding alongside pilgrims making their way to the holy shrine. I have to remind Sister Maria on an irritatingly frequent basis to restrict her conversation with those whom we pass. We sleep each night in welcoming houses of God, so that we can be assured of safety and of being watched over by a holy presence, in silence and comfort. I feel a small pang on the fourth day that we cannot visit the great city and pray in the cathedral, but it will only slow us down. There are still two more days' journey to go and so we pass by the city walls in the distance and continue on our journey, following the River Ulla down its southern side as it widens out into the Arousa Estuary.

"The sea!" exclaims Sister Maria.

"God be praised," I say. "We are almost at our destination."

"I have never been to the sea," says Sister Maria, almost standing in her stirrups to look farther ahead, shading her eyes.

"We are not here to sightsee," I tell her, but she and Alberte pay no attention, exclaiming together over every little thing they notice as we reach the coastline and the small village of A Lanzada. The sound of the waves lapping, the white-gold sand and the deep blue shade of the sea all catch their attention and it is left entirely to me to seek out the right household.

"I thought it would be bigger," says Alberte, looking a little forlorn at the sight of the huddled houses along the shoreline. Seagulls scream overhead. I have only ever seen them rarely, when the weather at sea is bad and they come inland to screech in the convent's fields.

"It is not the size of the village that matters to us, but that it chooses to give up one of its daughters to our holy life," I remind him.

"Is that the hermitage?" asks Sister Maria.

A rocky outcrop jutting into the sea from the shoreline holds a tiny building, like a miniature church, with a large tower to one side.

"Yes," I say. "We will give thanks there for our peaceful journey here and again when we leave with the girl, that we may have a safe journey home."

"What is the tower for?" wonders Sister Maria.

I do not answer her, for a boy has run up to greet us.

"Have you come for Catalina?"

I look down into his wide eyes. "I am Sister Juliana of the Convent of the Sacred Way," I tell him. "I and my Sister Maria here have come to take Catalina home."

The boy looks puzzled. "This is her home," he says.

"She has been promised as a bride of Christ," I say. "Her true home is at the convent now."

He only stares at me.

"Where is her father's house?" I ask.

He points, then runs alongside us as we make our way to the largest house in the village, where a woman is already standing waiting for us. Word of strangers spreads fast in a small village.

Catalina's father is a merchant of middling means. He is a chandler, supplying ropes and other such necessities to ships both large and small, although his trade is mostly with the smaller fishermen and merchants, not ocean-going craft or grand vessels. He finds himself in ill health, suffering from a growth in his stomach which is likely to kill him soon, for there is no cure. Therefore, he has been taking care of his affairs, including marrying off various sons and daughters who are old enough. He has a houseful of daughters, hence the dedication of Catalina to our convent.

The girl is thirteen years old. She looks nervous at the sight of me. I think of myself at her age, almost twenty years ago, although since I had been told I would come to the holy orders since I was a baby, I think I was more prepared.

"My dear girl," says Sister Maria, enfolding her in an unnecessary embrace. "We are so glad to see you! It is a great honour to have been chosen to journey here and bring you home to our convent. I am sure you will be happy there and you will become ordained one day yourself, praise be to God."

Catalina gives a weak smile, but she is brave enough when bidding goodbye to her family the next morning. Our departure is delayed by her mother insisting on us all eating a final and overly lavish breakfast together and her father fussing too much over ensuring her stirrups are well-set for her legs. She has very little in the way of belongings, but of course she will not need anything personal at the convent. Her brothers and sisters and what appears to be half the village have come to bid her farewell, which delays us still further. Catalina's lower lip trembles a little when her mother weeps while blessing her, but that is natural enough and shows a good heart and a familial devotion which I am sure will in due course become a devotion to the convent. She mounts the horse that Alberte has brought for her by herself and lifts one hand to her family. I see a little tear fall but I look away so that she need not be ashamed of her moment of weakness.

"We will pray at the hermitage for a safe journey home," I say.

We ride down to the shoreline and then walk past the tall tower to the tiny chapel. It is smaller than our refectory inside, but all places of worship bring me a sense of peace and we pray together, the three of us, while Alberte waits on the beach with the horses. When we emerge, he is staring open-mouthed at the way the waves rush onto the sand and then pull away again. Catalina, perhaps out of nerves, chatters incessantly.

"The tower was built as a lookout against the Norsemen," she informs us. "They use the estuary to sail upriver and come closer to Santiago de Compostela on their raiding parties."

"The Norsemen's raids were long ago," I point out.

She shakes her head. "They still go on now," she says, "just more rarely. They try to take women and children, to sell them for slaves."

Alberte and Sister Maria stare at her, fascinated.

"We need to begin our journey," I say. "It is already late."

We mount again and turn the horses inland, ready to journey home.

"Will you miss living by the sea?" asks Sister Maria.

Catalina looks back over her shoulder at the sea, sparkling in the mid-morning sun. "Yes," she admits. "There is so much to see, it changes every day. And they say it has healing properties."

"What kind of properties?" I ask.

"Women who are barren go down to the hermitage once a year at midnight for the Ritual of the Nine Waves," she says. "Once a woman has undressed and been washed in nine waves by the light of the moon, she will have children for sure."

"That is a pagan belief and practice," I say sharply. "I will not hear of such nonsense, nor should you repeat it." I hope the girl will not gossip all the way home; she is worse than Sister Maria. "We will not speak for the rest of the journey unless it is necessary," I tell her. "It is best to grow used to the rule of silence as quickly as possible, so that it will come to seem natural to you."

She nods, chastised. I give her a small smile of approval for showing her agreement and obedience without speaking.

Our late departure means that the midday sun burns down on us while we are still progressing along the banks of the estuary, passing small farms as we go. To our right, we pass a large apple orchard, the very first apples turning shining red. The sweetly tart fruits of early summer come as a welcome relief after the bitter greens and heavy chestnut flour of the winter. The breeze rustles through the branches and birds sing. It is a place of great peace, reminding me of my herb garden at the convent. I have missed the garden, even in these few days away from it, the silence and the scent, the mastery of my own little kingdom.

"May we rest, Sister Juliana?" asks Sister Maria.

I consider for a moment. We should ride on, but the sun is at its zenith and the rustling leaves and faint scent of apples calls to me. "Very well," I concede. "We will rest a little while. The shade will be cooling."

Sister Maria slides ungracefully down from her horse,

landing with a solid thud on her small feet. Her round face is beaming. "May we taste the fruits?"

"No," I say sharply. "They are not ours to pick, Sister. You should know better."

But Sister Maria is already holding a red apple in her hand. "A windfall," she says. "A gift of God to the needy."

"You are hardly in need, Sister," I say, looking with disapproval at her ample girth.

Sister Maria is not listening, of course, she is hunting for other windfalls in the long grass. She finds and offers one to Alberte, then another to Catalina, who looks to me for guidance. I am glad to see her hesitation; it speaks of humility and reverence for one's elders and superiors. "You may accept," I say. It would be a waste of God's bounty to let the windfall fruit rot in the field, after all. Alberte is sharing his apple with his horse, the foolish boy. When Sister Maria holds out a fruit to me, I hesitate but then take it with care, wiping a little mud off the red peel. Apples are easily digested by persons in good health, even when eaten raw, and the first apples of the season have a crisp sweetness that is pleasing to the palate. A little further down the slope is an old tree stump shaded by a young tree and I make my way to it, leaving the others behind. I sit down and look out over the fields, then lift my hand to my mouth. I bite, feel the sharp-sweet flesh crunch beneath my teeth and even as I do so, Catalina screams somewhere behind me.

I twist on my seat and look round, expecting the girl to have perhaps disturbed a snake in the long grass, but instead I am faced with Alberte, who is staggering towards me, his face ashen, eye wide, his neck ending in a scarlet slash from which blood is pouring. Even as I rise, he falls, so that behind him I can see Sister Maria struggling in the arms of a man and Catalina running back towards the road, pursued by another man. I open my mouth to cry out and a rough hand comes over my mouth, my left arm is pinned back so hard I think for a moment my shoulder is about to dislocate. I struggle and try to bite the hand and it is taken away for a moment, only to strike me so hard the world grows dark.

Something wakes me. My shoulders ache and my stomach hurts, for all my weight is pushed onto it, I am lying draped over something moving, my head hanging down, longer grass stems touching my face. I open my mouth and vomit spews from it, filling my mouth and nose with the sweet-bitter-sharp taste of apple mixed with bile. My head feels cold even in the sunlight and it takes me a moment to realise that the men who took me have removed my coif, wimple and veil, so that my shaven scalp is exposed to the air. My hands are tied behind my back, I have been thrown over a saddle and when I try to move, I realise I have also been bound to it, for I cannot slide down from the horse. Now I realise that I have also been stripped of my habit, I am now wearing only my shift and my shoes. In terror, I think that I have been violated, that our captors have defiled our bodies, but there is no pain between my legs.

I twist my head to the right and see a horse being ridden ahead of me, the high leather boots of a man, nothing more. I twist my head the other way and see more horses behind me: the first bearing the shaven and unconscious head of Sister Maria, the one behind that the long dark locks of

Catalina, whose face is turned towards mine, her eyes open in mute terror. I meet her gaze but only shake my head at her not to make a noise, for if we do, we may be struck again, or our mouths bound up. Beyond Catalina's horse, I can only make out the legs of two, perhaps three, horses and more leather boots. I cannot see the faces of the riders.

We are no longer on the road. Instead, the horses pick their way through fields, keeping to the rough overgrown borders or through wooded areas so that my face is scratched by shrubs and low-hanging branches. I keep my eyes shut, for there is not much to see and I am afraid of brambles. But my mind is racing. One word keeps coming back to me. *Rus.* As a child, my father told me of the Norsemen, whom the Arabs called Rus. They sailed great ships and raided our coastlines, kidnapping men and women, taking them as slaves for themselves or selling them to the Maghreb, across the sea south of Al-Andalus, in the lands of the Muslims. The worst of their attacks took place long before our time, but as Catalina told us, there are still the odd raids, brutal and quick, taking unwary women and children for slaves. I think of the moment of temptation to which I succumbed: the shade, the ripe fruit, the fresh scent of apples in the warm air and curse myself. Poor half-witted Alberte is already dead for my sin and the fate of Sister Maria and Catalina is my burden to carry now, for I cannot think how we might escape. Eyes still closed, I pray for help to Our Lady, though the pain in my shoulders and the ache in my head tells me that my prayers may go unanswered, that my temptation to stray from the path I had been commanded to follow is about to be punished more severely than I could have imagined.

The horses stop in a heavily wooded area, but I can hear the sea again, the rush of waves on the shore not far away and guess that we are somewhere back close to A Lanzada. I think of the watchtower by the hermitage and hope that someone is watching, that they will spot something amiss and come to our aid. It is full daylight, surely a Norse ship would be spotted at once?

But the men have other ideas. They yank us down from the horses, I hear the muffled yelps from Sister Maria and Catalina as they fall to the ground, their bound hands meaning they are unable to break their falls. When my turn comes, I try to brace myself, but it makes no difference, I am half-pulled, half-thrown into the shrubby undergrowth and left to lie there. I dare not move, expecting the men to force themselves on us, but instead I hear them move a few steps away, speaking to one another in a guttural tongue, their voices unafraid, one even laughs. I cannot see them, but I hear them sit down and then faintly smell food that they are eating, bread and apples, no doubt picked from the same orchard where they took us. I can hear them crunching, smell again the faint sweet fresh smell. I look carefully about me without moving. I can see Sister Maria's feet and some of Catalina's long hair. I can hear Catalina crying softly.

Time goes by. Occasionally I move a little, only to stop my limbs from going numb. I dare not draw attention by moving a great deal. The men continue to talk between themselves as though they were merely passing the time together in idleness. I hear one snore when he snoozes for a while. They are unhurried, unconcerned at being found out. They must know this place well, know that they are fully concealed. They are waiting for something, but I am not sure what. I see Sister Maria wriggle violently once and one of the men throws an apple core at her with a command, no doubt to be still and silent, then laughs.

They have been waiting for darkness.

The sun sinks. I cannot see it, but I feel the cool breeze of the evening, see the shadows fade and change to dusk. We have been here for many hours. My mouth is dry with the desire for water, for I have not drunk since late morning. At last one of the men squats near each of us and lets us drink from a waterbag. It is not enough to fully sate my thirst but the few gulps I am allowed are desperately welcome.

They wait a little longer, as dusk turns to night. I think of the watching tower and wonder if it has a light in it, how far out to sea that light might shine. I pray to Our Lady of the Lanzada, the hermitage in which we knelt only this morning, where we asked for a safe journey home. I pray for a miracle.

I am thrown back over my horse, my stomach pressed hard against the saddle, I hear the other two women served in the same manner before the Norsemen begin to lead us further through the woods and then out into an open space, I think we must be on a clifftop overlooking the sea, for I hear the waves closer than ever and beyond the ground I can only make out an empty nothingness of darkness. The stars shine brightly, but the moon is only a tiny crescent, I cannot make out any details by its pale glow. I twist my head this way and that, trying to make out anything, anything at all, the tiny lights of the village or even of a single house. One of the men cuffs my bare scalp and hisses something at me, no doubt an order to be still. I kick out at him and he cuffs me harder. I hang loose again, my face half against the hard leather saddle, half on the horse's warm flank.

This time, when we are pulled down, we land in soft sand, then are yanked to our feet and made to trudge through it, my feet slipping and sliding as the sand yields to my steps. I and my captor are leading the others closer to the sea. Twice I nearly fall, but the man behind me jerks me back to my feet, pulling my arm so hard it hurts.

When cold water washes over my feet I step back, but the Norseman has other ideas. He forces me forwards. I struggle, for a moment unreasonably fearing that he intends to drown me, which would be easy enough. If I were to fall now, knee-deep in water, my hands bound, I would drown in moments. I am pushed forwards again into the shallows of the sea, feel the wetness cover my feet, my ankles, my calves and the cold embrace of my shift as it becomes soaked, clinging to my thighs and waist. Now I see a moving shape close to us and realise there is a small rowing boat bobbing up and down. I am all but thrown into it, then pushed to take a seat on a rough wooden plank that serves as a bench. In the darkness, I make out the other men, Sister Maria and Catalina joining us. The boat rocks wildly and I want to clutch at the side but cannot. I wonder what is to become of the horses and wonder if perhaps these men have an accomplice here by the shore, a traitorous Galician who is well paid for his silence, trading the lives of good Christians for valuable horseflesh.

27

Two of the men take up oars and now there is the fast sound of wood against water and the boat begins to move across the waves. Far off along the shore, at last, I glimpse a cluster of tiny lights which may well be A Lanzada, but they are too far away to hear our screams, even were we able to scream.

I twist my head in the darkness and see a faint light in the endless dark waters. The men are rowing towards it. I feel a cold shudder pass through me, certain that a larger boat, a ship, is waiting for us, out there on the waves, showing only enough light to guide us towards it.

We draw closer and closer to the dim light. One of the men in our boat lets out a sudden call and at once, more lights appear ahead of us, illuminating what has been waiting all this time.

The ship fills my heart with fear. Its carved prow is surmounted with the head of a beast and it rocks slowly back and forth on the water as though it is alive. The lights now shining from it should reassure me, but they do not, they only tell me that these men, out here in the deep waters of the sea, are no longer afraid of being caught, that it is too late for the miraculous rescue I prayed for.

Each of us is tightly held by the men in the little boat and passed up to the many disembodied hands reaching over the sides of the ship. Lifted over the waters beneath us, we are then thrown onto the deck. I fall poorly, hitting one elbow so that pain shoots up my arm. I yelp in pain. A hand pulls me to my feet, a lantern is lifted. I come face to face with a man, his face a hand's breadth from mine.

His eyes are pale blue, like an early morning sky, a colour I have never seen before. His hair is dark yellow, long and coarse, pulled back from his head into a rough plait as though he were a peasant woman, though this is no woman. He towers over me, his shoulders massive and bare under a sleeveless leather jerkin, his muscled arms and even his neck marked with dark blue designs, shapes and whorls I do not know the meaning of. He pulls the gag from my mouth and then says something loudly into my face, but I do not know what he is saying. I turn my face to one side, and he slaps at me to look back at him. He repeats the words, but I only stare at him. He shrugs and drags me towards Sister Maria and Catalina, who are already sitting, their hands tied behind their backs, their tear-streaked faces turned towards me, eyes fixed on me as I stumble my way behind the man. Their captors have left them, gone to join the rest of the crew.

Suddenly I am fighting, hitting and biting, kicking and screaming, not words but only screeching fear. My composure has gone from me. My thoughts of caring for Sister Maria and Catalina are gone, at this moment I care only for myself and my safety, my ability to escape the man holding me prisoner.

But every bit of my strength and desperation is nothing to this man. He half-laughs, then pushes me so that I stagger backwards landing hard on my behind, almost in the laps of Sister Maria and Catalina, their bodies softening the blow.

"Sister Juliana," whispers Sister Maria, but I do not know what she was planning to say, for the man reaches over and gives her a hard slap to the face, so that she cries out and then hangs her head low, tears dripping from her face in silence. Catalina flinches and her shoulders shake with the effort of keeping her own sobs silent. I sit in silence, though no tears fall from my eyes. My mind goes over and over the moment when Sister Maria asked me if we might rest a while. I think of my hesitation, my agreement. I wonder, if I had said no and kept riding, would we be safe within the walls of the convent that would have hosted us tonight? Or would the Norsemen have taken us anyway? Were they on the road behind us, or hiding in the orchard? Had they already marked us as their victims, was our fate already written, or was there a moment when the wheel of destiny turned? Was it the moment when I reached out my hand for the sharp-sweet scarlet flesh and gave myself over to the pleasures of the world?

Above us, the beast-ship's head towers over us. I see its open mouth, the carved teeth within, a scarlet-painted tongue rippling out.

"Do not fight them," I whisper quickly. "They will only hurt you."

All around the ship orders are given and shouts come in response. I consider screaming for help but know already that it is too late for that now, we are far from the shore and I saw no other ships or even little boats. There is a heavy falling sound above our heads and craning upwards I catch sight of the bottom of a vast dark sail unfurling above us.

The Slave Block

They took away my veil.

Song of Solomon 5:7

*T*HROUGHOUT THAT NIGHT OUR PROGRESS is marked only by the occasional splash of oars, mostly by the billowing sound of the sail above us. The men do not talk much between themselves. The rise and fall of the sea makes me sick to my stomach and I hear Catalina retching over and over again, smell the bitter bile of her vomit, which in turn has me gagging until my stomach voids again. I taste, amidst the bitterness, the last sweet hint of apple and think of Eve's mouth, whether she could still taste the sweetness of the forbidden fruit on her tongue even as she stumbled out of the Garden of Eden. Perhaps she could. It would have been a bitter reproach, for all its sweetness.

At some time in the night, exhausted from all that has gone before, I begin to doze. I am awoken by a splash and the shouts of the men. There is a lot of noise and a torch is lit, but I cannot see much beyond the vomit-spattered deck. But shortly afterwards I am lifted up and carried over a man's shoulder as though I were a sack of grain, to a different part of the ship. I feel my bonds first loosened and then fastened to something. I seem to be tied to a heavy weight of some kind. I feel Catalina placed close by me, but I am so tired that the ensuing darkness calls to me again and I fall asleep not long after.

The half-light of early dawn wakes me. At last I can see. I look about me, see Catalina asleep at my feet, her long ropes bound to a metal ring set into the deck, as are mine. Above us is a small awning of heavy red silk, pulled low over us like a tiny shelter, so that I can hardly see out of the sides.

But Sister Maria is not with us.

Panicked, I try to stand but cannot, for the rope is not long enough. Instead, I kneel and try to scan the boat deck, wriggling to the edge of the awning and poking my head out. The light dazzles me.

I can see a few men on the deck. Two stand by the prow, one by the mast, a handful lie wrapped in rough blankets, sleeping. The oars are stacked by the sides, waiting for use. The ship rises and falls with the waves, but the motion is calmer than I feared. From low down, I cannot see a shoreline. There is no sign of Sister Maria.

"Sister Maria!" I call out.

The men at the prow turn to look at me and then look back at the sea, uninterested. I can hear them talking to one another, there is a brief laugh, then silence.

"Sister Maria!" I call more loudly, my voice higher than I would like, wavering.

Catalina's eyes open suddenly, she jerks awake and

struggles briefly against her bonds as though having forgotten what happened, before recalling where she is and what has gone before now. Seeing me, she begins to cry. "Sister Juliana," she gulps, "what will become of us? Will the convent send men to bring us home?"

Poor innocent. She has little knowledge of the world. No doubt she has heard heroic stories of knights rescuing their ladies, of noble men setting the world to rights. She does not know, has not thought, as I have done, that the convent may never even hear word of our whereabouts. Alberte's body may not be found, our horses may be sold to some disreputable dealer, our Mother Superior may believe that we have run away, or she may guess that bandits or Norsemen have robbed, raped, killed or kidnapped us, but certainly there is nothing she can do about it. The Norsemen have taken us onto the high seas without a soul seeing us and I am certain their destination is either their own homelands far to the north, or the Maghreb, to the south. I squint at the rising sun in the east. It is on my left. We are sailing south.

"Catalina," I say.

She continues to sob, but looks up at me.

"It is likely that we are sailing to the south of Al-Andalus, most likely to the Maghreb," I tell her. "We are to be sold as slaves to the Muslims."

She lets out a little cry and one of the men turns. Seeing us still bound, he looks away again.

"Catalina, if it is Al-Andalus and we are separated, then if you can ever run away, head north, back to Galicia."

"And the Maghreb?" she asks.

I have no answer. Already what I have suggested to her

is absurd, that a thirteen-year-old girl might escape her captors and travel safely from Al-Andalus to Galicia, but it is all the hope I can offer her. I wanted to give her something to cling to. But from the Maghreb? Who knows where we might be sold to? How would we escape and travel over the sea even to reach Al-Andalus?

"You must pray," I tell her at last. I do not know what else to tell her.

"For rescue?" she asks.

How can I tell her she will not be rescued? How can I tell her, looking at her long black hair and fine features, her large black eyes now rimmed red with tears, that she is a beautiful young girl, that she is likely to be sold to a rich man as a bedfellow, a whore?

"You must pray to the Virgin Mary for her guidance and protection," I say at last.

Catalina begins to mumble. "Hail Mary, Full of Grace, the Lord is with thee. Blessed art thou among women…"

I look about me, still fearful for Sister Maria. Where has she been taken? Has she been hurt, or taken by one of the men to… to…? I hardly dare think what I fear. But the deck is mostly uncovered, surely she should be visible to me. I twist my head this way and that and finally I open my mouth and scream her name as loud as I can. "Sister Maria!" I only want to hear her answer me once, if she can, just to know that she is here, with us.

I open my mouth to scream again and am cuffed sharply round the head. A Norseman has come close to us and he is scowling.

"Silentium," he says in oddly accented Latin, *silence*.

"Please," I say, kneeling up, staring up into his strange

blue eyes, replying in Latin, hopeful that we can speak together. "Please. Where is Sister Maria?"

He stares at me. I had thought perhaps he spoke Latin well, but it appears he does not.

I point at Catalina, at myself, at an invisible Sister Maria. "Where?"

He makes a gesture at the green-blue waves. "Transulto." Then he walks away, joining the men by the prow.

I stare at the man and then at the sea. I think through what I said, the exact words, the exact gestures I made for him to understand me. I think of his answer, *leapt*, of the gesture, the exact direction to which he indicated. I think through our brief exchange over and over again trying to find a different possible explanation.

There is none.

Sister Maria, in the night, jumped overboard and drowned.

That was the cause of the splash and shouts I heard in the night and the reason why Catalina and I were lifted to the middle of the ship and bound to the deck, so that we could not do the same. Fat little Sister Maria, too much in love with the outside world for my liking, who wished she might have had children of her own, who spoke cheerfully and too long with everyone she met, who ate greedily of nature's bounty, chose to die rather than face what might come and in so doing, has committed a mortal sin.

Catalina has not understood the conversation I had with the Norseman. She is still quietly sobbing and repeating Hail Marys; she has not reacted to the news. Perhaps she thinks Sister Maria is tied up somewhere behind us, perhaps she thinks she has been taken elsewhere on the ship. I sit in silence as the sun rises in the sky and listen to Catalina's whispered prayers. I do not speak again until night falls. In the darkness, after repeated questions, I have to tell Catalina what has become of Sister Maria, then listen to her weeping for the rest of the night.

I lose track of time, but the ship rises and falls on the water for one day after another, perhaps seven in all, perhaps ten, I cannot be sure. We are kept under the little shelter, the height of it meaning we cannot stand, only lie or sit. They change our bonds, so that we are tied around the waist with our hands free, this so that we can use a pail to relieve ourselves. The Norsemen care enough for us as cargo that they give us water and a little food during the voyage, enough to keep us alive but not enough to stop our endless thirst, our endless hunger. At night we have our hands bound again, they are not willing to risk the loss of another valuable commodity. We see daylight and darkness come and go but rarely see anything beyond our tiny red shelter: not the sea, nor the ship, nor the men, except for one or two who empty our pail of waste or throw food into our laps. But there comes a day when we make land, I can hear the men shout and I prepare myself to know to what shore we have come.

Our little awning is suddenly unfastened, rolled up and put away. Catalina and I shrink back, newly made afraid of the outside world, knowing our destiny is about to take on an as yet unknown shape.

Where our departure was secret and solitary, the Norsemen's beast-ship lying dark on the sea, hidden from any who might hinder their ungodly work, our arrival is its very opposite. The ship comes closer and closer to the shore, the great red sail now taken down, our progress made by the oarsmen aboard. The long neck and head of our beast glides past small fishing boats. The men aboard them are darker-skinned than we are, burnt browner still by the sun. They wear long robes in bright colours, some have their heads wrapped with cloths, a few even have their faces fully veiled with only their eyes visible. They watch our boat with interest but not with fear. I believe they know the Norsemen and their business here. These are the docks of a large city, beyond the quayside lie mud-coloured ramparts and rooftops, with high towers dotted here and there amongst them. Released from our crouched shelter, the sun beats down on us so hard that it makes my head swim.

"Where are we?" whispers Catalina beside me.

I shake my head. The Maghreb, I believe, but I do not know what port. There is the smell of rotting fish, of dung, of sweat. I feel my stomach roll and hope I will not disgrace myself by vomiting again. The Norsemen busy themselves with securing the ship alongside the dock, the oars now put away. The yellow-haired man comes towards us and with a quick movement unties us from the metal fastenings. I stand, unsteady, but already I am being pushed towards the edge of the ship with Catalina. One of the Norsemen has jumped ashore and now he places a rough plank between the ship and the dockside, which we both stagger across, followed by the yellow-haired man. Having my feet on the ground again makes tears start to my eyes, despite the circumstances. The Norseman pushes at me to walk forwards and I do so, Catalina clinging to my arm. There are men everywhere and there are few who do not leer at Catalina and I as we pass, our heads uncovered and dressed only in our by now filthy linen shifts.

"What is that?" whispers Catalina, cringing back against me.

A strange beast lumbers past us, its body like a horse but one spawned by the devil, warped in its nature. It is hairy, with a misshapen hump on its back and legs that look as though they were put on backwards, ending in soft cloven feet tipped with wide blunt claws.

"A camel," I say, having seen a picture of one once, an illustration in a book. I had thought it fanciful then but now I see that the artist was correct. They are everywhere across the docks, being laden with goods or unburdened. I see one or two horses also, a few mules and donkeys, but it is clear that the chief beast in use here is the camel. They make strange groaning noises when they are told to rise or sit, and both Catalina and I give them as wide a berth as we can when we pass by a group of them.

All around us, men shout and labour. But as we disembark a strange sound fills the air, a wailing, an unearthly cry emanating from the rooftops and on a sudden most of the men stop their work and kneel in the dust, all facing in the same direction. They hold their hands before their faces and bow their heads towards the dirt, again and again.

"What are they doing?" asks Catalina, wide-eyed at the spectacle.

"Praying," I say tightly. "It is not true prayer of course,"

I add, mindful that I am still all Catalina has in the way of spiritual guidance. "How can it be? Out here in the open, without even being in a sacred space nor with a holy man to direct the prayers. It is what passes for prayer amongst these people. They are Muslims, heathens."

She nods, cowed. The prayer seems to have finished, for the men rise and go about their business. The Norseman pushes us forwards, towards a low building at the back of the dockyard. We stagger towards it, our feet made unsteady by the heat, by fear, by the hard ground that does not rock beneath us.

There is an ill-painted door on which the Norseman hammers with his fist. It opens quickly, a short ugly man nodding when he sees us, as though we are expected. He waves us in, and we follow him into darkness and then into a dusty courtyard. A fat well-dressed man is sat under an awning and he gestures to our captor when he sees him, greets him as though they are old friends. The Norseman speaks with him for a few moments, then gestures towards us. The fat man shows little interest, only nods to his servant, the short man, who pushes me towards a door at one end of the courtyard. For a moment, ridiculously, I want to run to the Norseman from whom we are being taken. He is the only person who knows where we came from, who could, if he wished, takes us back to that same place, to the apple orchard where he and his men killed Alberte and took us women. If he leaves us, if we never see him again, how would anyone here ever take us home again? But the short man pushes me again and I know that there is nothing I can do to avoid the fate that has already been laid upon me, the fate I first glimpsed when I saw

Alberte stumbling towards me, already half-dead. Whether I ever see the Norseman again or not, makes no difference. I walk towards the door and the man opens it and pushes me through the doorway.

The room is mostly empty, apart from some old rags and a little straw. In a corner is a large vessel, perhaps for water. In another corner is a covered pail and from the smell in the room I can only imagine that it has already been used for bodily functions. The floor is made of bare tiles, dirty and chipped. There are thick iron links set into the walls, such as might be used to tie up a horse, were they outside. In here, they are no doubt used to tie up people. The door bangs shut behind us. I hear a lock turn and Catalina and I are alone for the first time since we first met. She begins to weep at once, clinging to me as a child might to its mother. I pat her stiffly. She will need to be stronger than this, will need to put her faith in God rather than in a fallible human such as myself.

"What will we do? Oh, what will we do?" she begs me.

"I do not know," I say, trying to sound as though there is no reason to wail. "First, we must drink." I make my way over to the vessel and am glad to see that I was right, it is half-filled with water. Just behind it lies a wooden cup, badly split but which I use to scoop up some of the water. I taste it cautiously and although it is not fresh or cold, at least it does not taste foul. I make Catalina drink three full cups and although her shrunken stomach makes her gag briefly at the sudden filling, still, she does not vomit, and I drink deeply myself. There is a window, which lets in light, but it has bars across it, and I do not trouble myself with checking whether they are solid. It is clear to me that we are in a room in which many unfortunates such as ourselves have been before. This is a room made for captives. For slaves.

Catalina has slumped to the floor. She looks up at me, her face white, her eyes rimmed with red, tears still falling. "If we could only speak their language," she whimpers. "My father is not very rich, but he would pay a goodly sum if he knew we were here. Would the convent pay for our release?"

I shake my head. "Your father will believe you to be safely at the convent by now," I say. "And the convent…" I stop. I wonder what they will think of me, if they will think that harm has befallen our little group, or whether they will think that we were tempted by the world, that we ran away. I hope that the Mother Superior will not think such a thing of us, that she will realise that something must have occurred. But even if she does… "No-one will know what has become of us," I say simply. "We have travelled too far, and the Norsemen made sure not to be seen. There is no way home."

Catalina bursts into noisy sobs and I hear her cry out for her mother. I gaze out of the window, but I can see nothing but a sky so blue it makes my eyes sting.

Later that day a squat serving woman opens the door and indicates we should follow her. We are taken outside, to a walled yard with pecking chickens scratching in the dirt and a tethered goat that bleats incessantly. There is a small tiled area on which the serving woman gestures that I should stand, then she tugs at my shift and makes a movement to show I should remove it. I shake my head. She pulls from her pocket a sharp knife and holds it up. I am unsure whether she means to threaten me or indicate that she will cut the shift, but I comply, lifting the shift over my head. She takes it from me and turns away. I have not been naked before another person since I was a child and my mother washed me. In the convent we bathed rarely, instead washing ourselves with a cloth and a basin of water. If we bathed it was done quickly and we kept our shifts on, so that we should not think on our mortal flesh. I have barely seen my own naked body as a grown woman. I stand naked in the hot sun, wondering on what saint I could possibly call that would not turn away in horror at what has become of me, a woman whose life should be devoted to holy service, an anointed bride of Christ, standing shamelessly naked in the open air.

The woman returns with two pails of water and some small rags and indicates that we should wash, which I do gladly, for I am still spattered with vomit and mud, seawater and urine. When I am clean, I use what is left of the water to wash my shift, placing it back on my body dripping wet but at least cleaner than it was. Catalina follows my example, her still half-formed body hunched and miserable. Afterwards, we are led back a different way and shown into a different room, this one far larger and already filled. Later I count more than sixty people, men, women and children. Most are dark skinned, the odd few here and there are lighter skinned. There are women weeping, clutching their children to them, knowing, no doubt, that they are to be separated. The women whisper to their older children, tears running down their faces, no doubt aware these are their last words to them. Beside them stand or squat their menfolk, faces closed up, one hand on their women's shoulders, their fingers digging deep into the flesh for one last touch, one last chance to make their feelings known. A few men and women stand or sit alone, friendless and without even the comfort of a desperate familiar touch. Their faces are closed in bitterness.

A young, light-skinned woman gestures to an empty space beside her. I nod to her with as much dignity and courtesy as I can manage, and she manages a small smile and a nod in return. Catalina and I lower ourselves to the floor by her. She says something that I do not understand. I shake my head.

"I do not speak your language," I say in Latin.

"My name is Rachel," she replies, her Latin passable.

"I am Sister Juliana," I tell her, relief at speaking flooding my voice. "This is Catalina."

"'Sister'?"

"I am a nun," I say. "Catalina was to be a novice in our convent."

"Where was your convent?"

"In Galicia."

Her eyes widen. "What are you doing here?"

"Where is here?" I ask, suddenly aware I still do not know.

"Tangier," she says.

I feel the heaviness in my belly from the confirmation that I was right. We are in the Maghreb. "We were kidnapped. Brought here by Norsemen," I say. "You?"

"The same, but from Al-Andalus," she says. "I lived by the sea on the Southern coast. I could see the shores of the

43

Maghreb from my home. I never thought I would cross the sea to come here."

I move closer and kneel by her, untie her hands from the tight leather strips that have been used to bind her. I chafe at her wrists which are badly marked from the ties and she smiles at me.

"Thank you," she says. "You are very kind."

I look her over. Her colouring is similar to mine, she has a Biblical name. "Are you a Christian?" I ask.

She shakes her head, hesitates for a moment. "I am a Jew."

I sit back. I had thought I was speaking with a woman of my own faith. I am among heathens twice over. I see that she understands my disapproval and reluctance to converse with her further, for she does not speak to me again that night. Sleep is impossible, it is a night of weeping in the darkness, one sob leading to another echoing around the stifling room, the stench of bodily waste growing stronger.

When morning comes the merchant and his servant return, accompanied by the Norseman. Judging by his colourful robes and the thick gold bracelet he wears, the merchant is well-off. No doubt trading in slaves has made him good money over the years.

The slave merchant looks the three of us over. He speaks with the Norseman.

"What language are they speaking? Do you understand them?" Catalina asks Rachel, who is paying attention to them.

She nods. "Arabic, although the accents are hard to

follow. I know it from my own land, from Al-Andalus. It sounds different here."

"What is he saying?" Catalina asks Rachel. I frown at Catalina to hold her tongue, but she does not look at me and I, too, wish to know what is said, although I do not wish to speak with the Jewess.

She looks uncomfortable but speaks in a whisper. "He says your hair is very fine and that you are very beautiful."

I feel a cold shudder go through me. I can already sense Catalina's fate and it is one of such depravity that I do not know how to erase it from my mind.

The merchant is looking at me and shaking his head. He jabbers at the Norseman and the Norseman replies with something that makes the merchant laugh.

"What did he say?" asks Catalina again.

Rachel shakes her head.

"Tell me," she insists.

"He said Sister Juliana is… not beautiful. Or young," she says, looking away.

He said I am ugly and old, I think to myself, guessing from her awkwardness that the merchant did not mince his words.

"Why did he laugh?"

"I would rather not say," she whispers.

"Please," says Catalina. "Perhaps it will help us."

"He asked why she had no hair, he said it makes her ugly. The Norseman said she is a holy woman, that she must be an untouched virgin even if she is old. He said her hair will grow soon enough and that virginity is worth a better price than hair." Rachel's cheeks are scarlet.

I look away, gaze at the painful blue sky.

Catalina yelps with pain. I look to see that the merchant has pulled her to her feet by her hair, she twists in his clutches so she can look to me.

"Help me!" she screams.

"Our Lady will protect you," I say loudly, as she struggles with the merchant.

"Our Lady has forgotten me!" she cries.

I do not reprimand her in her hour of need, it is natural that she should have doubts, even Our Lady's holy son doubted His father in His own hour of need. Instead, I pray out loud, so that she will hear holy words even as she is taken from us. "Hail Mary, full of grace, the Lord is with thee; blessed art thou amongst women, and blessed is the fruit of thy womb."

"Help me!" she screams again as they reach the door, but the merchant's servant has lifted her bodily and she cannot escape him, he carries her from the room and out of our sight. He returns swiftly for a girl so dark-skinned her skin seems to have glints of blue and another with pink-white skin and hair the colour of saffron. My heart sinks, for it is clear the three girls have been specially selected, being young and beautiful, perhaps for a harem, for I have heard of such places.

Beside me, Rachel is weeping. "Poor child," she says, turning to me and trying to embrace me. "To be violated…"

"What is done to her body will not dishonour her soul as long as she stays true to her faith," I say, extracting myself from her arms. "She will be a martyr to our faith. These heathens will go to hell for what they have done."

Rachel stares at me as though I am mad, but I ignore her. I cannot expect a Jewess to understand. Instead I pray for Catalina's soul, that it will rise above the treatment her body may receive. I pray for my own sin in failing to bring her home safely to the convent, this girl-child entrusted to my care whom I have failed to protect.

The slave merchant's servant returns after a little while and this time he takes Rachel.

"I will pray for you," she says to me as she is dragged from the room. I do not answer her. I am not sure I want the prayers of a Jewess, nor whether it would be right for me to pray for her.

There is a delay of perhaps some hours, but then the door opens, revealing the merchant's assistant with several armed men. There are commands given. Although I have no-one to tell me what is happening, it soon becomes clear that we are all to leave this room, to follow the assistant and his guards. The women begin to wail, their voices chiming and clashing together. One woman crawls on her knees to the merchant's assistant and clutches at his feet, speaking quickly. She opens her robe to show him her breasts, perhaps promising him the use of her body if he will not take away her children, but he only pushes her away with his foot and gestures to the armed men to accompany us. A few of the men are bound, but we women and the children are not. Where would we run to? We would be caught and beaten in moments, for we do not know the city, nor any people here, there would be no door to hide behind, no protection we might seek. The children cling to their mothers and fathers in desperate fear, they would not run even if their parents urged them to. We pass through the narrow streets, this sorry trail of men, women and children, bound to meet our fate.

Our walk is brief, we come to an open area, a large public square. There are stalls around the edges, many dozens of them. We are led to an empty space, facing the centre of the square, behind a small wooden platform.

The heat is like nothing I have ever felt before. I have grown used to the cool stone corridors of the convent, the shaded corners of the garden even in summer. Although it is autumn, still the sun rages down on us. I can feel my pale skin prickle and burn in the heat and see even the dark-skinned children shrink under its rays, their mothers trying to shield them from the worst of the heat by holding out their own arms to cover their children's heads, taking the burning into their own skins rather than let it hurt their offspring.

A crowd begins to gather at the sight of us and now the merchant steps forwards. He is dressed in bright red and yellow robes, no doubt the better to be seen and he speaks at length, gesturing towards us, a beaming smile on his face as he enumerates our qualities as future slaves. He holds up a woman's long hair, he pats the muscles of the largest, strongest men, he exposes the breasts and thighs of the best-looking women. He pushes the older children forwards, showing their teeth and height, their potential to grow and serve for many years to come. I watch him and see only the Devil himself, his forked tongue calling come buy, come buy, to the watching crowd.

The bidding, when it begins, is brisk enough. The

merchant knows his business, he has spoken long enough for the crowd to have already made their choices. The strongest, tallest men go quickly and the wails of their womenfolk as they are led away make me shudder. The children go quickly also, their mothers screaming as they are dragged away, tears running down their terrified faces, slapped and kicked for struggling against their new owners in their efforts to run back to their mothers. Now the women go, the most beautiful first, shaking as they reach their new masters, then the mothers, who follow their bidders without question, their bodies already broken by their hearts, shuffling as though only half living. I wonder how many of them will even live for long, such is their pain.

Now the merchant indicates me and speaks quickly, pointing to my shaven head and laughing as he makes some bawdy joke, at which the crowd titters. One man calls out something and the crowd laughs harder. I wait, silent. The merchant brushes my arm, perhaps to draw attention to my pale skin, although it is more pink than white just now, burnt by the sun. I have no doubt that he has already mentioned my provenance, suggested that I must be a virgin, since I have been a holy woman until now. I think that only a beast of a man would even find pleasure in the idea of defiling a woman dedicated to God, even the God of another. But now two men are bidding for me, one a sallow-skinned man who looks ill, the other a fat man in richly made robes, who quickly outbids the other. The merchant is delighted, for all that he said I was old and ugly, he has sold me to a wealthy man for a price with which he seems pleased. He pushes me forwards and I find myself eye to eye with the fat man. I am almost as tall as he, despite being only of average height myself. He grins at the sight of me, reaches out and runs his hand over my bare scalp, letting his fingers linger over it. I stiffen at his touch, but he has already turned away. I think for a moment that I could run while his back is turned but suddenly realise that he is not alone, he has an armed man beside him, a black skinned bodyguard who now grips my elbow and steers me through the crowd after my new owner. I think of Catalina as she was taken from me, her face full of misery. I doubt I will ever see her again and I dread to think what will happen to a girl as young as she is, as beautiful. I know that she can only expect to be defiled, to be used as a plaything by a heathen Moor. I wonder what possible sin she can have committed in her short life, to be punished like this by God. For myself, I know that I have been punished because of my temptation in the apple orchard, for my arrogance in believing that I was above the worldly desires such as gluttony, that I could travel safely out into the world and not be ensnared by all it could offer. I thought myself better than my sisters because I did not have my head turned by a handsome young nobleman in my care, believed I might be destined for a senior role within the convent and yet the temptation of a crisp sweet fruit on a tree turned my head, even as it did Eve in the Garden. I know that all of my life I will hold Catalina's face in my mind, knowing that I and I alone brought her to this place. I should have brought her safely home to our holy house, even as I was taken there by my mother, who would have died rather than see me here now, her daughter in a land of heathen Moors, torn from her holy devotions.

I should have trodden in the footsteps of the saints. Instead, I am now a slave.

I am put in a tiny locked room for the night, given a flat bread and some kind of bean stew, too heavily spiced with cumin, but I eat it in great gulping mouthfuls, not having eaten hot food for many days now. I have plentiful water, too, and I drink as much as I can hold, afraid of what the future may hold. I have been given a small length of cloth, which I wrap around my head to protect it further from the burning sun. I wish I had some salve, for I can tell that the delicate skin of my head has been sunburnt, but all I can do is put cold water on it and hope the wrap will allow it to heal. Covering my scalp gives me some small comfort. I wait for a summons, for my new owner to call for me, but nothing and no one comes, and I fall asleep, huddled on the floor, my dreams full of an endless screaming by the women and children sold today. I do not know if I, too, scream in my sleep, but no-one would care even if I did.

I am woken before dawn, stumble my way behind the man who brought me here. It is colder than I expected outside, and I shiver, standing in my shift and bare feet. All around us echoes, over and over again, the strange, warbling call echoing from the rooftops. I think it must be a call to prayer, for I see shadows here and there, kneeling in the dirt. The bodyguard, though, does not pray. He pulls me forwards and from the darkness emerge five more men, their skins so black I had not noticed them in the half light.

Behind them come more than twenty camels, a few loaded up, many without burdens, but instead saddled for riding. I shrink back from the men, but the bodyguard pushes me forwards and one of the men takes my wrist. His grip is not hard, but his hand is large, and I do not doubt that if I were to fight or flee, I would not get very far.

He says something and suddenly I am in the air and then find myself sat on the back of a camel, the wide saddle spreading my legs in an obscene manner. I try to find a better way of seating, but this saddle is not made for riding sideways and my shift is not made for riding astride. The men watch me as I struggle and there are a few chuckles that make my skin feel colder than the grey light. At last something lands on me, a crumpled robe such as I have seen people here wearing, which I gratefully pull over my shift, covering my shame.

Within moments the men are also mounted. The lead bodyguard makes a clicking sound with his mouth and the camels begin to move. I clutch at the neck of my own mount, but have been given no reins, there is only the broad saddle made of cloth to hang on to. The camel's gait is slow, swaying, but it is not difficult to remain seated, even for a novice rider such as I. I am sat higher than I would be on a horse, there can be no question of slipping to the ground and trying to escape. My hands and feet are free, but I am bound to go wherever these men intend to take me. I find my lips trembling as I whisper a prayer for safety. I do not know where the man is who bought me, I know only that he owns me. I do not know my destination; I know only that I am to make another journey.

Days and days and days pass. I do not know how many, and by the time I have thought of counting them, too many have passed to remember. The heat here is unlike anything I have ever felt before. It is dry, so dry that sometimes I feel as though my lungs cannot draw breath, as though all the moisture has been sucked from my mouth and nose. I drink water when it is given to me, greedily, desperately. It does not taste like the pure cool water of the convent, kept in stone jars. This water tastes of goatskin, it is warm and fetid, but I drink it anyway. I am more grateful than ever that I was given the robe I wear, which covers most of my skin, for I would have been burnt beyond repair otherwise, my skin being pale and unused to long periods of time in the sun. My hair has begun to grow back. I touch it in wonder in the early mornings, when I retie my headwrap. It is a soft downy fuzz, like a new-born baby, like a cat or dog. I stroke it at night and wonder how soon I will be able to cut it again, shave it back to the skin as it should be.

I grow used to the endless swaying walk of the camels, they are a different kind of beast to a horse, having neither their skittishness nor their elegance. They are bad-tempered and slow, groaning in protest when they are made to sit and stand. I suppose I should be grateful that I am allowed to ride them at all, for to walk this distance each day in this heat would kill me. I do not know where we are going, I do not know how far away our destination is. I know only that the landscape through which we travel is so different to the one I am used to that it feels as though I am in a dream, or some fantastical tale told by a storyteller. If I were one amongst many slaves, I would assume that I was being taken elsewhere, to be traded onwards. But I am the only one. I try to ask the men with whom I travel where we're going, who they are, but they speak only what I suppose is Arabic and I do not understand their gestures.

One thing I give grateful thanks for each night, however, is that my body has not yet been sullied. I have not been dishonoured. I know from what Rachel said that my virginity was seen as a valuable commodity, which explains why the Norsemen did not touch me, as I expected them to. I can only suppose that these men, with whom I travel, have been instructed not to tarnish me, for they leave me alone, only touching me to help me gain my seat or leave it each day. I give thanks to Our Lady for this, for in her purity she has protected mine. I do not know how long this protection will last, nor for whom my virginity is intended, for I cannot help but think that if it has been respected so far, it is not because of my faith, but rather because I am the property of one man. I do not know if the man is the one who walked around me in the marketplace, whose fingers crawled across my bare scalp, or whether he was only choosing me for another.

At night I watch the sky and the stars, knowing that we are travelling south-west, further and further from my home. By day, I sway endlessly on my mount and wonder whether this journey will continue to the ends of the earth. Much of the land here is like a desert, reminding me of passages from the Bible, of Jesus' time in the wilderness, of His fasting and prayer, of the Devil's temptations and His refusals to be tempted. I think that perhaps I, too, should fast, but when I am offered hard bread and sweet dates, I am too afraid of possible future deprivations to refuse. I eat what is given to me, I drink as much water as I can. Whatever is to come, I must be prepared for it.

The dread in my heart is lifted only by a few tiny moments each day, when I recognise some plant or tree. The olive trees at first, for they are large and easy to recognise. But later on, smaller plants come to my attention. I see wild thyme and smell it as we trample over it along tiny paths and the smell gives me courage, for it signals to me that, even in this strange new land, in this unknown world, in what is to be my unwilling new life, there are things I know. That my knowledge has sailed here with me, is travelling with me even as we make our way through desert dunes and treacherous mountain paths. And all the time I am learning things about this new world. I see chattering monkeys for the first time, which I have only ever seen before in paintings, see date palms up close, look across desert sands.

I grow accustomed to the camels and their ways, sometimes pat my own mount, who huffs and nuzzles my hand, the only touch of kindness I can expect.

Once or twice we stop on the outskirts of the city, and on those days, we eat better food. I eat hot stews, flavoured in ways I have never thought of, but with plants which I recognise. I taste cumin, which I had previously used mixed with flour and egg yolk, baked in a hot oven and given to patients to avoid nausea in their intestines. Here, it is being used for flavour only. I smell rose water and wonder if they use it for cramps, as I would have done. There is much use of cinnamon and fennel, both of which bring heat, and I wonder at their use in a country already so hot. After the first days, I felt the fear inside me lessen a little, for the men surrounding me at least seemed to bear me no ill will nor to have evil intentions towards me. They are even, perhaps, slaves, as I am, doing only what they have been told to do, bound to the same invisible and unknown master.

One morning there is much chatter amongst the men, and one of them even turns to me, smiling broadly.

"Aghmat," he says.

I frown and shake my head.

"Aghmat," he says again, very clearly and carefully, as though this is a word I should know.

I shake my head again and he turns away, disappointed, his companions only shrugging their shoulders. I wonder what the word means, whether it is our destination, or his name perhaps, although he did not gesture to himself. There is nothing I can do but wait.

Later that day, on the horizon, we see the outline of the city. It is a large city, as large as the city the Norsemen sold me into.

The man who spoke to me earlier turns in his saddle and points to the horizon. "Aghmat," he says, with insistence.

It is the name of the city, then, I suppose. And, since no one has bothered to tell me the name of any other of our destinations along this route, I can only suppose it to be our final destination. I feel my belly clench, wondering what fate has in store for me in this place, this Aghmat. I say the name over and over quietly to myself, my tongue struggling with the sound, this, my first word in the language I will no doubt have to learn to speak, if I am to be kept here. It has a guttural sound, like the rest of their tongue, like a patient bringing up phlegm from congested lungs.

Aghmat is a large city. The walls, when we reach them, tower high above us and from the many traders coming and going through the main gates, I can see that it is also wealthy. Only a large and wealthy city has need of so many merchants visiting it along the trade routes. There are gold merchants surrounded by guards, silk merchants whose wares must be packed with care, merchants whose trade includes herbs and spices, for I can smell them in their camels' packs as we pass close by. And there are all the smaller local traders, mostly farmers, bringing fruit and vegetables, livestock and the other goods needed to feed a city of this size.

The men know their way, they guide the camels down one street after another, until we come to a narrow street, where three of the men remove any camels without burdens and walk away with them. Meanwhile the rest of the men and I, along with the six camels that carry packs, make our way further down the narrow street and one of the men hammers at a large gate set into the wall, which is opened promptly. There is what sounds like jovial banter between the men and the person opening the door, a woman's voice.

The camels have their burdens removed and passed from man to man until they disappear through the open gate and into whatever space lies beyond. I wait, high on my camel, uncertain if I, too, am to be passed through this gate.

It seems I am to be unpacked. The camel is ordered to

kneel, and I hold on tightly as it lowers itself to the ground. I have already learnt that camels possess no grace when preparing for dismount. I dismount and stand up, grateful to be on my feet again, although my knees are weak, having sat in the same place for many hours.

Now I see the woman. It is her voice I heard speaking with the men, but now that she sees me, her chattering stops. She looks me over, from my wrapped head to my bare feet, sliding over my crumpled robe. I look her over in turn. She has very black skin and tightly curled hair, cut short. She wears a faded yellow robe. But it is her height that is most noticeable. She is a dwarf. I have not seen many in my lifetime. There was one, when I was a child, servant to a local noble. He was a man. And there was another, once, on a pilgrimage, who stayed overnight in our convent. I have never seen a female dwarf. She carries herself with confidence, as though she is a person of some standing in the household, approaching me with frank curiosity. She points at me and asks a question and when the men answer her face falls a little. She looks at me and smiles, as though she pities me.

"Aisha," she says, indicating herself to me.

I keep my face still. I do not know her well enough to respond and I do not know what she has been told to make her look at me with pity. Whatever it is, I will find out for myself before I return her smile.

She says other things, but I do not understand her, do not respond. She falls silent.

I stand still in the narrow street but when she gestures me to enter the doorway, I do so, following her slightly lurching, waddling, gait.

The house is built on three storeys around a courtyard, which is planted like a garden. There are trees, reaching high into the sky, and a fountain with splashing water. The whole of the floor is made up of tiny tiles, repeating over and over again a starred pattern in green and white. This is a house of extraordinary decoration. Everywhere are carved wooden doors, brightened with paint and featuring many artistic flourishes, such as fruits and flowers. Each of the storeys above us has an open walkway, like a balcony, around it. From the uppermost walkway, the faces of four women look down on us, curious and silent. This must be the house of my new master, whoever he is. I am, suddenly, more afraid than I have ever been, more afraid even than when the Norsemen took us and I thought that someone might rescue us before we reached the coast. Now I know that this is my destination, that someone is waiting for me in this house and I am so afraid that I forget to pray.

I turn and run.

I hear shouts behind me as I run out of the gate into the alleyway and then as fast as I can down first one street and then another, tiny narrow alleyways, with high walls on either side, closed gates and doors everywhere, no place to hide, no place to duck down and hope that my captors will pass me. No, they are close behind me, shouting. I burst out into a wider street but now my appearance and the shouts of the men behind me only draw more attention to my flight. I feel a sudden cramp in my leg, my limbs unused to movement after all these days sat atop a camel. The cramp is so hard that I stumble and fall and as soon as I do so I feel a hand on my leg and know that my attempt at escape was futile, laughable.

They pull me back to the house, dragging me along. I do not try to turn and run again, that would be useless. But I resist, being taken back the same way I have come step-by-step, my reluctance clear. When they get me back to the same doorway, I feel a hand between my shoulder blades before I am roughly shoved, falling forwards into the courtyard space again, landing this time on my hands and knees. I look up and meet the gaze of the dwarf, who shakes her head and looks at the man who brought me back. They talk between themselves and at last she nods, as though reluctantly. I find myself forced to my feet and pushed down a small walkway and through a door. Ahead are stairs, heading downwards. I baulk but am pushed forwards in no uncertain terms and make my way down the steps, which are shallow. At the bottom of the steps is a door. The man with me pushes it open.

It is a small room and bare, it smells of stale air, having no window, only the door. I hesitate but I am pushed forwards again and hear the door crash behind me. The door, I now see, is made of a plain wood, no painted flourishes here. In the centre, rather than a window, or plain wood, it has a small open space, fitted with bars, through which a small amount of light comes, although when I edge close to it and look out there is hardly anything to see, only the corridor I have just walked down. This room is a form of prison, there is no doubt about that. And I, in it, am a prisoner. The thought ought to frighten me, but there is something about the room, so silent, so empty, so without luxuries, that somehow reminds me of the convent. Slowly, I kneel, feel the cold stone floor against my legs, my palms touching one another, and the words come unbidden, Our

Fathers followed by Hail Marys, each prayer turning my prison into a holy sanctuary.

Some time passes before they bring me a pot for my bodily needs, a water jar and dipper. I am given bread and a rough stew of some sort of beans mixed with vegetables, heavily spiced. I eat all of it. Later, as the light fades from the door, it opens briefly, and a rough woollen blanket is thrown towards me. Perhaps God has reached out his hand and blessed me, reminded me of my vows by meeting my simplest needs and putting me in this silent space.

This idea at least stops me thinking of the obvious question: what sort of a house needs a prison?

The House of Women

Fair as the moon…

Song of Solomon 6:10

I AM NOT SURE HOW MANY days I have been in the room. I have almost grown used to the silence, the small dark space, the unending prayers I offer up, having nothing else to do and no way of knowing what the outside world holds for my future. I almost begin to think of myself as an anchorite, locked up forever to pray for the world's sins, this tiny room my reclusory. Perhaps it is a life I could grow used to, although I would miss my garden, miss tending both plants and people.

But I am only fooling myself with such ideas. Instead, after a handful of days, the door opens and rather than a quick silhouette appearing to bring me food and dispose of my waste, it stays open and I have to adjust my blinded eyes to the light streaming in, until I can see who has come for me.

There are two women. One is the black-skinned dwarf, behind her a sturdy older woman, wrinkled with age. Behind the both of them towers a strange looking woman, taller than any I have ever seen before, her heavy shape lowering over the dwarf, making both of their heights more extreme through contrast.

The dwarf gestures that I should follow her. I shake my head. She shrugs and points to the tall woman, who takes a step forward, hands held in menacing fists.

I hold up my hands in submission. "I will come," I say, my voice cracking from disuse.

I allow myself to be led through the doorway and along a narrow corridor. At the end of it is a fantastically painted door, bright colours swirled around a heavy metal handle. The giantess steps forwards and pushes the door open. We follow.

The room is dimly lit and hot, so hot that I gasp. The air is thick with moisture, my lungs feel as though I am drowning with every breath I take. I am reminded of the steam I would make my convent sisters breath in if they were afflicted with hoarseness and coughs. The giantess lingers in the doorway for a moment but now that we are inside the room the dwarf waves her away and she closes the door behind her, leaving the room with even less light. She has barely gone when the older woman has lifted my robe and shift over my head. I clutch at them, but I am too late.Now I am entirely naked, standing before the women. I hunch my shoulders and try to cover my nakedness with my hands, mortified. I am about to speak, to request something to cover my modesty with, when a wave of hot water crashes over my head, overwhelms me, fills my half-open mouth. I bend over double with the shock, coughing and spluttering as I seek to clear my lungs. But another wave comes, then another. It takes me this long to realise that the older woman is throwing pail after pail of what feels like near-boiling water over me. Even when I stand and turn to face her, my hands extended in front of me to make her stop, she does not cease. She must throw more than eight pails of water at me before she stops, so that in the end I give up, eyes and mouth shut, trying only to remain upright in the face of her onslaught. I fail and sink to my knees.

At once she stops, but the dwarf, standing behind me, quickly has her hands on my head, rubbing vigorously across my scalp and then continuing over the whole of my body, much to my shame. The sensation of hands against my bare flesh is shocking to me and at first, I push her away, but at last I realise that she will not be stopped, that I can succumb or fight but the end result will be the same. The substance in her hands is a slippery kind of black soap, which has a strong smell, reminding me of olive oil when it is first pressed, the sharp fresh smell of the crushed fruit like fresh-cut grass at haying time. She rubs this all over me and then takes a small rough cloth and proceeds to scrub me with it, so fiercely that I can see my own skin peeling away, the new skin beneath it scarlet with the heat and her rough treatment.

I feel faint. The heat, the drowning sensation of my lungs, the excess of sensation across my untouched body. I stagger and the women catch me, then lower me to the floor, murmuring to one another. I feel something hard scrape against my skull and realise they are shaving my head of what little hair had grown back. I am happy for this, at least, to be done, it feels like the only familiar thing that has happened to me since I was taken. When they are done, I lie on the warm wet floor tiles and hope that they have finished.

They have not. Now they crouch by my side and suddenly there is a ripping pain moving across my leg. I shriek but the older woman holds me down. I try to raise my head and see the dwarf doing something strange with a thread in her mouth and hands, moving back and forth across my leg. It takes me a moment to realise that she is, with her thread, somehow pulling out all the hairs on my legs. My head spins again and I have to lower it back to the hard floor. I lie there, held by one woman while the other pulls out every hair on my legs. When she has finished, I feel my shoulders slump in relief as the pain stops, before, to my horror, she begins the same work on my most intimate parts. The pain is indescribable. I scream aloud and at once, a rough warm hand presses down over my mouth as the pain continues.

Then comes cold water, thrown over my prone and shaking body. They roll me onto my stomach so that they can throw more cold water, then hoist me to my feet and rub a scented oil over every part of me, which I believe contains rose perfume in it. They wrap me in a large cloth, which I clutch at. I stare at them, seeking an answer for their behaviour in their faces, but they are busy with their work. Now they lead me out of the darkness through the doorway and upstairs into an enclosed courtyard, with a bright blue sky above it. I do not even think that I am half-naked except for the cloth, for I am still shaking with the cold, or perhaps with my own fear.

We pass quickly through the tiled sunny courtyard. I am in such shock from my treatment that I can barely see properly, only enough to stop myself falling as we ascend more stairs and find ourselves on the upper level, looking down on the courtyard. A door opens to my right and I am pushed into it.

The room is large. After my prison and the bathing room downstairs, it is so bright that I blink as I look around it. There are long drapes at the window, through which I can see rooftops beyond, yellow-brown layers of different heights.

A push on my shoulder leads me to sit. I look down and see that I am sitting on the edge of a large bed, covered with bright blankets. My bare feet rest on soft rugs. The room contains little else other than a large chest in carved wood.

The dwarf opens and then rummages in the chest, removing several garments in bright silks, scarlet and orange trimmed in tiny discs of beaten silver. She holds them out but I only stare at her as though my wits have left me and so she stands before me and begins to dress me as though I were a small child, tugging at my limbs, pulling me upright, pushing me back down onto the bed. The silks feel very strange, touching yet not touching, warming instantly to my skin as they slip over me. One foot and then another is pushed into a yellow leather slipper and then after consultation with her older companion, a long piece of yellow silk is wrapped tightly about my head. The feel of it, the knowledge that my bare scalp is once again modestly covered, as it should be, brings tears suddenly spilling down my cheeks. The dwarf reaches out and wipes them away, making a grimace as she does so, whether a smile or a reproach I am uncertain. The older woman dabs something on me and a strong smell of rose perfume fills the air.

The headwrap brings me such comfort I barely realise what the dwarf is now doing to my face, working with a little tray of pots and a pointed wooden stick. She rubs and pokes, then there is a sudden sharp pain through one earlobe and, before I can think, another in the other earlobe. I yelp, but she and the older woman only shrug me away. When I touch my lobes, I feel a hard, dangling, circle and look down in disbelief at blood on my fingertips. They have pierced my ears.

Warily I look beyond my bloodied fingers. Down at my waist, now encircled with a thick silken belt dangling with larger silver discs. There is no mirror here, but I am horribly aware that I have been dressed as some kind of rich man's fancy, in bright silks and chiming jewellery. I touch my lips and see that there is a red paint on them, rub my eyes and see blackness on my knuckles. The women tut at my actions and take pains to tidy up the damage I have done to the make-up they had applied to my face. I slap at their hands, wipe my mouth against the silk sleeves I am wearing and note with satisfaction that the red smear will stain the orange silk. I will not be painted like a whore, paraded in gauzy silks as though I were suggesting to a man what might lie beneath them.

But the older woman has grown tired of my antics. From her pocket she holds up leather thongs. Her words are a stream of gibberish, but her face makes it clear that she is threatening me with being imprisoned again in the tiny room downstairs, with my hands being bound. I stop trying to remove the paint and allow the dwarf to repair whatever damage I have done to their handiwork. The older woman nods when it is done and then the two of them simply walk out of the door, leaving me alone. I think for a moment that I could run out of the door, but I can hear a heavy lock turning and know that I am still a prisoner, however I am dressed. I make my way to the large window and look down, onto a narrow street below. I take a sheet from the bed and think to tie it, to let myself down, but then I see a guard standing below the window and know that if I do so I will swiftly find myself caught and brought back to the tiny room downstairs.

I kneel and pray. I cannot formulate any kind of meaningful thoughts and so instead I only repeat the Hail Mary over and over again, the prayer I learnt when I was only a child, from my mother. In the midst of this I open my eyes and see the bed. A dread cold comes over me, an understanding of what lies ahead. I have been bought as a slave and now, in a rich man's house, have been dressed in silks and jewels, have been washed and perfumed and painted... only a fool would not understand what is to become of me. I think of the narrow street below and wonder, if I leapt, whether I would break my neck and so join Maria in her mortal sin, or whether I would only be crippled. Behind me, the door opens, and at last I see my master.

I was right. It is the man from the slave market, the fat man who turned me around and touched my head, who laughed as he spoke with the trader of slaves. He is almost as round as he is tall, indeed he stands shorter than I, and has to look up to me, which he does not seem to care about. He lets out a laugh when he sees me, as though

I am of amusement to him. He walks around me and then says something which I do not understand. I do not speak. I simply stand still and wait. He pulls at my head wrap, so that it falls to the ground and once again my scalp is exposed. He rubs his hand over the skin, grinning broadly, saying something like "Kamra", which I do not understand. Even his touch on my skin is a violation, I shudder against it. My heart is beating so hard I think I may die; I think that perhaps its speed will cause me great pain in my chest and that I will fall to the floor and die.

But this does not happen. What does happen is that the merchant places one fat hand, thick with golden rings, over my breast and squeezes it hard. I step backwards, unable to help myself. He slaps me round the head, and places his hand on my other breast, while a second reaches round to fondle my buttocks. The silk I am wearing does nothing to protect me, it is too fine, too delicate. I shake my head and step backwards again and again, quickly find myself pressed up against a wall, at which he laughs, and slips his hand between my legs. I turn my head and bite the arm closest to me, the one whose hand is currently touching my neck. He yelps and I take advantage of his surprise to climb across the bed away from him, but he grabs my ankle and with surprising strength pulls me towards him, belly down. He kneels on one of my legs, so that I cannot move, his great weight bearing down on me so that I think my leg bone may snap. I cannot move, can only struggle, face down, as he places one hand over the silken trousers I am wearing and rips them downwards, a tearing sound exposing my buttocks. I scream, but he only laughs and slaps me across the buttocks, as though I were a wicked child. He is speaking throughout, but none of the words mean anything to me, only that he sounds happy enough, even as he attempts to defile me.

And for one moment, one tiny moment, he releases my leg and I am across the bed and crumpled to the floor, jumping up again and clutching at the drapes around the window shutters, which have been closed, the light streaming through them, tinting the room yellow-red. He shouts behind me, but I have already made up my mind without even thinking about it, even as I fumble with the drapes and pull open the shutters. I do not climb, I simply lean forwards, tipping the whole of my bodyweight towards the street below, hoping for a quick death. It is an unholy death of course, but it is better than what is to come if I stay in this room.

There is one fleeting moment when I am free, when only the air can touch me. Then there is a thud that reverberates through me and the *crack* sound as my thigh bone snaps as I hit the hard-cobbled street below. Then pain, only pain, such pain. I scream because I cannot do anything else, because the pain bursts out of my mouth. Above me I hear shouting, look up to see the merchant's angry red face, before darkness descends over me.

When I open my eyes, I am in a darkened room, and too hot. It takes a moment before I realise I am in the kitchen of the house, that over me are standing the dwarf and the older woman, a moment before the pain comes back in such terrible waves that I cry out again and again, putting my hand over my own mouth to stop my cries and failing. The dwarf is weeping, holding my other hand and tentatively dabbing at my face with something cold. It hurts every time she touches me, which I do not understand, as nothing has happened to my face. I am close to the open cooking fire, it is this that is making me too hot, I am sure of it. I look down at my thigh, I can see the unnatural crookedness of it, the flesh failing to hide the fault within. I look around me, hoping that a physician has been sent for, although inside I know full well that this is not the case. I have defied my master, I have not subjected myself to his evil desires, I leapt into the air rather than be touched by him, I have broken his property.

I try to push the dwarf away, but as soon as she stops dabbing the cold cloth onto my face heat rages through it. I try to touch my face, to touch the heat and the resulting pain is so bad that I whimper. Something has been done to my face. I look at the dwarf, gesture to my face, my eyes asking the question I have no words for. She shakes her head, looking at me with fear, but the older woman, standing behind her, has understood me and knows that I will find out, sooner or later. She walks away and returns shortly holding up a little mirror. It is very small, and the image is blurred, but one look in it reflects back to me what has happened.

I have been branded, burned, over and over again across my face, welts of red raised flesh, blisters already forming. I know that no remedy I may use, no unguent, will ever entirely remove such scars. My leg is broken, my face is forever scarred.

An irate shout comes from the courtyard. I cower, recognising my master's voice. But the older woman shakes her head quickly. He is not calling for me, he is calling for someone else, he is done with me. This scarring, this raging heat in my face, is his punishment, inflicted whilst I was in the darkness of pain, unaware of what was happening. So be it. I will be scarred, there is nothing I can do. But my leg… my leg fills me with fear. It must be set. I know how to do it, but once bound I must stay still for many, many days, months even. I do not know if I will be allowed this, and even if I am, whether it will heal straight or crooked. I look up at the older woman and then down at my leg, gesture to it as tears flow down my cheeks. She nods, a serious nod, filled with understanding of the gravity of my injury. She grimaces at the danger of it, the likelihood that it will not heal well. But then she points to a corner of the kitchen, she indicates sitting there, points to vegetables and a knife. She is suggesting that I may stay here, in her kitchen, for I believe her to be the cook here. She is suggesting I could be given little tasks to do, in the hopes that staying still will aid my recovery. I bow my head to her, still weeping, and reach for her hands. I kiss each of them, giving thanks to God out loud that there is someone here who will protect me as much as her position in this household allows. She can tell, perhaps, from my weeping and the seriousness of my tone, that I am blessing her, and she nods, places one of her hands over her heart in return.

The dwarf points to herself and says "Aisha," then points to the older woman.

"Maadah," she says and the cook nods, then points at me in turn. She does not wait for me to say my own name, instead she says "Kamra".

I do the best I can. I ask, with gestures, for what I need.

Maadah brings me strips of cloth, that my leg may be tightly bound, alongside a few short pieces of wood. With her help, and Aisha's, we bind my leg as tightly and straight as possible. They cut away my ripped silken apparel and to my relief I am given a plain loose robe in a faded green, which is far too big for me and therefore falls comfortably over my awkwardly straight leg. I know that I must drink the root of cornflower, but I do not know how to ask for it. I make gestures to ask for writing implements. It takes a day before Aisha can lay her hands on ink and a sheet of something which I think is vellum at first, although it is not quite like it. At any rate, I can draw on it and I do my best to draw a cornflower, indicating that the petals should be blue by touching Maadah's robe, which is of a similar colour. I draw the little dangling purple flowers of comfrey also, known as knitbone, for its ability to do just that. Aisha nods at this, and takes away my drawing, I think she goes to the market with it to show to a seller of such remedies and sure enough returns with roots and leaves which I recognise. I embrace her as best I can, so grateful am I for her help. I drink the cornflower root daily, wrap comfrey around my leg and meanwhile Maadah smears some kind of mixture on my face, which eases the burns. I try to smell it, to find out what is in it, but I am not sure I recognise all the ingredients, some of them may be local to here. After several days Maadah nods approvingly at my face and tries to show me the progress of my burns in the mirror, but I only shake my head and look away. It is vanity to be more concerned with my face than with my ability to walk in the future. I am a bride of Christ, and Christ looks only at our hearts. He does not concern Himself with a woman's good looks or otherwise.

Time passes. I live all of my life in the kitchen. Early on, we find a way that I may relieve myself, with much pain and difficulty, but Maadah and Aisha do not shy away from such crude matters, only helping me when needed and disposing of my bodily waste without comment. A corner of the kitchen becomes mine, they place a sack stuffed with straw under me and give me a blanket to lie under at night. I know that my legs will grow wasted if I do not use them, so I try to move a little each day, even from my sitting position, half-crawling across the kitchen floor, folding and straightening the good leg.

I try to make myself useful. I peel and chop vegetables, butcher meats, grind spices and herbs for the meals. I learn one dish after another, until Maadah nods and smiles at my efforts in making them myself, without her input. I learn to roll tiny grains until they are made into something called *couscous*, to be buttered and salted, then topped with the thick stews they like to eat here. Once or twice I suggest, by pointing, a different spice or herb and Maadah nods, acknowledging that my choices are good. By night, I sleep by the last embers of the fire, wrapped in my blanket, and wake to find a little basin of water and a cloth laid out for me by Aisha so that I may keep myself clean.

I do not see my master, for which I am grateful. Day by day I learn new words, now that I can hear Aisha's chatter and Maadah's responses all day, alongside the other women who visit the kitchen. I begin by pointing to each herb and spice, for I know what they are, and to know their name in this new language is a comfort to me. Then I point to other things: the fire, the wood, a pot, water. Slowly, slowly, my leg heals, slowly, slowly, I learn to speak. Finally, the day comes when I can stand, leaning heavily on two sturdy sticks Aisha has found and brought to me. I look down. My work was not perfect, the leg is twisted. I will always limp. But I am standing, I am walking again, and I give thanks for this, grateful that God has not entirely deserted me, even here.

I work harder to learn the language. Aisha laughs at me when I speak, for she says my accent makes their words sound strange, but at least I begin to understand those around me and make myself understood in turn. Once I can ask questions and comprehend the answers to some degree an endless stream of them falls from my lips. I ask about the city, about the country, about our master.

"We sit on the trade routes," she explains, "that is what has brought the Master riches."

"What does the Master trade in?"

She makes a face, as she always does when he is mentioned. "Gold," she says curtly. "He trades with the Dark Kingdoms, to the south. He used to trade in slaves, but then he found that gold was easier. Gold does not die if you mistreat it," she adds.

I nod. This makes sense of our master's riches: the silk robes, the dark-skinned and heavily armed bodyguards he surrounds himself with on his journeys, this large and elegant house.

"Caravans come and go from Aghmat all the time," she tells me. "They are vast, you will have seen them on your journey here."

I nod. Traders can have more than a hundred camels, I have learnt. The caravans go on and on into the distance, and because they all follow the same trade routes, one caravan will often join in close with another, for there is safety in numbers, from bandits and other dangers. When crossing the deserts, there is the danger of getting lost and so many of the caravans follow one another.

"What other traders are there?" I ask.

"Oh, all kinds. Cloth: wool and linen of course, but also silks, and those that have been decorated are worth a great deal, the merchants who trade in them are rich. The cloth destined for the nobles will have been decorated with embroidery, or silver – they like to put little silver discs on some clothes, or twisted threads of gold. And there is jewellery of course, made with silver, or gold. Some of it is very fine, it is embedded with pearls or precious gems and woods. Have you seen ebony? It is black as night, black like a coal. And prized, of course."

I continue my work, but Aisha has sat back on her heels, with a dreamy expression on her face.

"Imagine being a queen," she says, a faraway smile on her face. "Imagine sitting on a throne while the best merchants bring you their wares. You could choose any jewellery you wanted, you could have glass cups and the best rose perfume. You wouldn't just chew on a stick of sugarcane, or peel an orange yourself, you'd have cooks, to make all kinds of delicacies and sweetmeats." She puffs out her cheeks and blows out a sigh. "Well, I suppose I can dream of such a day," she adds, laughing. "There is no chance Maadah will make such things for us, she's a good cook but not fancy."

"Are there many traders in spices?" I ask. "And in the ingredients for healing?"

"There are plenty," she says. "Although some seem a little frightening."

"Frightening?"

"Such things they have! Skulls from snakes and creatures pickled in jars, as though they were radishes. And teeth, so many teeth! They pull them right out of your head, if they hurt."

I nod, my tongue creeping over my own teeth, which thankfully I still have all of. Sister Rosa was always insistent on cleaning them with salt and a little stick, although she also kept a good supply of cloves for toothache and had a sturdy pair of pliers for pulling out any teeth that had gone rotten. Her own teeth were healthier than most, so I followed her example.

"Why am I called Kamra?" I ask her. "What does it mean?"

"Moon," she says.

"Why did the Master call me that?" I ask. "He could have called me anything."

She looks awkward. "It is just a name," she says.

"But why that name?" I persist.

She gestures vaguely towards me, at my head. "He said your head was like the moon," she half mutters.

I frown and then think about what she has said. My clean-shaven scalp, when he first saw me, the skin on my head whiter than white from the many years' protection from the sun, the lack of hair. It is a cruel nickname then, a name he chose to refer to the distinctive thing about me. The name was both accurate and intended as a jest, a jeering. My white scalp earned me the name of moon. I think for a moment of telling Aisha what my real name is, or at least one of them, but then I think that this name is good enough. It is a reminder of who I really am, that my scalp should have remained shaven, it has something of my past to it and is easy enough to pronounce, amidst these other words that I find so difficult. So, I remain Kamra, not challenging the name.

"Why did he buy me? He obviously did not think me beautiful. And there were beautiful women on the slave block, he could have bought them." I think of Catalina.

Aisha sits back on her heels from scrubbing the tiled floor. "The Master often brings women home from his travels," she says. "He likes them to look different."

"Different?"

"Different colours, different sizes, different ages. He says he likes variety," she adds, grimacing. "He has had many women in the rooms upstairs," she adds. "Old women, girls not yet past childhood, even one or two men."

I am appalled by such depravity but Aisha only shrugs. They have all grown used to their master's ways by now, know that they must bow their heads and ensure he is happy when he is here, that it is not their place to refuse him anything. He travels a great deal, Aisha tells me, so that much of the time the household is relatively ungoverned, for there is no mistress. "There was one, once, but after she had borne him two sons she died, and he never replaced her. He preferred to hire nursemaids for his sons and take his own pleasures where he wished. His sons are now grown men, both traders of Aghmat in their own rights, one deals in silks, one in gemstones. We do not often see them; they have their own households."

"Why would he choose me?"

"He said you were a religious woman, he had never seen one for sale before, he would have found that interesting."

I shake my head at the kind of man who would even think that. "Where are the other women?" I ask.

"Most are sold on, if they are worth selling. One ran away. A few of us he could not sell on, so we are still here."

I stop what I am doing and think about what she has said. By now I know that the household is made up of six women: myself, elderly Maadah, tiny Aisha, a very young girl named Ranya, barely out of childhood, who stays in the shadows of giantess Dalia. And Faiza, whose skin is mottled, half brown and half white, in patches like a leopard. And now I see what we are. A household of discarded playthings, a house of women who are too odd to be resold, kept only to carry out domestic chores, ready for the Master's rare visits.

Aisha watches me at my work. When she sees me pause when watering a plant to touch its leaves and smell it, she brings me a little potted plant of my own, though I have no idea where she got it from. It is mint, the mint they use here in their tea, which they drink copious amounts of, laced with honey. I take it in my hands and look at her. She indicates that it is mine, and reluctantly I nod my head to her and give her something approaching a smile. She beams back at me as though I have embraced her and she must say something to Maadah, who then seeks me out.

"You know plants?" she says.

"Yes," says Aisha, standing beside her.

"Be quiet," she says. She looks more directly at me, shapes her words carefully and clearly. "You know plants?"

"Yes," I say without adding anything more.

She nods her head, as though confirming what Aisha has told her. She asks something else, but I do not understand.

I shake my head.

"Can you heal sick people?" she asks.

I nod my head.

She calls for young Ranya, who has a bad cough. She makes her stand in front of me and then asks her to cough, which she does, a thick hacking sound. Maadah looks at me. "Can you help?" she asks.

I turn away from her and walk to where the lavender flowers are growing. I pick a few, then make my way to the kitchen, where I take honey and water and mix all of them into a little pot, which I set on the fire. Maadah, Aisha and Ranya watch me, curious. When the mixture has bubbled for a little while I pour it carefully into a cup, straining out the flowers as I do so. I hand the cup to Ranya and say, in my awkward accent, "Drink this, every day. It will drive out the stuffiness in your chest." Privately, I also think that it will drive out malign spirits and that perhaps this girl, who has been through such hardships here, may suffer from them also.

I make the mixture every day for four days and by the fourth day Ranya is smiling at me, and Maadah nods her head as she can hear for herself that the cough is abating, becoming lighter.

Now I have a function in the household. I am given the care of all the plants in the courtyard, and I rearrange them to my liking, placing the ones who enjoy the sun in the centre and those that prefer a cooler, shadier location at the edges, where they are sheltered from the blazing rays of the midday sun. The various members of the household come to me with their ailments and Maadah lets me have a pestle and mortar of my own, along with a few other little implements and pots that I may use when creating my remedies. When I ask for ingredients that I do not grow myself in the courtyard, at first she tries to give instructions to Aisha, who shops in the market for the household. But after a little while this becomes difficult, I cannot adequately explain everything I need. And so one day I am given leave to go with Aisha to the marketplace and told that I may select my own herbs and other ingredients.

I am nervous. Since the first day I arrived in Aghmat, I have not left this house, its courtyard, its walls. I have looked out over the rooftops, and seen the wide stretch of the city, but I have never ventured outside of the closed courtyard gate. But now I want to see more of this world in which I live, and so, tentatively, I follow Aisha out. I remember the narrow street in which I am standing, the street that brought me here and where I tried to run away. As we walk on, I see the narrow side street where I tried to jump from the window and fell. I will remember that street forever, I think bitterly. I will limp forever because of that one moment, my leg twisted and broken, the pain of it and the knowledge that it saved only my chastity. It did not release me from slavery, it did not return me home. I wonder briefly if the price I paid was too high, but by now we are joining the main street towards the market square and my thoughts are distracted by the world around us.

The marketplace is very large. Aghmat is a rich city and it displays its riches here, in a wide-open square, entirely surrounded by market stalls, and further behind it, dark warrens, tiny side streets making up the maze of further shops. There is a large mosque, where the people of the city pray. The stalls and shops offer everything one might wish for. From luxurious carpets, laid out on vast racks to show their beauty, down to tiny vials of rose perfume, so rich and sweet a scent that it makes your head spin. There are food stalls where merchants call their wares, offering stuffed dates, roasted meats, fresh breads, tiny sweetmeats and juices freshly squeezed to take away the day's heat. I can hear the metalworkers, the constant clang-clang-clang of their work, metal against metal as spoons and jugs and platters are created in their burnished hands. No doubt there are other metalworkers, those who make weapons, but they are needed less than daily utensils. Everywhere we walk our paths are blocked by beasts of burden, camels, mules, donkeys, horses, carrying everything from water jars to fruits and vegetables, even struggling livestock bound for slaughter. We have to start and stop with every step, allowing the traders to make their way towards stalls and the souks through narrow streets, pausing at the houses of well-known customers. There is every kind of person here. Little children run past us, shrieking as they play games, occasionally I spot one clasping stolen fruit or sweetmeats, a stallholder raising their voice behind them in indignation. There are old traders, sucking on pipes, swilling back sweet teas as they call out to passers-by, inviting them to look more closely at their goods: carpets, blankets, woven hangings. They promise shade and tea in return for a customer's attention.

There are those who make other kinds of promises. Whilst most of the women here dress in long robes, with little flesh on show, the colours of their fabrics bright but not gaudy, there are other women. These wear golden beads strung into their hair, their lips are painted bright shades of red, their arms are full of jangling bangles which they make sure to shake as they move, their robes, while long, seem somehow to offer glimpses of an arm, a leg, to gape open for a tantalising glimpse of their necklines. They laugh and joke amongst themselves, they call out to the men who pass by, something about sweetness, about honey, although they have nothing for sale but themselves.

There are jewellers, leather workers, and a slave trading block, which I move away from as soon as I recognise what it is, as though the trader might suddenly grab me and sell me onwards.

Aisha winks at me and puts one finger to her lips, indicating a secret, before using a small coin to pay for fresh oranges, cut and sprinkled with cinnamon and rosewater. After we have enjoyed their sweet taste, she busies herself buying fresh butter and cheese. She points to a lamb and a pair of chickens and they are slaughtered for us there and then, the blood spilling on the ground while a blessing of sorts is spoken over them. Behind the butcher sits an old man, his father perhaps, now too old for such a violent trade, whittling away at a wooden spoon he is creating. He nods and smiles to me and says something, but I do not understand and so I only nod and move away, once the meat has been parcelled up for us. Our baskets have grown heavy by the time we reach a small store to which Aisha nods and points, smiling.

And here at last are all the remedies which I have been lacking. Cumin and fennel seeds, cinnamon and ginger, pepper and rose. There is Java pepper and black hellebore, fenugreek and fern. I find dried hops and fresh sage, caperberries and dill. There is mallow and mustard, poppy and plantain, as well as thistle. I touch wormwood and clover, henbane and horseradish. Aisha laughs. I look at her and she indicates my own face and makes a face indicating extreme happiness, a ludicrous grin. I cannot help but laugh a little, knowing full well that she caught me smiling at the sight of these ingredients, so well-known to me. I touch one or two of the ingredients and raise my eyebrows at her, asking permission to buy them. I do not know what Maadah has told her, what I am allowed. But Aisha nods at everything I touch, she waves her hands to indicate more, that I must not be stinted. Maadah is being generous, now that she knows that I have healing skills, she seems determined to make use of them. I return to the house with one tiny packet after another spilling from my basket and Maadah smiles, well pleased. I beg some little jars from her and set up a shelf within the kitchen in which to store my remedies and ingredients. Seeing what I am doing she even clears a second shelf when it becomes obvious that my collection will not fit on one shelf alone.

I grow so busy with my remedies that I half begin to think myself at home. I do not just treat the household, for Maadah begins to spread word of my skills further afield, her friends and neighbours arriving at our gate and being shown to me, my name being called as soon as they appear. They are grateful to me, these slaves and other servants, they bring me little gifts when they are cured, perhaps a little bunch of dates still on the branch, a fistful of olives, such gifts as one slave can offer to another. When a woman brings a new-born child who seems to have difficulty breathing, and I cure it, she returns to ask for my name, that she may give the child the same. It is a girl, and Aisha, understanding the woman, tells her the name by which I am known, Kamra. The woman is happy with the name and goes away clutching her baby daughter to her.

I do not forget my prayers. Even though I live among these people, learn their language and eat their food, even though I have accepted a name in their own tongue, still I keep to my own prayers. I try to find a quiet place in which to pray each day, I try to follow, as best I can, the correct prayers for the right part of the day. And I turn my face away when the servants of the household pray in turn, preferring not to see their heathen practice. I look away from their devotions and continue to work even as I see them put away their work and obey the call to prayer that rings out across the rooftops of Aghmat five times each day. It would be all too easy to feel the need to be one of them, to convert so as to be accepted. It is not a temptation I intend to give into. For their part, they watch me pray at first with curiosity and later with disinterest, as they grow used to it.

The Master does not visit often. He travels various trade routes, making connections, seeking out those rich enough to need his gold. And perhaps he travels so that he may visit more than one slave market, so that he may look for those women who are strange, different, who give him the thrill of the new. When he does return home, our household is on high alert. We women shrink back from his presence, afraid that his time away will have tarnished us with new, will have reminded him of our difference and what he sought in us. We scurry to do as we are bid, we hurry to please him in any other way than the purpose for which we were bought. The house is immaculate, each room is luxurious and perfectly clean, we serve meals full of exotic and exquisitely made delicacies, for which we scour the market even as he scours markets for other pleasures. We arrange for dancing girls, for musicians, for jugglers and other such entertainers, in the hopes that they will draw his attention away from us. No matter what happens, when he is in the house, his attention must be drawn away from us. It is an unspoken pact between us, each woman protecting the others in any way she can. When he is in residence, his sons also visit, and they, too must be warded off. They have straying hands, each of us has felt their fingers on our arm, our legs, our behind, caressing and poking, pinching or lightly slapping. Each of us knows not to stand too close, to move gracefully away, to offer something else to keep their prying hands busy: a hot drink, sweetmeats, fresh fruits, anything but ourselves. When their father is gone, the sons do not seem to visit us, for which I am grateful. No doubt they have their own households to torment. I wonder what their wives make of them, these men who seek elsewhere. Perhaps they are grateful to be left alone.

And of course, the inevitable day comes, when a new girl is delivered to this household. There is no mistaking what she has been chosen for, her skin is a warm golden colour, but it is the bulk of her that draws the eye. The flesh of her body ripples when she moves, her breasts are larger than any woman I have ever seen, her vast behind balancing them perfectly. Her triple chins set off a rounded face with high fat cheeks tinged with pink and large black eyes, a rosebud mouth too small for the rest of her. She arrives, as I did, with a commotion in the street, the heavy battering of our gate and when it is opened there she is, sat atop a camel, eyes wide and frightened. She is pulled down from the camel's saddle and lands ungracefully, clutching the beast as though it is her only friend. It probably has been, for the past few days. Aisha exchanges glances with me and I nod, I understand what she is here for. She stumbles forwards, shuffling ungracefully as she seeks to regain her balance after so long astride the camel's swaying gait.

She does not fight so is not locked away in the room downstairs. She does not jump from the open window as I did. We wash and dress her, she sleeps obediently where we tell her to, and when the Master arrives, a few days later, we can see from her face and the slump of her shoulders that she knows full well what is to come. She submits. In silence, for we hear no screams. The Master, it seems, is pleased enough with her, for he gives her a necklace and when he leaves, orders that she be sold on, he is tired of her now, she is no longer a novelty. But it seems she is not that easy to sell and so she re-joins us, returns to our house of women and tells us her name, Nilah, bringing our total to seven. And we, this household, await the next woman to arrive, the next novelty that has caught our master's eye. There is a slave girl in Aghmat whom I have seen once or twice, for she is easy to spot in a crowd. Her hair is the colour of saffron, her skin extraordinarily pale, her eyes are blue like cornflowers. I am quite certain that once, however long ago, she made up part of our household. I wonder if this is my new destiny. If I am to live in a household of strange sisters, welcoming one novice after another to be fed to our Master and then discarded, as I lost Catalina whom I should have delivered safely home to the convent. I wonder if I will ever forget Catalina, if I will ever see her again to beg her forgiveness.

I avoid the Master's straying hands several times and as the seasons change, I begin almost to feel myself safe.

There is a festival once a year here, where birds of prey are displayed and then some are set free. The Master is away and so I stand with the other women in the crowd and watch the birds as their leather anklets are unclipped or cut loose and they are thrown forwards into the sky, the way they circle above their masters before realising that they are free, that they need not return to the commands they have been trained to but instead may return to the forests and deserts whence they came, to seek out their long-lost mates and their favourite hunting grounds. They test the air and feel the wind turn their wings towards freedom, away from the minarets and rooftops that have so long held them captive. We watch as they leave the city's sky, turning from large to small, then disappearing altogether from sight. I hear Nilah sigh to herself.

"Let's go home," I say.

Aisha clutches my arm. "Do you not want to see Zaynab?"

"Who is Zaynab?" I ask.

She widens her eyes at my ignorance. "The queen of Aghmat," she tells me. "She is the most beautiful woman in the world, so they say."

I shrug.

"Come with me," she says. "The procession of the nobles will pass by the main street on their way back to the palace and we will see her."

"Haven't you seen her before, if she is the queen?" I ask. I have little interest in seeing the procession, nor a woman who is no doubt vain as well as being a heathen.

"She does not often go out in public," says Aisha, still tugging at me. "Come on!"

I follow, dragging my feet, hoping that we will miss the procession after all. But when we reach the main street there are big crowds lining the road on both sides, eager to see King Luqut as well as Queen Zaynab.

"She had a vision," breathes Aisha.

"Who?"

"Zaynab. She said she would marry the man who would rule all of the Maghreb."

"Is that why Luqut wanted to marry her?" I ask.

"Yes. He made her divorce her first husband so he could have her for himself."

I am appalled. "He took her from her lawful husband?"

"Yes," says Aisha, with all the gusto of one telling a fantastical tale. "She was only a girl and married to a man she loved, but because of her vision, Luqut took her for himself. They say she screamed when she was told. But now she is the queen of Aghmat and Luqut says that with her by his side there can be no doubt that her vision will come true."

I am about to ask more questions but there are shouts and cheers from our right and Aisha grips my arm, pulling me forward so that we will see better. Already we can see the fine horses of the royal guards who are leading the procession. Behind them, I can see two riders, a man and a woman.

"There they are!" whispers Aisha in excitement.

The two riders come abreast of us and I see an older man, broad of shoulder, his face turning this way and that to acknowledge the crowd with a confident smile, a man certain of acclaim. Closer to us is the queen, Zaynab. The procession slows, as guards ahead clear the crowds out of the way and so I see her for longer than I might otherwise have done.

She is far younger than her husband, she is probably a few years younger than I am. Her face does not turn this way and that. Instead she looks straight ahead, her eyes unwavering, as though she were a statue. She is certainly beautiful, and I note the absurd lavishness of her clothing and jewels, rich silks tumbling all around her, ropes of gemstones and heavy gold weighing her down. But I have to concede that perhaps to suppose her vain may be a mistake. She does not look as though she is revelling in her beauty, in the opulence of her clothing and heavy gold headdress. She looks unhappy. It makes me sad to look at her. I wonder whether we share the same pain, this queen and I, a slave. Torn from our vows, she from her husband, I from God's own son, forced to live another life at another's whim.

"I have had enough," I say to Aisha, and I turn for home, away from Queen Zaynab's sad face.

The Beat of Drums

Terrible as an army with banners.

Song of Solomon 6:4

I AM LAYING OUT HERBS ON the airy rooftop to dry them, turning each bundle, each leaf and flower every day under a shaded awning, to avoid them turning musty. The awning shelters them from the too-hot sun which would diminish their powers. I hear footsteps and panting, and Aisha joins me. She drags me away from my chores, to the edge of the rooftop.

"They say an army is coming," she says, pointing beyond Aghmat's city walls.

I look out at the empty plain and then back at Aisha. "An army? What do you mean, an army?"

"The Almoravids!"

"Who are they?"

"Desert warriors," breathes Aisha. "From the south."

"Should we be afraid?"

"They tried to cross the mountains before, years ago, but they failed. But now they say there are more of them, and that they have a greater leader, named Abu Bakr."

"If they failed before, it is likely they will fail again," I say, exasperated with Aisha's gossiping. "I have work to do."

But it is not long before fear spreads in the city. The Almoravids have succeeded in crossing the mountains. It seems that their new leader Abu Bakr is indeed a strong man, and word has it that his second-in-command, a man named Yusuf, is also a redoubtable warrior and leader of men. Their army has taken Taroundant, a strong city, a city almost as big as Aghmat.

Suddenly armed men are everywhere in the streets. The Amir's army prepares for battle, we see guards and soldiers in the streets, we hear of their preparations, the armourers in the markets deafen passers-by with their hammering, sharpening swords and fashioning spears.

"King Luqut will beat them," says Aisha, with certainty.

"How can you be sure?" I ask. "Everyone says they are stronger this time."

"He had better beat them," says Aisha, looking less certain. "No woman will be safe if an army conquers this city."

I think that anyway, no woman is safe in our own household, considering the Master's behaviour. I want to say that I will take my chances with a new army, although I know that this is nonsense. A conquering army, soldiers, will certainly be worse than a single man.

"Well, there is nothing we can do," I say. "It is God's will what will happen."

"Allah be praised," says Aisha. "I give thanks that we have a strong Amir, he will protect us."

We hear whispers, rumours, gossip, nonsense. But at last

there comes a day when the nonsense becomes truth. The Amir and his army are heading out to fight the Almoravids. He is a fearsome warrior, this land is his, he knows it well. He has a strong army, there is no reason why he should lose the coming battle. Still, I find myself whispering prayers under my breath as I work, praying for this heathen king to defeat the coming army. I should not care what happens to him, but certainly if he loses, I and all of this household, this city, will be at risk.

The city withdraws into itself. People retreat to their houses, close their shops, the market falls silent. We gather on the rooftops, straining our eyes to look out over the plain to see anything, though we can see nothing. The army rides out at dawn. Aisha and I buy food at the market, as always, but there are only a few stalls open. The main shops are shuttered, the merchants are hurrying either back to their own homes or to places of safety, herding their animals with brisk shouts. One by one the gates set into the high city walls close, pushed to by guards who stand waiting, hoping to welcome our army back into the safety of the city, once they have defeated the Almoravids.

Darkness falls. The Master is still away on a trading trip and we are unsure whether this is of benefit to us or not. For once, perhaps, we would have liked to have had a man in the house. If, God forbid, Luqut is defeated, what will a conquering army do to a houseful of unprotected women? We stay inside, keeping only a couple of lanterns with us, but first one and then another of us hears a sound, looks to the others to see if they, too, can hear it. It is a low sound, so far away that it is hard to hear it. We can only feel it, as though it were a heartbeat. It comes again and again and again, like a heartbeat indeed. We look from one to another and when it becomes clear that all of us can hear it, we make our way up the stairs, moving towards the windows, which we dare not open, looking upwards to the stairs which would take us to the rooftops, which we dare not ascend. It is a beat. It comes regularly, repetitively, so deep that it sounds in our bellies and our feet rather than in our ears.

"What can it be?" whimpers Dalia, shoulders hunched, making her smaller than usual.

"Drums," says Aisha in a whisper.

"Drums?"

"The Almoravids carry drums in battle," she says. "They will drum all night and all through the battle, however long it lasts."

They do. The beat continues, coming closer and closer, until it feels as though even the city walls must be reverberating. In the darkness of the night, Aisha and I open a shuttered window one tiny crack and hear the sound come louder.

"They must be just outside the city walls," I say, horrified.

"The Amir must have retreated," says Aisha, squatting on the ground. She sits in grim silence for a little while. "If they storm the city, we must find a way out of here," she says.

"There is no way out," I say. "If a conquering army enters the city, we are all dead. Or worse," I add.

She nods and is silent for a while longer. "We could dress as men," she says.

"Then they will sever our heads from our bodies," I say.

One by one, the other women of the household find us, seeking us from room to room. When they do find us, they huddle on the floor, robes wrapped around cold feet, in terrified silence occasionally broken by small whispers to one another.

The drums continue all night. When dawn breaks, there is no call to prayer, its absence deafening. Still the drumbeat goes on. The city walls have not yet been breached, but the drums are so close that we know that Luqut's army must be failing, that the men of Aghmat, the husbands and sons, fathers and brothers the city sent out to battle, are being killed, one by one. We relieve ourselves in a pot and carry it at night down to the courtyard. We take furniture from other rooms and push it against the door of the room in which we are huddled. The seven of us wait, certain of a hammering at the gate below, certain that the door of this room will be shattered open, to reveal the Almoravids, these unknown and powerful desert warriors. We do not even know what they look like, although Maadah says that she has heard that they wear only dark robes, carry shields almost as big as themselves and that all the men veil their faces. Although there are plenty of local men who veil their faces, somehow the thought of conquerors whose faces we cannot even see is more frightening than if they were to show themselves.

In the end it takes three days and three nights. By the third day, the city walls are breached. We hear running and shouts, screams of people dying, both men and women. We hear things being broken, whether by the city people throwing things such as pots to protect themselves or deliberate damage being caused by the conquering army. It is clear that we are overrun, that our army has lost, and that we are now in the hands of the Almoravids. We no longer dare to leave the room in which we have locked ourselves. We relieve ourselves in a pot which has a lid, but as the hours go by without emptying it, the room begins to smell fetid from the waste of our bodies and our stale breath, tainted with our growing fear.

Sometime in the late afternoon, the room grown hot, our bellies crying out with hunger, our mouths dry with thirst, we hear shouts from the streets. Not shouts of panic, as we heard before, but rather announcements, orders. We stand close to the shuttered window and hear, over and over again, that there is a curfew being placed over the whole city. No one is to leave their houses after darkness, on pain of death.

"Will we be safe tonight, do you think?" asks Maadah. "Can we leave the room once darkness falls?"

None of us are sure. On the one hand, perhaps the curfew means that our conquerors will leave us alone, so long as we obey their rule. On the other hand, perhaps they wish for all of us to be shuttered in our houses so that they may visit each house in turn, take what they want, rape and loot at will. Perhaps it is convenient for all of us to be immured within our walls. Perhaps they wish to burn us to death.

But night comes and the streets are silent. After much whispered debate, Aisha and I push open the shuttered window and look down into the street below, holding ourselves back a little, afraid of being seen. In the dark night, there is little light in which to see anything, but there is a dark shadow at the end of the street, holding a tall spear. It stays motionless, even when we watch it for some time, and at last we can only surmise that it is an Almoravid guard, that there are guards set all over the city tonight to ensure curfew is being respected. The open shutter allows in some fresh cold air, which all of us gulp in greedily, taking turns to stand close to the window, tiptoeing across the floor to exchange places.

The moon is fully high in the sky before we dare to leave the room. It takes all of us to lift the furniture fully off the ground before we can move it, to minimise the sounds we make. At last we edge the door open, creep out onto the balcony and look down into the courtyard below. There is no one there, the gate is still closed, as we left it. It seems that the curfew is indeed a peaceful one.

We tiptoe down the stairs, bare feet on cold tiles and creep into the kitchen, where we gulp cold water and share stale bread, dried dates, handfuls of nuts. We cram our fasting bellies with as much food as we can, not knowing what tomorrow will bring. We empty our waste, clean ourselves a little. We are free to sit in the courtyard of course, but we find ourselves retreating back to the room we have spent the past few days in, it feels like a place of safety. We pull blankets and rugs over ourselves and sleep fitfully, every little creak or too-loud snore jolting us awake in fear.

Dawn brings the sound we have not heard for three days, the call to prayer has been reinstated. We can only assume that the Almoravids have ordered the holy men of the city to take up their usual routines. The women pray and for once, I do not turn away or find something else to do. I kneel and clasp my hands, pray alongside them, only with my own words. I am not sure what to pray for, only that we be spared whatever harm the Almoravids intend to do to us.

Once again, loud voices from the street tell us that we are free to go about our daily business. The Almoravids now rule the city, we are told, but mean us no harm, if we treat them as our new masters. The night-time curfew will stay in place, otherwise, our lives may go on as they did before.

"As if we could go about our daily business as though nothing is happened," sniffs Maadah.

"We should at least eat and bathe," says Aisha, ever practical. "We cannot know what will happen from one day to the next. If we are safe within these walls, then let us make the most of it for now."

We spend the day in silence, as though I were back in the convent. There is nothing to say, nor anything much to do. We eat, we bathe, we sit in the quiet courtyard and listen, our ears ever ready for sound, our feet ever ready to run.

While there is still light, before the curfew takes place, I gesture to Aisha and point to the stairs leading to the roof. The others shake their heads, but she nods and together we climbed the stairs, reaching the rooftops step-by-step, crouched down in fear.

We are almost surprised to see the city's rooftops still there, as though nothing has happened. But that is not quite true. We can see a part of the city walls that is damaged, we can see fires here and there, sullen smoke still rising after the flames have been put out. The streets are too quiet, the odd animal wanders, lost without a master, harnesses trailing. We see two bodies, lying in the street at the back of the house, daggers still in hand and no one come to collect them, men too eager to protect their city when it was already too late to do so. I cross myself and utter words of blessing, wondering if they are any use to a Muslim, although Aisha nods at what I am doing and mutters some words of her own.

"You are safe then," comes a hiss.

We jump and clutch at each other, but it is only a woman from the next house, on the rooftop of her own house, barely a jump away.

"Thanks be to Allah, we are safe," says Aisha. "And you?"

The woman gives a quick nod. "My husband was fighting," she says. "But he escaped, came back here. Allah be praised."

"Has he been injured?" I ask.

"No, praise be," she says. "But he said it was terrible."

"What happened? asks Aisha.

"He said that they had barely left the city walls when the amir became confused, as though ill, that his sword arm grew weak. He fell almost at once. The generals soon afterwards, they lost their courage with Luqut gone. He said the Almoravids were like no army he has ever seen, and his father fought them last time, he saw them as a boy.

He said that they have changed beyond recognition. He said they arrange themselves into line upon line, stretching to the horizon. They beat their drums without stopping, hour after hour, day after day as the men advance. They do not stop, they do not break rank, they only advance, one step at a time, side-by-side, no gaps between them. He said the drums made our men feel dizzy and sick, that they could find no gap in the lines through which to attack. The Almoravids would not retreat, only advance so slowly it seemed imperceptible and then our soldiers found themselves backed up against the city walls and it was too late. They must die or submit. Many men died, until it became clear that the only thing left to do was surrender. The remaining nobles and officers laid down their weapons and told the men to do the same. My husband said he was filled with shame, but what else could he do? He knew he would not return to me and to his children if he did not. The nobles swore loyalty to Abu Bakr and ordered the city gates to be opened, so that the city might not be further damaged. The army was too terrible, there was no chance of winning, they were lucky to escape with only a third of the men killed. There will be families grieving all over Aghmat, but at least some men have been saved."

There is a heavy hammering at the outer gate, the sound we have been waiting for. We look to one another, even look to the woman as though we might leap to safety, from one rooftop to another, but it is too far for me, let alone Aisha.

"Hide," says the woman and retreats into the safety of her own house.

Aisha and I make our way back down the stairs, cautious, slow, before Aisha suddenly clutches my arm.

"It is the Master!" she says.

I stare at her, but her ears are better than mine, more accustomed to his voice, for she is right, I can hear him now.

"Open this accursed gate or I will have you all strangled!"

We run down the second flight of stairs, across the courtyard, pull back the gate to see the Master with six of his bodyguards, all of them pale with fear, pushing too hard to get through the tight gateway.

"I should have you all beaten," he blusters. "What is the meaning of this, barricading the gate against me, eh?"

"We were afraid of the Almoravids, Master," cringes Aisha, ducking out of the way of his flailing hands as he attempts to strike us. I am not so quick, he ends up half-smacking my cheek, a glancing blow that hardly satisfies him.

"Well close it again now we are in!" he yells at his bodyguards, who move quickly to do his bidding. I hear fear in the Master's voice now, feel it in his shouts and blows. He is unnerved by what has happened to this city in his absence, what it may mean for him, for his business, his family.

We women are commanded to bring water to wash, food at once, no matter that we have few supplies. Later his two sons arrive, slipping through the streets with hooded robes borrowed from servants rather than their usual finery.

We all, even the Master, peep from closed windows, watching the dark shadows patrolling the streets, tall men, their faces fully veiled, long spears and vast shields held at their sides. We hear the clatter of horses' hooves and brace ourselves for what is to come.

The Master, and no doubt others from amongst the richest merchants, have been summoned to visit the amir's palace, now the stronghold of our conquerors. He sets out alone, without the safety and comfort of his bodyguards. We wait for his return.

He returns shaking, his usual arrogant demeanour broken. It seems the conquerors have stripped the palace of its decorations and finery. We huddle in the corners of the courtyard and staircases, eavesdrop on him speaking with his sons.

"They claim to disdain luxury," he says. "Their leader looks like a common soldier. You would not be able to tell him from his men."

"What did they want with you?" asks one of his sons.

"They want gold," says the Master, shoulders drooping. "They want more gold than can be imagined."

"For what?"

"For men, for armour, for horses. For a kingdom. They intend to control all the trade routes; they will tax us to get what they need."

The three men sit in silence for a while, digesting the news, trying to foresee their future in all of this. On the one hand, as merchants, their trade is needed. On the other hand, there is a risk that they will be taxed so harshly that their trading will barely be worthwhile. They cannot tell yet, they can only wait and discover how these, their new masters, will treat them. They are cowed by the news, wary of their futures, afraid to put a foot wrong, not knowing how this new regime will treat any failure to comply. I have never seen the Master so shrunken, so defeated.

The hammering we were afraid of comes again and this time at night. The Master is dragged from his bed by the dark-robed men, spluttering and cursing them as he goes, leaving us alone, untouched, the house unstripped of its goods. It seems he tried to hide the extent of his wealth from our new rulers, that he did not pay what was promised and they, in turn, have shown that they will not be defied. We are uncertain whether he has been killed, but it seems likely when he does not return. Our household falls empty and silent. We wait to know our fate, expecting one of his sons to take his place, to command us. But they do not come. Eventually we hear whispers that they, too, defied the Almoravids and paid the price.

We stay indoors for several more days, too afraid to venture out, too afraid to believe the Almoravids when they say the citizens of Aghmat should go about our business. The fountain brings water to the house, so that we may drink and bathe, the kitchen has enough dried foodstuffs that we can eat, albeit plain fare. None of us desires fresh fruit and vegetables enough to risk going into the unknown new world outside our gate.

The rooftops become our source of knowledge, of gossip, rumours and whispers. The men and women of the city gather on the rooftops before the curfew comes each day, exchanging sources of knowledge which may or may not be true.

The new regime allows us to leave the house by day, although the curfew by night still stands. At last the day comes when Aisha and I must leave the house, for we are without food and no one else in the household dares to venture out. We wrap ourselves in winter cloaks, as though the heavy cloth might somehow protect us. Clutching a basket, we creep out of the main gate and into the narrow street. There should be children running, the clip clop of mules and donkeys, the huffing of camels. But the city is quiet, our neighbours still afraid to venture out if they can avoid it.

"Let's go back," begs Aisha.

"We need food," I remind her. "And we are allowed to go to market, so long as we do not defy the curfew." Even so, I hold her hand tightly in mine as we come to the end of our street and make our way onto the wider road that leads to the market.

There are people about, here and there, although they walk quickly and quietly. The men do not look about them, the women walk with their heads down. No one chatters or stops to greet one another. They go about their business quickly. Not all the market stalls that should be open are trading, only a few, here and there, those of which people have most need. There is a stall selling vegetables and we make our way there and, in half whispers, make our purchases, not even daring to gossip. Next to them is a dried goods stall, and we purchase dried fruit, lentils, chickpeas. I find myself buying more than is necessary, more than we would usually buy, so that we will not need to venture out again in a hurry. There is no meat for sale today, no spices, nor fresh cheese and butter. We will have to make do without.

We turn to leave and suddenly see our first Almoravid up close. A tall man, wrapped in a long dark cloak, a spear in one hand, a sword at his belt. His face is fully veiled, I can see only his eyes, and only his eyes follow our movement. He does not move, only watches as we pass and then turns his attention back to the rest of the market square, no doubt searching for any signs of unrest. But this is a cowed city, a city that has recognised its defeat. The days pass and there is no sign of disobedience, no sign of reprisals. The merchants who escaped punishments pay the heavy taxes demanded of them and are grateful they are not higher. The people begin to go out and about again, quietly at first and then more boldly, until the city chatters again and it is as though nothing had ever happened.

But there are stories emerging, which Aisha, of course, quickly finds out about.

"Queen Zaynab is to marry Abu Bakr!" she says.

Maadah stops what she's doing, and all the women gather together to relish this gossip.

"Is this one of your nonsense stories, again, Aisha?" I ask.

"It is the truth!" she says. "May Allah strike me down if it is not true!"

"She is marrying him?" I say.

"Yes! They say that she met with him, and took him, blindfolded – "

"Aisha," I say warningly.

"I swear! She took him blindfolded to a secret place, where she showed him untold riches. Gems and gold beyond counting. 'All this is yours,' she told him, and now they are to be married. She will be the queen of the Almoravids. And they wish to create a new city."

"Not very loyal," comments Maadah.

I think of the only time I have seen Queen Zaynab, how beautiful she was, but also how unhappy she looked. I am not sure that she felt much loyalty towards Luqut, who took her from her first husband when she was still a young bride. Perhaps she hopes for a better marriage with Abu Bakr. Perhaps showing him whatever riches Luqut had in his treasury is her way of securing her future.

Aisha's news is proven to be correct. Zaynab marries Abu Bakr with great pomp and ceremony and the people of our city repeat again the story of her vision, that she would marry the man who would rule the Maghreb.

"Her vision has come true. It was foretold that she would be wife to the man who would rule all of the Maghreb."

"It was not Luqut's destiny to rule. It was the Almoravids, her vision is coming true at last."

"How ridiculous," I say, when I hear this. "Did her vision require her to marry three times before it came true?"

"It was foretold," says the stallholder, speaking with conviction while weighing out barley.

I roll my eyes. I do not believe in Zaynab's so-called vision, it seems too convenient to me. Too much like convincing a conquering warlord to spare her life and treat her with dignity rather than take her as a common prisoner of war or indeed simply end her life. She has protected herself by creating a legend.

A young girl, her hand sought by so many. Who chose to travel across the Maghreb, far, far away from her home and her family, to her first husband. A woman who had a great vision and was demanded as queen by the Amir of Aghmat. Whose city was destroyed and yet who cast a spell over the commander of the conquering army, showing him riches such as are only dreamed of in this life. Made queen again from the rubble of a ruined city, lifted once again to greatness. Her vision coming true at last as the army prepares for domination.

The people begin to think that perhaps their amir's fall was destined, that Allah always meant for the Almoravids to take over this city, that he guided them to this place, to marry their queen, and fulfil her holy vision. No doubt this idea is welcomed and encouraged by the Almoravids. I do not know what to think. But I give thanks to God that this army has not yet brought harm to myself and the other women of our household, as we once feared. We are not sure how long we will be left alone in this household, or even if the small amount of money we have will last us more than a month or two, but for now, at least, what we were afraid of has not befallen us.

A new piety sweeps the city. The people dress with more sobriety, dance and flirt less, sacrifice more animals and say their prayers with renewed conviction. It is a way to survive, I suppose, to believe that what has happened, the suffering caused by losing so many men of the city, was intended. That Aghmat, rather than being humiliated, is part of a grander plan, one approved by Allah, who has guided the Almoravids this far. The people choose to believe this. The metalworkers set to making new weapons, the merchants feed and clothe their conquerors, although the Almoravids take little pleasure in the riches and comforts that a city like this one might offer them. They seem to disdain the luxuries of the world to a degree that surprises. We hear that every room of the palace has been stripped bare, that generals and common foot soldiers alike lie on the bare floors, wrapped in coarse blankets to sleep, that the servants grow idle, not called upon to provide rich foods and sweet drinks, massages and bathing that were required by the former amir. Now they need only bake bread and roast plain meets, serve dried dates without adornment and pour cold water to drink. I wonder whether Queen Zaynab approves this new austerity in her life, or whether she is still served as she once was.

Perhaps for the first time since I came here, our household relaxes. The conquerors have shown no interest in us. The Master and his sons, who made all of us nervous, are gone. Apparently, we have been forgotten. We eat, we pray, we sleep. We clean the house and ourselves, we speak of small matters. I gather leaves and roots from the plants in the courtyard and make remedies for such minor ailments as afflict us or our neighbours, which we barter for vegetables and grains to eke out our food stores, which are running low.

I begin to think that I have somehow found myself in a new convent, peopled with this strange array of women collected by our late master. I wonder, even, if I might convert them, if somehow this household might become a nunnery, under my guidance. It seems unlikely, for all of them cling to their own faith, as I do to mine and who could imagine a nunnery here of all places? And yet the rhythm of the day seems familiar to me, and it brings me an unexpected peace. There are days when I hope this time will last for ever, that no one will come to disturb this fragile peace we have somehow made between us in this uncertain time.

But it seems God has other plans for me.

I am watering the plants in the courtyard, squatting down to remove dead flowers and leaves, touching the earth in each pot to see if it is dry or damp, when a shadow falls over me. I look up, expecting Maadah or some other known person and find myself at the feet of an Almoravid soldier. I freeze, waiting for a blow or worse, but the man only stands there, looking down on me.

"Stand," he says. His voice is calm, unhurried, unconcerned.

I let go of the pot of water and slowly, slowly stand before him, his dark eyes staying steady on mine. We are very close, there is less than a hand's breadth between us. I wait. To be grabbed, to be forced in some way.

But instead he takes a step backwards, away from me, as though he, too, finds the closeness disconcerting, although his eyes do not leave mine. "You are a member of this household?" he asks.

"Yes," I say. I do not say anything more. When it

becomes clear that I am not about to speak again without prompting, he speaks.

"You are a slave?"

"Yes," I say.

"How many others are here?"

I tell him. He nods.

"Gather them."

I step away from him and walk slowly away, aware of having my back to him, of not knowing what he's doing when I cannot see him. I make my way to the kitchen, and whisper to Maadah. Her face drains white. One by one, we gather together the other women and make our way back into the courtyard.

The Almoravid is standing where I left him, he has barely moved. We stand before him, leaving a fearful distance between us.

"Are you all women here?" he asks.

I nod.

"I am Yusuf bin Tashfin," he says. "I will be your new master and you will be my new household."

Nobody speaks. We stand in silence.

"Show me to a bedroom," he says. "And bring me water and bread."

Maadah finds her voice first. "I am the cook here. Shall I make a meal, Master?" she asks, her voice a little shaky.

He shakes his head. "Just water and bread," he repeats.

She nods, and scuttles away, followed by the rest of the household, none of whom wish to lead this man, our new master, anywhere.

"You," he says, addressing me.

"Yes, Master," I say.

"A bedroom," he says.

I turn my back on him and walk away, hear his footsteps behind me across the courtyard and up the stairs, trying not to tremble at the thought that, once we reach a bedroom, he may well choose to have his sport with me. I wonder which room to take him to, but decide that, if he is our new master, then he must be taken to the master's bedchamber. I open the door, and step back, hoping he will not drag me in with him. But he only walks through the doorway and looks around the room. "Very well," he says. "You may bring me the bread and water when it is ready."

"Yes, Master," I say, quickly shutting the door and running down the stairs to the relative safety of the kitchen. The other women are huddled there, their faces afraid.

Maadah's hands shake when she passes me the tray to carry upstairs. "Be careful," she says.

I nod and take the tray.

"He is their second in command," breathes Aisha. "Why would he come alone?"

I stop halfway to the door. "What do you mean," I ask, "their second-in-command?"

"Yusuf bin Tashfin," she says, repeating the name he gave. "He is Abu Bakr's second-in-command."

"He can't be," I object. "Why would he not have men with him?" I think of our amir and his nobles, even our late Master, how they would go nowhere without an entourage of guards, lesser nobles, bodyguards, servants, slaves.

"Never mind that now," hisses Maadah. "Take that food up to him." The tray she has given me contains fresh-baked bread from this morning, cool water in a jug with a cup ready to fill, dates and slices of fresh orange, as well as little cakes.

"He didn't ask for all this," I say.

"If he is our new master," says Maadah, "then it's our business to please him. And the way to please a man is to fill his belly."

I shake my head and hurry away from her, across the courtyard and back up the stairs, until I reach his door. I want to leave the tray here, do not want to face him again, but I know that I must. I tap gently on the door.

"Come," I hear.

Tentatively, I open the door.

In the brief time I have been gone, he has managed to transform the room. He has removed the silken drapes, the bright blankets, decorative objects. The bed has been stripped bare, only a yellow blanket remains, the plainest of them all, woven in wool. The rest of the room's hangings and covers have been piled in a corner, as though they were rags for washing. His sword has been left on the floor beside the bed, where he now lies, a dark figure in this light room.

"You may leave the food there," he says, indicating the low table by the bed.

I do so. He looks at the tray, eyebrows raised. "You may tell the cook that when I ask for bread and water, I mean bread and water," he says. He sounds amused. "There is no need to try and impress me," he adds. "Only to obey me."

I nod my head in silence. I stand, waiting for further orders, while he props himself up on one arm and pours himself a cup of water, which he drinks quickly, then fills again.

"You needn't hover there," he tells me. "I will call for you if I want something. I need to sleep."

I move towards the door.

"Wait," he says.

I stop.

"What is your name?" he asks.

I hesitate. "Kamra," I say at last.

His eyes travel over me, from my crooked leg and the limp he has already seen, up to my face and the scars it bears. "Kamra? Where are you from?"

"Galicia," I say.

He frowns. "Kamra is not a Galician name. What was your name before you were taken as a slave?"

I do not speak. Am I to give this man the name I was born with? Or the name I took as a nun? Neither seems right, neither seems suited to this world in which I find myself. "You may call me whatever you wish," I say.

"Stubbornness is not usually a desirable trait in a slave," he says. There is something teasing about his tone, as though he finds this conversation amusing. It raises my hackles.

"You may call me whatever you wish," I say again.

He nods, but still does not use any name. "You may go now," he says.

Now a new life begins for all of us. We are relieved not to have been left destitute and certainly now we are protected, but we struggle to adapt to his ways, at first. Our new master eats bread and water, a little meat. He sleeps like the dead, I can hear him softly snoring sometimes, if I pass by his bedchamber. He has the house stripped bare of all superfluous decorations, telling me, when I ask what to do with them, to give them to the poor, the needy. I stand, with my hands full of silks and precious trinkets and stare at him.

"There are no poor and needy in Aghmat?" he asks me, amused again.

"Every city has poor and needy people," I say.

"Then seek them out," he says and turns away, wrapping the yellow blanket about him and preparing to sleep.

Somehow, I become his personal servant. It is to me he gives his orders, barely speaking to the rest of the household. It is I who have to repeat his commands to Maadah, who feels underused, to the other women, who regard me with uncertainty at first, as though I am making up the odd orders he gives. Sometimes he does not even sleep in his bedchamber. I find him in the courtyard, in the early hours, saying the dawn prayers. He kneels amidst my plant pots, a rough mat on the tiled floor beneath him. The first time I see him like this, I stand silently watching him. It takes me a little while to think who he reminds me of and when I realise, I shake my head. Surely, I am mistaken. He reminds me of the Mother Superior in the convent, so long ago, in my other life. She had a way of praying that seemed truly holy, as though she could hear God's voice speaking to her while she was on her knees, her eyes uplifted, her face filled with a kind of joy. It seems strange to see the same joy in the face of a man, a Muslim, a heathen praying to a god who does not exist. The strangeness of it draws me somehow, and from then on when I see him at prayer, I pause to watch him, hidden in the shadows. I do not think he sees me, until the morning when he addresses me as he stands.

"You do not pray?" he asks me, without turning his head towards me, near the kitchen doorway.

I am silent for a moment, before I realise that he has indeed seen me, and is speaking to me. "No," I say.

"Why not?"

"I am a Christian," I say stiffly.

"He turns to look at me more directly. "Even Christians pray," he says.

"I pray in my room," I say.

"You could convert," he says.

I am so shocked I do not say anything, and he suddenly laughs out loud, the first time I've heard him do so. "I see your faith is more important to you than I thought," he says. "I meant no disrespect."

I say nothing.

"My apologies," he says again, more seriously. "You are a woman of faith, then?"

"I am a nun," I tell him.

He looks up, his hands busy making the mat into a neat roll. "You are a slave," he reminds me.

"I am a nun," I repeat. "I have not renounced my vows."

"How did a nun end up as a slave in Aghmat?" he asks, stepping closer to me.

"The Norsemen took me," I say.

"From a holy place?" he asks, frowning.

I shake my head. "I was on a journey," I say.

"Alone?"

I shake my head. I am not about to describe what happened to me, to us, to this man.

He nods, grave now. "I am sorry," he says simply,

handing me the mat to be put away. Then he turns and leaves, the gate closing behind him.

Aisha has more news. I swear the girl is nothing but a gossip sometimes. Although I have to admit her gossip often brings us valuable information.

"We are to leave Aghmat," she says.

"Leave?"

"Yes. The Almoravids want to build a new capital city. It is to be on the plain and they will call it *Murakush*, land of God."

"But there's nothing there," objects Maadah. "Where are we to live?"

"Tents," says Aisha.

"Tents?" echoes Maadah. "Don't be ridiculous, girl."

"Well they don't care, do they?" says Aisha. "Look at the Master, sleeping on the floor in the courtyard when he could be in a silken bed."

"I'm not living in a tent, and that's an end to it," says Maadah.

But we find out soon enough that Aisha is right. A new city is to be built, a fortified garrison city, where the army will be based. But a city cannot be built without food, water, labourers, and their families.

"Gather the household," Yusuf says to me. When we are all grouped before him in the courtyard, he looks at our expectant faces. "Aghmat is finished as a city," he says. "It will become smaller and less important once Murakush is built. Henceforth I will need only two slaves to serve me." His finger briefly indicates Aisha and me. "The rest of you will be given to new masters." He looks at the other women's worried faces. "I will choose your new masters myself," he adds. "And I will do so with care."

The women choose to stay in Aghmat. By now it is their city. They cannot believe that its glory will fade as Yusuf suggests. They cannot ally themselves to this invisible city, this *Murakush* that exists in name only, as a thought, an idea. They need walls and streets, they need the stalls of the traders they have frequented, they need one another. Yusuf tells us that this house, and the women, will be given to an older officer in his army, one who wishes to take up a quieter administrative position in charge of Aghmat, while the army continues on its way to greater conquests. "He is a good man," he says. "He will treat you well. He has a wife and family; he is not one to mistreat nor take advantage of his slaves."

He surprises us by setting Maadah free.

"I think perhaps you have served as a slave long enough," he says, looking at her wrinkled face. "I have agreed a paid position for you here, as a cook. I am sure your cooking is better than I have allowed it to be."

She kneels at his feet and blesses him, promises to pray for him and for his glory in coming battles.

"So, I am left with only two slaves," he says, looking at Aisha and me. "I daresay that will be enough. I am a man of few needs."

The two of us stare at each other, wondering what our new life will be like.

The army is sent ahead, Aisha and I are told to join Yusuf in a few days' time. In the meantime, we are charged with clearing the house, giving anything not yet donated to the poor to them now. The officer will bring his own family goods to fill the house, we are told.

"What do we do with your plants?" asks Aisha.

"I don't know," I confess. I hate to leave them behind, but I am a slave, they are not mine. It is not for me to request that they come with us, to a strange and rough new life.

But Aisha is bolder. She goes to Yusuf and tells him, rather than asks him, that I must keep my herbs, that they are important.

"I told him he may well have need of a slave who is also a healer," she says to me, her face beaming when he gives permission to take the plants with us, and gives her coins so that she can hire a man and his beasts to carry them. "He says it is your business to find water for them, the new city will not have a proper irrigation system for a long time," she adds. "He says you may have to work hard to carry enough for them."

We all cry when it is time to leave. Maadah, Dalia, Ranya, Faiza and Nilah stand in the narrow street, watching as Aisha and I climb awkwardly onto two old mules, followed by several more loaded down with crates of plants. Their owner looks surprised at the cargo he is to carry, but he knows we serve the second-in command of the new rulers and so he only nods brusquely, clicks his tongue to start the beasts walking, ignoring our endless waving and last words called out to one another.

When we reach the plain after a jolting ride, I forget to dismount, astonished at the sight before us. It is a city of tents, laid out as though around a central square, with streets marked out between them. There are huge tents, fit for a large family, there are smaller tents. Then there are tents so tiny they seem to be made of nothing more than a blanket and some poles. All around the edge of this cloth city are soldiers, currently engaged in digging, building, carrying, lifting. Water must be brought from nearby, there must be places to relieve ourselves, there must be firmly trodden paths so that traders may visit this sudden city that has appeared almost overnight. No trader worth the name would miss the opportunity to serve such an army.

I had never realised the true scale of Yusuf's troops, there are thousands, tens of thousands of men of every hue and size, both battle-scarred and still fresh, creating this new garrison camp for their leaders to call home.

"Come," Aisha exhorts me. "We must find Yusuf's tent."

I could have described his tent before even seeing it, it is as plain as he is. A dirty brown in colour, ragged at the edges, yet large enough to comfortably hold the three of us. I hesitate a little at the idea that we will sleep so close to him, fearing perhaps that his demeanour so far may not hold true for ever. But I swallow my fears, unpack the plants, which I place around the borders of the tent's outer walls as though creating a tiny garden in circular form, and busy myself, with Aisha's help, in making the interior comfortable. We find a source of water, order large water jars to keep our supply cool, create a little campfire outside where we can cook evening meals. We have brought some basic provisions, but we will need to find traders. We walk around the camp, finding our way in this new home.

There are people here from all over the Maghreb and beyond. I see men and women with hair the colour of the yellow Norsemen, who make me nervous despite myself. I see men with skin so black they all but disappear into their black robes. I even see a woman with hair like fire, who knows full well the value of her scarcity. She has decked herself out with cheap jewellery and robes which leave nothing to be imagined. I turn my face away.

It turns out to be easy enough to find stallholders, even if their stalls are no longer as elaborate or permanent as they might have been in Aghmat. Here, they make do with displaying their goods in woven baskets on the ground, squatting beside them in the open space at the centre of the tents. It does not take long for vendors of food to arrive when there is an army to feed. There is need of grain, legumes, meat, vegetables and fruit. Yusuf has been generous with the money we are given to care for him, considering how basic his own tastes are. We buy what we have need of and carry it back towards his tent.

In the centre of the camp, not far away from Yusuf's, stands a tent like no other. Larger than any family tent, it looks newly made and is black, a deep strong black. It towers over the other tents, a tall man could stand within it and keep his head high, indeed, raise his arms above his head.

"Queen Zaynab's tent," whispers Aisha as we pass it. "She had it built specially."

"Why does she not share Abu Bakr's tent?" I ask.

Aisha shrugs. "He is used to a rough life," she says. "She is used to a palace."

I wonder if we will see her, but the only person standing nearby is an older woman, with dark eyes, who watches us pass, her gaze lingering on the plants around Yusuf's tent.

"Who is she?" I ask.

"Hela," whispers Aisha. "Queen Zaynab's handmaiden."

"Why is she staring at the plants?"

"They say she is a healer," says Aisha. "Like you. Perhaps you could work together."

We have reached Yusuf's tent with our purchases. "I doubt it," I say, looking back at the woman's dark eyes, her unsmiling face even when she meets my eye. "Besides, I am not a healer. I am a slave."

I begin to wish I was indeed able to practice as a healer, for Yusuf certainly does not keep us busy enough. He has no need of two slaves, for he barely eats anything requiring much work. We bake flatbreads and sometimes roast a little meat; he will eat a few dates or nuts and consider it a meal. He drinks water, there is no need to prepare fresh juices. Aisha and I eat well enough, indeed sometimes I think we eat better than our master. We keep the tent clean and fresh; we wash his clothes when he gives them to us, we water the plants and watch the world go by.

But after a little while a change comes over Aisha. She spends time on the outer edges of the city of tents, watching the soldiers practice their war skills. She dresses with more care; she offers to do all the purchases from the market. At last I ask her what is going on and she confesses.

"He is such a man," she breathes. "So kind. So strong. He says he will buy my freedom."

I think that Yusuf will refuse, but to my amazement it turns out that Aisha has caught the eye of one of his bodyguards, a special troop of men, all from the Dark Kingdom, chosen to match one another in height and breadth, in their black skin. Deliberately clad in matching armour, they make a fearsome force around Yusuf when he is in battle. Imari is a man who would dwarf a woman twice Aisha's height. When Yusuf hears of his desire to marry Aisha, he gives Aisha her freedom as a wedding gift. Suddenly she is a free woman with a husband, all within a few days. I gather herbs for her, herbs that will bring her the child that she so dearly wishes for and tell her how to prepare them. I embrace her and watch her as she says her vows, as she is promised to this man forever.

"I am going nowhere, though," she tells me. "Else how will you know all the camp gossip?"

"It is a sin to gossip," I say. "But I will miss you."

"You will see me every day," she promises and she is true enough to her word, not a day passes but she comes to see me, even if only briefly, and I am glad not to have lost her altogether, I have come to think of her as a good friend.

"I am not sure there is a need for another slave," says Yusuf to me after a few days. He has finished his evening prayers and is sharpening his sword, sat on his blankets on the floor of the tent. He still does not wish for a bed. "I have you, you are enough."

I am not sure how to answer. I am uncertain of

properness surrounding the two of us sharing this tent, alone together. I only bow my head in agreement with his decision and wait to see what will happen.

What happens is nothing, at first. Things go on as they did before. But slowly a new intimacy grows between us. Where before, Aisha and I would sit together sewing, weaving, cooking or only speaking together, now I am alone and Yusuf begins to talk to me, in the evenings.

"Tell me about the convent you lived in," he says one evening.

I stiffen a little. I cannot imagine what a Muslim would want to know about living in a convent. I mention a few of the prayers, the readings that our Mother Superior would relate during evening mealtimes, but he waves this aside.

"I mean daily life," he says.

And so instead I talk of the sparrows who nested in a crumbling wall in the garden, the herbs I planted and cared for. The cool stillroom where I prepared and stored remedies, the pilgrims who came and went and the stories they told us of the outside world. I tell him about Sister Rosa, the wheezing old nun who taught me everything I know and who died in my arms, all the remedies she had taught me useless at that last moment. How she looked at me and smiled, as I busily ground some new attempt at a cure, how she reached out from her bed and took my hand away from the pestle and told me that it was time to stop, that she was ready to leave. I feel my voice grow choked as I describe this and stop speaking.

"She was right," he says, keeping his eyes steady on

me. "There is a time to stay and fight, and there is a time to leave. And it is Allah Himself who must tell us which is which, for we are not always wise enough to know for ourselves."

I nod and wait for my eyes to clear. "My name was Sister Juliana in the convent," I tell him.

"And before that? As a child?"

I hesitate, then speak my Christian name, the name my mother and father gave me. "Isabella."

He nods gravely at what I have shared.

"Tell me more," he says. "Tell me of happy times."

I tell him of spring, the plants leaping back into life, of summer, when the cool chapel walls were a blessing sheltering us from the heat of the day. Of autumn, when we gave thanks for a good harvest and kept our hands busy with preserving. And harsh winters, when we were warmed by the sense of sisterhood, of community.

He begins to tell me things about himself. He tells me of his life as a child, roaming the sweeping desert dunes far to the south. He tells me of joining forces with his cousin Abu Bakr and their realisation of what might be, when they succeeded where others had failed and took Aghmat.

"You do not have a wife?" I ask, wondering at my boldness in asking.

"I do," he says, chuckling as though this is an amusement to him.

"Where is she?" I ask.

"On the other side of the mountains," he says. "She will come here soon enough, but I would want a more comfortable life ready for her. She is very young, and I was afraid to bring her with me whilst there was a chance that

I would fall in battle. I would not want anything bad to happen to her."

"Who is she?" I ask, surprised by him describing a young woman.

"A runaway," he says, chuckling again. "A girl from my own people, who lived a strange life as a child, dressed as a boy of all things, trading along the routes with her father and brothers. They tried to make her settle down and learn women's skills, but she would have none of it. She dressed as a man again and followed my army."

I stare at him. "How did you find out?"

He laughs out loud at the memory. "Oh, I saw her at once. I waited to see how long she would follow us, but when she'd been with us a whole day and night, I had to find out why."

"Was she badly treated at home?"

"No, she was treated well enough. But she had a spirit for adventure that could not be contained." He looks away, thinking about her, his eyes warm at the thought. "I liked her spirit; I liked her desire for adventure. And I thought she would be safer with me than if she ran away again alone. I thought she might make a good wife when we founded a new kingdom. I married her then and there."

I try to reconcile this severe leader with a man who finds a runaway girl amusing and takes her as a bride without further thought. "When will she come?" I ask, thinking that it will be strange to have a mistress instead of just a master.

"I will wait a little longer to send for her," he says. "There is much to do here, and I want to be able to give her some attention when she does arrive."

I want to ask what will become of me when she arrives, but I assume that I will be given a little tent close by and will serve both of them. I wonder what she will be like, this woman from his tribal lands, this wayward adventurer who sought out a life of war and travel, of excitement, when I tried so hard to avoid such things, safe in my convent. And yet somehow, we will have arrived in the same place, at the same time, finding ourselves living in a city of cloth that will one day turn into a city of towering rooftops, if Yusuf and Abu Bakr have their way.

City of Cloth

The flowers appear on the earth…

Song of Solomon 2:12

*T*HE CAMP CONTINUES TO GROW, as more soldiers join the army and their families, if they have them, follow them. More and more tents continue to be erected, on the outskirts of the tents already here. This strange cloth city grows day by day.

"I think you must be bored," says Yusuf to me one night.

"Why do you say that?" I ask.

"Your garden of plants is growing," he says. "It is almost a field."

"Does it bother you?" I ask.

"Not at all, why should it?" he asks. "They are useful, both for our meals," he gestures at the food I have laid out, rich with herbs and seasonings, "and for healing, in battle. One never knows when one may need such skills."

"Do you wish me to move them?"

"I think perhaps you need a bigger space," he says, still eating.

"We would not use all the herbs I could grow in a larger space," I say.

"You may sell them, if you wish," he says. "This is still a new city, there is need for fresh grown food."

"Sell them?"

He shrugs. "You may keep the money," he says. "Use it as you wish," he adds.

I stare at him, but he is drinking a cup of water, and then he leaves me, muttering something about needing to speak with Abu Bakr.

I take him at his word. I find a small piece of land on the outskirts of the camp and claim it for my own, murmuring Yusuf's name to the only person who queries what I am doing. It has an immediate effect. I move many of my plants to the space and let them grow more vigorously, especially the mint, which grows wild and rampant, popping up here and there where least expected in vibrant clumps. Even though I must haul water to keep the plants green, I grow so fond of my little garden that sometimes I forget the passing of time and have to run back to Yusuf's tent to prepare a meal. The plants grow well and soon I can make up little bunches of parsley, coriander, sage, cumin, fennel tops and other herbs and vegetables. Yusuf was right, the people of our cloth city long for freshness. The traders come often but they bring food that can be stored, not the bright green tendrils that bring flavour and freshness to a dish. The women reach out eagerly for what I can give them, and my bundles of herbs are used up every day well before the midday sun strikes. With the first coins I begin to accumulate, I buy a hoe, so that I can work the ground more easily. The rest of the money, I put into a little stitched bag, kept under my blanket. I do not know what it is for, yet, whether I might one day be able to buy my freedom, or whether that will never be allowed. Aisha comes to watch me at work sometimes, helps me to thin out seedlings. One day she tells me, her smile lighting up her face, that she is with child. I embrace her, truly happy for my friend.

Occasionally I see a beggar woman making her way around the camp, her feet bare, her long dark hair dirty and lank. Despite her appearance, I think she is still young, perhaps barely twenty. Sometimes she is given a little work to do by a trader or one of the women, perhaps carrying water or washing clothes and I see that she does it well, she is a hard worker but somehow has found herself here, lost and alone, with no one to protect her. I notice she has no shoes and give her a coin so that she can buy simple shoes to protect her feet from the rough ground.

"May God bless you," she says.

Her accent is odd. "What is your name?" I ask.

"Rebecca," she says.

"Are you a Christian?" I ask.

She shakes her head.

"A Jew?" I ask, a little disappointed.

"I was born and raised Jewish, in Al-Andalus," she says, looking away. "But I fell in love with a Muslim when I was very young, and my family disowned me when we married. I was his second wife and his first wife hated me. When my husband died, she threw me out of the house and my family would not take me back, they said I was dead to them." She swallows. "I offered myself as a slave, for I had no way to make a living. Then my master sold me to a man in the Maghreb and I ended up here. He died, so I suppose I am free, but still, I have no way to make a living. The camp allows me to scrape by, there is always someone who needs willing hands."

I nod. Once I might have turned away, knowing her for a Jewess, but she has been turned away from often enough already in her young life. There can be no harm in showing her a little charity, I decide. I give her the odd bunch of herbs or greens and she always thanks and blesses me. The law states a Jew cannot live in the city, they may trade here but must sleep beyond the city walls, so those Jews who do trade here often live at a little distance from Murakush and travel here each day to work. Rebecca, I find out, sleeps just beyond the encampment.

The tent flaps are yanked aside so hard that I hear one of them rip at the top. I look up in consternation, as Yusuf storms into the tent. He does not sit down in his usual place, only stands, fuming, in the middle of the tent. I had been seated, sewing. Now I am uncertain whether to stand or not, he looks so angry that I am a little afraid to come any closer to him. Staying low to the ground seems safer.

"Is all well?" I venture, finally.

"No," he snaps.

He does not offer anything else and I do not enquire further. I have never seen him so angry, he has never been so abrupt with me. I continue my work, keeping a cautious eye on him, my stitches growing erratic with my lack of attention. Some time goes by before I dare to look up at him directly again. He's still standing, staring at the tent walls, what I can see of his face somewhat flushed, his brows lowered.

"Tea," he orders, in a manner he has never spoken to me before.

I stand, see to the fire outside, bring water to the boil and make tea. When I return, a cup in my hands, he is now seated, arms wrapped around his knees, his brows lowered. He takes the tea without a word of thanks and I retreat to my place and my sewing.

"It is madness!" he suddenly exclaims, startling me a little, for I had expected him to remain quiet.

"What is?" I venture carefully.

"Abu Bakr has decided to quell the rebels in the south himself, instead of sending one of the generals. It is absurd and unnecessary!"

I nod, not daring to speak. Then I think that he requires more comfort than this. "It does seem strange," I say. "Surely there is no need for him to go himself?"

"Exactly! It is madness!"

He goes back to brooding for a while and I continue sewing, unpicking most of the stitches I have made since he entered the tent and starting again. Although Yusuf is right, in that it seems odd that Abu Bakr himself should need to go to the south to quell what is, by all accounts, a fairly minor rebellion, I cannot help but wonder why Yusuf is so angry about it. Perhaps he wished to go himself, though I have never heard him talk about any interest in going south. His focus always seems to be on conquering more of the Maghreb rather than any southern kingdoms. "Did you wish to go yourself?" I ask, finally.

"Of course not! Neither of us should go. An officer can go, a minor general. There is no need to take such a step."

"And he will not listen to reason?" I ask.

"Oh, he has lost his mind," spits Yusuf. "There is no reasoning with him."

I am surprised at both his insulting tone and words. Yusuf is usually very loyal to Abu Bakr; he speaks of him only in the highest tones of praise and respect. For some reason, this choice by Abu Bakr has riled him.

"And who is to manage the army while he is gone?" I ask finally, wondering if perhaps Abu Bakr has gone so far as to overlook Yusuf and give this role to a more minor general, which would certainly explain Yusuf's current behaviour, although it seems a very unlikely proposition: Yusuf is known to all as Abu Bakr's right-hand man, he would be the only possible choice of leader in Abu Bakr's absence.

"I am, of course," says Yusuf. There is a pause. "With the she-bitch at my side," he adds in a half mutter.

"What?" I think I have misheard him, it is not like Yusuf to speak disrespectfully of a woman and besides I have no idea who he is talking about.

"Abu Bakr, in his infinite wisdom, has decided to divorce Zaynab."

I stare at him.

"And he wishes me to marry her."

It takes me a while to find my voice. "But – but you have a wife," I manage at last.

He shrugs. "He wishes me to take another. Zaynab. Of all people."

"Why?"

"He says Zaynab is not fit for a rough life in tents in the middle of the desert."

"But she has been living in a tent all this time," I object weakly. "And she does not complain of it, does she?"

"How would I know what she complains of? She is not my wife. Yet," he adds grimly.

"But your first wife…"

He gestures impatiently. "That is not the issue. I may take more than one wife. And Kella will just have to accept it when she arrives. That is not the point. I would never have chosen Zaynab. Never. She is untrustworthy."

"I thought she pleased Abu Bakr," I say. "I heard she was allowed to sit in Council, that she had knowledge of the Maghreb, of the politics between the tribes."

"Abu Bakr killed her husband," snarls Yusuf. "Who is not to say she is biding her time, tricking us, waiting for Abu Bakr to trust her and then follow her lead into a trap?"

I think of her face, riding alongside her husband the amir, the sadness in it, the unhappiness. "Did she love Luqut?" I ask.

"How should I know? All I know is, our army defeated his, she was taken as a prisoner of war, and then managed to worm her way into marrying Abu Bakr, thus becoming our queen. I don't trust her. She is like a cat, landing on her feet after a fall."

I realise something about myself, something which I can only regard as a sin. That I am pleased that Yusuf does not wish to marry Zaynab, when whether he marries or not should be of no regard to me. I am finding myself pleased that he does not desire her, that he does not love her. I am pleased that he is reluctant to take her as a wife, that he has so far not even summoned his first wife. I know that this is a sin on my part, that there is something in me that wishes Yusuf to remain, to all intents and purposes, unwed. That for now, for these past months, I have been the only woman in his life, in his tent, by his bed. I have enjoyed the intimacy of our evening conversations. I bow my head to my sewing, resolving to no longer take part in this conversation, to pray on my sins and ask for God's forgiveness later, when Yusuf is gone. We sit in silence for some time before he speaks again.

"And he has the audacity to tell me that we will be an excellent team together, she and I! He said something ridiculous about her reading the maps and me leading the men, that together we would be unstoppable. I have no desire to be allied to that woman."

"You could refuse," I say and immediately bite my tongue. Why am I trying to encourage Yusuf not to marry Zaynab? There is no reason why he should not marry her, if his leader so wishes it and believes that together they would make a good match. Abu Bakr, after all, has been married to Zaynab for these past months and must know her better than any of us. If he admires her and believes her a suitable match for Yusuf, then who am I to speak for or against her? It should be no concern of mine, and yet the words keep coming out of my mouth. "You could say that you do not wish to marry her, that she should marry someone else."

"My leader commands it," he says, but I can still hear the anger in his voice at the path he is being set on.

He leaves the tent then, and I do not see him for the rest of the day. As soon as he leaves, I kneel and spend many hours in prayer, asking forgiveness for the feelings springing up in me, the absurd jealousy over Zaynab. I ask for greater guidance, to be set on a righteous path, to be reminded daily of my vows.

He returns later on but is still restless during the evening meal, which he eats angrily, stuffing the food into his face, with no remark on whether it is good or not, nor any conversation. I realise that I have grown used to our evenings together, talking about this and that, about nothing in particular, perhaps the day's events. Now we sit in tense silence and I am not sure if there is any topic I can broach that will put him in a better mood.

"Is the army's training going well?" I ask at last. Usually, talk of his men and their training puts him in a good mood, he will talk for hours about this or that training strategy, about which men seem to be proving themselves as possible future leaders, the most reliable warriors. Now he only grunts.

I return to silence. If this, his favourite topic, has only brought out of him a grunt, then I am wasting my time trying to think of any other conversation.

After dinner, he sits hunched, his face stuck in a scowl. I tidy the tent, clean away the food, and still he sits there.

"Perhaps a walk in the night air will refresh you after your difficult day," I say at last. It is all I can do not to tell him to stop being so sulky, as though he were a small child. At any rate, he nods, then gets up and leaves. I hope that he will come back in a better mood.

He is gone a long time. I lie down to sleep, but sleep will not come. I lie first on one side and then the other, neither of which feels comfortable. I try to think of calming things, such as listing the names of herbs, or the uses for one root or another. But this does not work. At last I give up, and lie awake, wondering where Yusuf is, for he has been gone a long time.

Sometime very late, he returns. And instead of taking to his bed, he kneels and prays. I have never seen him do this before, so late at night. I wonder whether I have always been asleep when he has prayed at this time, but I doubt it. There is something still preying on his mind.

Both of us sleep poorly that night. I hear him toss and turn even as I lie sleepless till the dawn. The notion of a marriage to Zaynab seems to have deeply affected him. Something in me, a voice I do not wish to answer, nor hear, asks whether in fact, despite his protestations, he already has feelings for her.

"Marry Yusuf? That would be her fourth marriage!" exclaims Aisha, as we make our way round the market together. "First she was a concubine, they say she married for love. Then after her vision, Luqut took her as his queen. Then Abu Bakr after she was their prisoner of war and now, he intends to turn her over to Yusuf? I have never heard of a woman being married so many times."

"Is she pleased, do you think?" I ask. The thought of Zaynab desiring Yusuf still unsettles me, despite my prayers.

"Who knows? I would have thought she would be grateful of a younger husband than Abu Bakr, at any rate," says Aisha. "He is old enough to be her grandfather. Perhaps they will make a good team," she adds, turning her attention to the vegetables she is purchasing, prodding them to see if they are fresh. "Yusuf will be the leader of our army while Abu Bakr is away, and she is a great beauty, whatever her character is like. Perhaps she will bear some children."

The thought of children only brings to mind what must be done to create them, and I shy away from the thought, hastily smelling one fruit after another, touching more items than I need to, confused and failing to select what I need to buy. "Surely not," I say. "She has been married three times and borne none. She must be barren." The thought gives me comfort and I chastise myself for it. My list of penances is growing longer by the moment.

"Perhaps she has never been married to the right man," says Aisha with a broad wink.

"Don't be vulgar," I say.

But it seems that Zaynab does indeed intend for Yusuf to desire her, not merely marry her to please his leader.

"Have you seen what she is doing?" asks Aisha, standing in the doorway of the tent.

I look up at her, framed in the light, her belly broadening before her. "Who?"

"Zaynab."

"What about her?"

"Have you *seen* it?"

"Seen what?"

"You have to see it for yourself," says Aisha, half giggling. "Come with me," she adds, holding out her hand.

"I am busy," I say.

"Not busy enough to miss seeing this," says Aisha firmly.

She will not accept my refusal. I get up and follow her, expecting some foolishness, uncomfortable with seeking out Zaynab.

Outside of Zaynab's vast black tent there is a little crowd gathered, mostly made up of children, two known prostitutes and a couple of young men, who seem to be blushing furiously.

"Look!" hisses Aisha, as we approach.

There is a carpenter at work, on a wooden bed. The bed is very large, and the man is currently carving its headboard. I frown at what I'm seeing, then take a step backwards. Beside me, Aisha giggles.

The bed is obscene. The man is carving a series of images, of couples consorting. There is no detail left to the imagination. The bodies writhe together as though alive, the most intimate parts of male and female bodies rising out of the wood as though desiring to be touched. I turn my face away, and one of the prostitutes laughs.

"I told you!" says Aisha, still giggling.

I walk away, my feet too fast for my head, which is still whirling. I nearly trip twice. "What is she thinking, making something like that?"

"Oh, I think she is thinking that if she is to marry him, she must make Yusuf a little more interested in her," says Aisha.

"He has been commanded to marry her," I say, my voice sharp. "She does not need to woo him, as though she were a harlot. It has been arranged; it is a marriage of convenience."

"It may be convenient for Abu Bakr," says Aisha. "But I think our queen wants there to be more than just convenience in her marriage bed."

I look down at her and she gives me a broad wink. I look away and continue walking, aware that Aisha can barely keep up with my pace, and not caring. I am tired of her prattling.

"She has changed the way she dresses, too," comments Aisha, panting a little behind me.

"What are you talking about?"

"Oh, have you not seen her since the marriage was announced?"

"No."

"She has got rid of all her jewellery. And all her bright silks. And her face is no longer painted. Not that that makes much difference," Aisha adds generously. "I've never seen a woman so beautiful, even without paint."

I think of how Zaynab usually dresses, the vibrant silks draped becomingly about her, the heavy strings of gems, the golden headdresses. Her painted lips, her dark-ringed eyes. "What is she wearing, then?" I ask, slowing down despite myself.

"Black," says Aisha.

I stop and turn to look at her. "Black?"

Aisha nods, catching her breath. "Black all over. Clothes, shoes. No jewellery. Of course," she adds, smirking slightly, "it's still the best silk and leather money can buy. She is hardly dressed in rags. But I'd say she had an eye to pleasing Yusuf, he's the one that doesn't like ostentation, Abu Bakr never complained about how she was dressed."

Again, something in me turns over at the thought of

Zaynab deliberately wooing Yusuf, shaping herself to his desires, seeking to please him. "You always did like to gossip," I say. "What do we care how she dresses?"

Aisha put her head on one side, regarding me without answering.

"Well?"

"He is your master," she reminds me. "When he marries her, she will be your mistress. I thought you would like to know how she is treating this marriage."

I give an exaggerated shrug. "I am a slave," I say, my tone bitter. "I have no say in who my master marries, nor who my mistress is. I certainly have no views on whether their marriage will be a good one or not. It has been commanded, so it will be."

Aisha nods, but it is as though she is nodding herself, rather than at my words, as though she has confirmed something she thought about me.

"What?" I snap at her.

She smiles more broadly. "Perhaps Yusuf might let you serve elsewhere, when he marries her," she says. "If you do not wish to serve her."

"I doubt I will be given the choice."

"There are always choices," says Aisha. "It is just that we do not always know what we wish for."

"I do not know what you are talking about," I say. "And now I must tend the plants."

"Your plants are always a good refuge," says Aisha. "I will bid you farewell then, until we next speak."

"Farewell," I say, already turning my shoulders to her. I do not know why I spend so much time with her, she is nothing but a busybody.

The Cup of Love

Jealousy… the coals thereof are coals of fire,
which hath a most vehement flame.

Song of Solomon 8:6

I AM PREPARING YUSUF'S FOOD WHEN the tent darkens.
I look up and see Hela, Zaynab's handmaid, standing in
the doorway, blocking the light.

"My mistress sends a drink for your master, to be taken
with his evening meal," she says. Her voice is deep for a
woman.

"What drink?" I ask, standing to face her.

"This," she says, holding out a wooden cup. It is worn,
perhaps it used to be red once but much of the colour has
been rubbed away with time.

I don't reach out for it. "He only drinks water. What is
it?" I repeat.

Her mouth twists a little, as though she is suppressing a
smile. "Ah yes," she says. "You are trained in herbs. Perhaps
you can tell what it is for yourself."

I reach out and take the cup. For a brief moment I hear
what I think is a sigh, feel a heat within me, rising upwards.
I would let go of the cup, but Hela has already released it, it

would fall and break if I did so. She is watching me closely. I smell the contents, then set the cup against my lips.

"Careful," she says.

I allow the liquid only to touch my tongue.

Hela watches me. "Well?" she asks.

I frown. "Houseleek? Cow parsnip? Lady's Mantle?"

Hela smiles. "And more."

I hold the cup back out to her. "These inflame lust," I say.

"Indeed," she says.

"My master has no need of this remedy," I say.

Her eyebrows raise up. "Is that so? Are you speaking from experience?"

I can feel heat rush to my cheeks. "I have taken holy vows of chastity," I say.

She nods. "So I understand. Then you will hardly object if my lady wishes your lord to drink this before their marriage. It can be no concern of yours, what goes on between them."

"Take it away," I say.

She shakes her head. "Give it to him each day when I bring it," she says. "I will know whether he has drunk it or not. If you do not give it to him, I will. And I will make it stronger. Tell him it is from Zaynab and he will drink it."

I want to refuse, but I am afraid of both Hela and Zaynab. Of what they could do to me, if they wished. I am a slave, they could get rid of me in an instant, on no pretext at all. I think that perhaps if I give this lust-inducing drink to Yusuf myself I could also lessen its powers. "Very well," I say, reluctantly.

Hela smiles a slow smile that makes my skin cold.

"Thank you," she says. "I will bring it each day until the wedding takes place, less than three months from now. You will return the cup to me each night." She pauses, as though waiting for me to say something else, but I stay silent. "Do not interfere with what you do not understand," she adds, her face grave.

"I know herbs as well as you," I say boldly.

"You are a gifted healer," she says. "I know this. But there are other things you do not understand."

"Such as?" I challenge.

"Why I serve Zaynab. Why Zaynab desires your master. What the…" she pauses, looking at the cup I am holding, then swallows, as though suddenly afraid. "…What the drink may do if you interfere with it," she finishes.

"I have agreed to what you want me to do," I say. "You may go."

She does so without speaking further and I am left holding the cup at arm's length. Yusuf will be back soon and in an effort to diminish the power of what Hela has made I add plantain, which can cool a man's lust, to a syrup of pomegranates and dates I already possess. I wonder, as I do so, why Zaynab wishes to increase Yusuf's lust. It can only be because she does not believe he actually desires her. I find some comfort in this. One cannot simply increase a man's lust for a woman he does not already desire, love philtres are only nonsense, as Zaynab will no doubt discover for herself.

I am about to pour away half of the cup's contents and add my own mixture to refill it, when I hear footsteps and, fearing Yusuf's approach, I hold the cup to my lips and drink half of its contents myself, then hastily stir in the syrup. The drink will be warm rather than cool, but I cannot help that.

I give Yusuf the cup. I tell him it is from Zaynab and hope he will refuse it but instead he takes it without question and I watch him drain it, although he makes a face at the excessive sweetness and follows it with water while I hurry to serve his evening meal.

Night comes and I cannot sleep. I try to say my prayers, to still my mind and yet all that comes to mind are my over-keen senses. I can hear Yusuf turn first one way and then the other in his bed, can hear his breath as it rises and falls, smell the scent of him in these close quarters. Images run through my mind, of Yusuf when he laughs, of how his eyes, which seem so dark on first sight, hold within them tiny glints of golden brown next to darker tones, which are only noticed in the sunlight. How his eyes crease at the corners when he is amused, how his mouth, which I have never seen, hidden as it always is under a veil, must curve when he smiles. The glimpses I have had of an ankle, a calf, of his forearms, which are sinewy with muscles, when he reaches out to me to take food or drink. My mind will not let go of these images; it will not let me sleep. In my mouth I can taste the drink that was in the cup and I wonder, if Yusuf's lips were set against mine, if our mouths would taste the same. I turn away in my bed, clasp my hands together even as I lie under the blankets and pray for God's help in setting such sinful thoughts aside. But God is not listening. I wonder whether He has stopped listening to me forever or whether, if I were to somehow atone, if He would make His voice heard again, find a way to set my feet back on a righteous path.

I am trying so hard to pray that I am startled when I hear Yusuf rise from his bed in the darkness. I think that he may be going outside to relieve himself but instead there is a long silent pause. I am about to turn over and see what he is doing when I hear him move again and then feel his hand on my hair. I freeze. Yusuf has never touched me, never allowed more than a finger to brush mine by accident if I pass him a dish of food. Now his hand is on my hair and he is stroking my cheek. My heart is beating so hard I think he must hear it. And then, just when I think that I cannot pretend to be asleep, I hear him curse under his breath and his touch is gone from me. I hear the tent flaps draw apart and when I roll over, he is gone into the night.

In the morning, when there is a cool breeze and Yusuf has left the tent, I try to pray. I kneel, I fold my hands together. I try to pray, and nothing comes. Nothing that would be acceptable to God. All that comes, unbidden, are images in my mind and sensations across my body. I close my eyes so tightly I see stars; I clasp my hands so fervently my knuckles turn white. And yet all I feel is Yusuf's touch on my hair and cheek, and all I see are his eyes. When I take deep breaths, trying to still my beating heart, all I smell is his scent, too well-known to me. I stay on my knees as the sun rises and sets, and still I cannot pray. Still I feel his hand upon me, I smell his scent. And then I smell something else. Something that reminds me of myself, the smell of herbs and roots that lingers around a healer.

"You must not drink from the cup."

I nearly scream. I open my eyes and stumble backwards, ending up on my behind, looking up at Hela, who is standing in my room, without my having heard her enter. She regards me with her large dark eyes, her emotionless face. I clamber awkwardly to my feet, so that I may face her. "What are you doing here?"

"You must not drink from the cup. It is not intended for you."

"I know that you are trying to drug my master," I say, trying to regain my dignity.

"Do not interfere. The drink is a matter between my mistress and your master."

"How can it be a matter between my master and your mistress, if my master does not know what he is being asked to drink?"

"He desires her. The drink will only enhance what is there already. As you already know."

"I know only that you have made a love potion for my master, that you intend to make him drink it every day, without his knowing."

"And I know that you drank from it," she says.

"How would you know that?"

"I know."

"How?"

She does not answer. Instead, she reaches out her hand and touches mine, only for a moment, her fingers cool. She nods, as though this has told her something, as though I have spoken to her.

"What?" I ask.

"You burn for him," she says. She speaks as though

what she has said is of no consequence, as though it were simply a statement of fact.

"I have taken a vow of chastity," I say. But even as I speak, I can feel the heat in my cheeks.

"Then stop drinking from the cup," she says. "You are only making your own life harder; your vows will be impossible to keep if you continue to drink from it."

"You think you are so gifted with herbs?"

She shakes her head. "I am warning you," she says. "Take heed of what I say."

"Or what?" I ask, trying to sound bold. "What will you do to me?"

Her eyebrows go up. "I? I will do nothing. You are doing it to yourself."

"Doing what?"

"Building up lust within yourself for a man who is not yours, for a man whose company you have forsworn. You say you have taken vows of chastity. The cup will make you break them, if you continue to drink from it."

"Why do you keep saying 'the cup' will make me lust for him?" I ask. "It is what you have put in the cup that might lead me astray."

"If you say so," she says. There is a heaviness to her voice, a weariness. "I am only warning you not to drink from it. Let Yusuf desire Zaynab. They can be no harm in it. They are betrothed, they are to be married, they may as well desire one another. Why would you seek otherwise?"

She has asked the question I cannot answer, of course. There is no reason why I should drink from the cup, no reason I should not let Yusuf drink from it, since I know full well what it contains and what its intended purpose is.

I look away. "I do not wish my master to be drugged," I say.

"It only enhances what is already there," she says. "You might want to think on that."

"Meaning what?"

"Meaning that you feel what you feel for your master already," she says. "The cup did not put that feeling there. It has only forced you to acknowledge that it exists. Stop drinking from it. Go back to your prayers. Keep your distance from Yusuf. In time, the feelings will fade. If you let them."

"Leave me," I say.

"Do not touch the cup again," she says.

"Is that a threat?" I ask.

"It is a warning," she says. She has already turned away from me, is already out of the door before I can think how to reply.

I stand, uncertain for a moment, then kneel again, my hands tight together, my eyes closed. I mumble a prayer by rote, without meaning, without any feeling attached to it, knowing as I do so that it is meaningless to pray like this.

That night the cup is brought for Yusuf again, this time by a servant. I do not touch it, I turn my face away and pretend not to have seen it. I tell myself that this is my choice, that I have not been influenced by Hela. Which I know is a lie. I keep away from Yusuf, I try to be busy elsewhere when he is nearby, I avoid our conversations in the evenings, claiming to be busy, to be tired. I hear him toss and turn at night as I lie awake, forcing myself to stay where I am rather than reach out to him. I may have stopped drinking from the cup, but I have to admit to myself, to no-one else, that Hela was right in what she said. The cup only enhances what was already there.

"My marriage will take place soon," Yusuf says suddenly one evening.

I try not to look at him, continue stirring the stew I am making. I want to tell him that 'soon' is precisely ten days away, that I know the number of days till the day of his marriage at all times, that if a stranger were to stop me in the street and ask me, I could tell him not just the days but the very hours until the ceremony that will bind Yusuf and Zaynab together. I am like a candle, burning down to the appointed time, knowing darkness is coming soon. I only nod, staying silent.

"You already know I am a man of simple needs," he says. He sounds awkward, his words circuitous coming from a man who usually speaks his mind plainly and without decoration.

I look up at him briefly, nod to show I am listening.

"Some small buildings have already been built," he says. "Soon there will be many more." He pauses, as though I should comment, as though he has made himself clear already.

I say nothing.

"I have arranged for you to have a small house," he says, looking down at his sword, which he is unnecessarily polishing. "It is nothing elaborate, only a room in a little courtyard, but you will be safe there and can live as you wish."

I stare at him. "Live as I wish?"

He shrugs. "Tend your plants, pray, whatever makes you happy." He swallows, turns the sword over in his lap, begins polishing the other side. "I would like you to be happy."

I want to reach out. I want to touch his face, pull aside his veil so that I may see what is hidden from me. I want to thank him and at the same time, I want to refuse. He is pushing me away; he is giving me a home so that he can go to Zaynab unimpeded. It is a hugely generous gesture towards a slave, and yet it fills me with anguish. I do not want to serve Zaynab, but I cannot bear to be separated from Yusuf. I say nothing, I do not know what to say, and what I do want to say is impossible.

"I have told Imari where it is, Aisha can take you there tomorrow. If you need help to move your plants, Imari can arrange it."

I should say something. I should express gratitude. Instead, I spoon out the stew into a bowl and pass it to him, in silence.

Aisha does not comment. For once, she is silent. She stands in the doorway of the tent and nods to me. Behind her are two men with mules, ready to load up my plants and follow behind us. I stand and follow her, walking through the city of tents, towards one of the small areas where building has already begun. She pushes open a little gate in a high wall, showing me into a tiny courtyard, off of which are two rooms. One is a tiny kitchen, in which I can just about turn around. The other is a larger plain room, without any hint of decoration.

Aisha watches the men unloading the plants, scattering them haphazardly around the courtyard space. "Useless," she comments. "You will have to rearrange them all when they've gone."

I nod.

"Well at least I can visit you here and not in Zaynab's tent," she says. "I wasn't looking forward to that."

I nod.

"Will you be all right?" she asks.

"Yes," I say. "Yusuf has been very generous."

"But is it what you wanted?" she asks. She does not meet my eye, she looks away, as though to allow me the freedom to answer without having to meet her gaze.

"I am a nun and a slave," I say. "I am sworn to obedience twice over. My own desires are not important."

"It depends how strong they are," says Aisha, still looking away. "The stronger they are, the harder it is to contain them."

She leaves me then, and I spend the rest of the day rearranging the plants to my satisfaction. The sun is almost setting when I look up to see Yusuf standing in the gateway.

"I am sorry," I say, springing to my feet. "I will prepare dinner at once."

He looks amused. "I have not come to chastise you," he says. "I came to see if all was well here." He walks around the courtyard, sticks his head into the tiny kitchen and then the room next door to it. "Bare enough for you?" he asks, teasing.

"I am more grateful than I can say," I say. I try to keep

my voice and words formal, but I am aware that my eyes are welling up with tears. "But I am sorry to no longer serve you."

"You will see me again," he says. "I am still your master; you cannot rid yourself of me that easily. You have served me well and you may be of use to me in the future. Having a healer to hand is no bad thing, when you must go into battle."

My heart lurches at the thought of him in battle. "I am sure Zaynab's healer is very accomplished," I say.

"I'm sure she is," he says. "But sometimes one would rather have one's own healer." He pauses. "I hope you will be happy here," he says.

"I am so grateful," I repeat. "I am sure I will be happy here. But…"

"But what?" he asks.

"I will miss our conversations," I say, stumbling over the words, feeling myself flush.

He looks around the tiny courtyard, gestures to the plants and a rough block of building stone left discarded. "I may have need of a quiet place, sometimes, where I can sit peacefully and talk to someone about small matters," he says. "It is tiring to speak only of great matters."

"I will be here," I say. I look away, I cannot meet his gaze, but the words still come. "I will be here whenever you wish to come."

He takes a step closer to me, pauses as though uncertain of his own movements, then lifts one hand and lightly strokes my cheek, his fingers brushing over my scars. Then, suddenly, he turns and in a moment is gone, the gate closing behind him with a shudder.

I let out the breath I did not know I was holding.

Preparations have been going on in the camp for many days, but today they reached their zenith. From before dawn, great piles of wood were assembled, ready for fires later. Women rose earlier than usual to knead bread and have it at the bakeries to be cooked in time. Yesterday the blood of hundreds of animals spilled across the earth, today they will be roasted, served on great platters to the whole of the camp.

Today is Yusuf's wedding. Today, he will marry Zaynab.

I wake and listen to the call to prayer. I wonder whether I could simply stay here all day, and see nothing of the ceremony, nothing of the feasting that will go on later. But Aisha is already at my door.

"Are you coming?" she asks and there is nothing I can say that would be acceptable. I only nod and follow her.

In the absence of a mosque, the ceremony is held in the open air, in the central space amongst this city of tents and half made buildings. Zaynab is dressed as plainly as though she were a slave, her robes all in black, her shoes black, her long black hair falling down over her shoulders. She is bereft of jewellery, although there is a tiny glint of something around her neck, half hidden by her robes, perhaps a very small necklace, although I cannot see it well. A contract has been drawn up, which is signed after Yusuf, before the crowd, asks for Zaynab's hand in marriage, having already presented many gifts to her. Both of them declare their acceptance three times. From where I am standing, I can barely hear their voices, only see how their eyes never leave one another, how Yusuf's hand trembles as he offers Zaynab a date to eat and receives one from her, the sharing of sweetness a wish for their marriage. They stand together while prayers are read over the pair of them, from the first surah of the Qu'ran.

"In the name of Allah, Most Gracious, Most Merciful. Praise be to Allah The Cherisher and Sustainer of the Worlds; Most Gracious, Most Merciful; Master of the Day of Judgement. Thee do we worship and Thine aid we seek. Show us the straight way, The way of those on whom Thou has bestowed Thy Grace, those whose portion is not wrath, and who go not astray."

This first prayer, which can be heard above the crowd, since the officiant has a carrying voice and is determined to be heard, is followed by many and varied blessings over the couple, everything from wishes for them to bear children to having a peaceful household. I tug at Aisha, wishing to leave. After all, the marriage is done now, these are only niceties, and I cannot find it in my heart to echo these blessings.

"Oh Allah," intones the officiant, "Bless this couple with faith, love and happiness in this world and the Next. Oh Allah, You are the Loving and the Merciful. Put love and mercy in the hearts of this couple for each other. Our Creator, strengthen the hearts of the bride and groom with faith, and let them increase in their love and commitment to You through their bond. Oh Lord of the Universe, all power is with You. Let this couple's marriage become a beautiful example to other couples. My God, protect this couple from the misguidance and planning of Shaytan. Help them resist his call to break their bond. Oh Allah, bless this couple with children who will be a source of happiness and joy to them and the world."

I slip my hand from Aisha's grasp and turn and walk away, unable to listen any longer. It is difficult to make my way through the crowd and the words of blessing continue to reach me, even as I struggle to leave the ceremony behind me and return to the barren peacefulness of my own empty room.

"Oh Allah, unite the couple and their families in faith and love. Oh Lord, You are the Just. Let this couple live their lives being fair and just to each other. Oh Forgiver, bless this couple with the strength to forgive each other's shortcomings. Oh Allah, give them the loving relationship which Muhammad and Aisha had. May Allah be pleased with them."

By the time I have left the crowd, I am almost running, making my way through the little mazes between the tents and outwards to where the first buildings lie, past stone and mud, wooden planks and half-erected scaffolding. I push open the gate to my own home, ignore my plants and make my way into the dark recess of the kitchen, the only space I can bear right now.

I kneel in the gloom and ask God to relieve me of the thoughts I am having, to take away the pain I should not even acknowledge, nor be feeling. The commander of our army is marrying a queen. It should not, must not, be of any matter to me. And yet it is.

Here in the darkness, here all alone, I acknowledge to myself and to God that I love Yusuf, that I desire him as a man, that I am jealous of Zaynab. That, watching them just now, all I wished for was to stand in Zaynab's place.

To take Yusuf's hands in mine, to place the sweet date in his mouth, to know that tonight, when the ceremonies, the celebrations and the feasting are all complete, Yusuf will make his way, not to the great black tent and Zaynab's lustful bed but to my empty room, in this quiet part of the city, and take me in his arms.

Aisha seeks me out later, finding me amidst my plants, tending to them one by one in an effort to still my mind.

"Yusuf's first wife arrived, but too late to stop the ceremony, even if she could have done."

I stare up at her. "What?"

"His wife arrived!"

"Kella?"

"How do you know her name?"

"He mentioned her," I say, thinking of how Yusuf described an adventurous young girl, seeking freedom, willing to risk joining an army, dressed as a man.

"Well she is here now, and she is miserable."

I think of my own feelings, watching Yusuf take Zaynab's hands in his, and feel nothing but a common sorrow with this unknown woman. "She did not arrive in time for the ceremony."

"No," says Aisha, squatting down and beginning to deadhead a chamomile plant. "She arrived only a little time ago, and was taken straight to Zaynab, no doubt against her wishes."

"What does she look like?" I ask.

"Miserable," repeats Aisha. "Young. Much younger than Zaynab. But not as beautiful."

I nod, continue watering a few of the drier plants.

"You don't look so happy yourself," says Aisha.

I say nothing. I keep my head down, but unbidden tears roll down my cheeks, attempting to water the plants.

"I know you care for him," says Aisha softly.

"I have no right to care for him," I say.

"We none of us choose who to care for," says Aisha.

"I have taken vows," I say.

"Vows are hard to keep," says Aisha.

"My temptation has been taken from me," I say.

"Has it?" she asks. "Temptation does not need to stand by our side to make itself felt."

"Then the path before me will be hard," I say.

The House of Secrets

Turn away thine eyes from me...

Song of Solomon 6:5

ALTHOUGH I TRY TO KEEP away from the main market square, eventually I see Yusuf's first wife for myself. Aisha was right, she is very young, younger than myself and Zaynab. She ought to outshine Zaynab, but she does not. When I see her, her skin looks very pale and she seems either ill or very tired. Or perhaps she is just unhappy, I think. Perhaps the sight of Yusuf with another woman, this unexpected queen holding the position Kella might have thought to take, is too much for her. She dresses in the bright colours that come from her tribe in the desert, but instead of illuminating her face, they only drain away its colour. She looks small and pale, tired and meek. I struggle to recognise the woman Yusuf described: an adventurer, someone bold enough to seek a life of freedom and to take it even when the odds were against her. All I see is defeat, in the slump of her shoulders, in her dull skin, in her eyes which do not look up and about but down at her feet. I tell myself that this is not my business, that how Yusuf chooses to manage the relationship between his first and second wife is not for me to either judge or even think about. He does not visit me, he has left me to my own devices. I should leave him to his.

I keep the little house bare, austere, trying to emulate the life I once led. I use the money I make selling herbs, not for fine robes or elaborate meals, for they are only worldly affectations. Instead I save them and buy writing implements. Here, what I first mistook for a strange kind of parchment is something called paper, made from beating rags or waste fibres from plants. It is thinner and finer than parchment and is in use everywhere, even by small traders. I resolve to spend my time writing down all the remedies I can recall, how to make them and store them, their uses and counter uses. I use my best script, I take a long time over each letter, each word. There is little to fill my days with, I may as well do the best work I can. I think that perhaps if I can remember all of the remedies I was taught, I will at least have made use of these days, created something that might be used by myself and others. I continue to grow herbs, to sell them.

"Are you well?" asks Aisha.

"Yes," I say. I always say this, I do not tell her that I am lonely. I see less of her than I would like to, now that she has her own household and her first baby has been born, a son, on whom Imari dotes. I see Yusuf mostly at a distance. And as I have no one else in this city, so I remain lonely.

"Zaynab has given her handmaiden Hela to Kella, as a servant," says Aisha.

"Why?" I cannot imagine why she would do this, it is clear that Hela is no mere servant to Zaynab. She is her personal healer, her confidante, why would she so easily hand her over to Kella?

Aisha shrugs. "Who knows?"

I walk through the market on a route that passes Kella's tent. I try to give the impression of looking elsewhere, but my eyes slide towards the sight of Hela standing outside the tent, cooking. I have never seen her cook before, I am surprised to see her doing it. Whatever she is making, it is heavily scented with parsley, I can smell it even at this distance. I hope, for Kella's sake, that she is not with child. Parsley in such great quantities would not be beneficial to an early pregnancy. But the thought of Kella being with child only makes me think of Yusuf lying with her, and I try to turn my thoughts elsewhere. She is his wife, he may lie with her if he so chooses, although I am aware that the rumours say that he does not, as he should, split his time evenly between the two of them, but rather favours Zaynab. I chastise myself for my interest in his affairs and turn my face away, focusing only on the purchases that I must make.

But my attempt at disinterest is about to be challenged.

The day is hotter than usual, and I am sweating. I wipe my forehead and under my eyes, my upper lip, then crouch down to take a drink of water from the pail I have beneath my stall.

"I need parsley."

I stand and find Kella standing before me. Her bright clothing is making her face look even whiter than it is, she looks ill and also as though she has not been much outside. She stands, waiting.

I fumble with the herbs but collect myself and pick up a large bunch of parsley, which I hand to her.

She shakes her head. "More."

I add another bunch and then another before she nods. She holds out payment, but her hand is shaking. I think of the rumours that she was with child. I think of the food I saw Hela prepare, how I thought then that it contained too much parsley. I look at her shaking hand and have a sudden intuition that she already knows, that she is not seeking to buy herbs from me but instead to have confirmed what she has already guessed. "Do not eat too much."

She looks at me as though she has waited for these words. In coming here and buying the herbs she has asked me a question, which I am now answering. "Why not?" she asks, and her voice shakes just as her hands do.

I want to make her sit down, for I am afraid she will faint. But her waiting eyes are fixed on me, there is a fear in them that frightens me.

"Parsley can take away life from within the womb," I say.

Her shaking hand falls, the coins she had brought as payment bouncing and striking the wooden surface of my stall even as she drops the parsley into the choking dust of the path. I step forward but she is already walking away, her feet shuffling as though she cannot even lift them, such is the weight of the burden she carries, the knowledge I have just given her. Something dark has been done to her, of this

I am certain. I can prove nothing. But if I had to seek out that darkness, I know that I would find it in the great dark tent that sits in the centre of this rising city. I would find blackness seeping from Zaynab's heart and through Hela's hands. I am fearful for Kella, even though I barely know her. And I wonder if even Yusuf is safe by Zaynab's side.

I have begun to add my own remedies to the fresh herbs I sell, little jars of ointments or packets of dried leaves. People tell me of their ailments, and I help them if I can, sometimes asking them to return another day so that I can bring what is needed.

It is early in the morning and I finish dealing with one customer, then see that Kella has returned to my stall. She chooses dried nettles and then looks at me doubtfully. I nod and add red clover and the leaves of raspberries.

"For a child," I say, and she nods without replying, her eyes filling with tears.

I want to say more but I do not know her well enough, cannot warn her to be more careful, but then I suppose she knows this already. I watch her walk away and say a small prayer for her. Perhaps Our Lady will look kindly on this woman who seeks only to bear a child to her husband. I hope that if she does so, her marriage with Yusuf will be strengthened and Zaynab's power over him will be lessened. I hope that if he is happy with these two wives I will be taught a lesson in humility, return to my own chaste life and think no more of him.

I hoe the field, water the plants, pick the herbs, sell them. I write down my remedies, creating a stack of paper that grows day by day. I pray. I eat, I sleep. My loneliness grows. This pale imitation of the life I once led, that I am now trying to recreate, does not come with the same sense of contentment and peace that I had then, it has neither the community of my sisters around me nor the calm of knowing that my path lies bright before me, clear and well-trodden. I feel adrift, uncertain of what I am doing, clinging to the remnants of a past that cannot be replicated here. I ask for a carpenter to carve a wooden cross to hang on my wall and he does so, for money overrides faith, it seems. I hoped its presence on my bare wall would bring me comfort, but it feels more like a reminder that I am very far from home.

There is a knocking at my gate when darkness has already fallen and I open it cautiously, to see the face of the Jewess, Rebecca, her cheeks streaked with tears, her hands bloodied.

"What has happened?" I ask.

"I was attacked," she says, in a half whisper, looking over her shoulder. "I was – I was violated."

I pull her inside and tend to her, giving her the means to clean herself and then bandaging her hands. "How did this happen?"

"I fought them," she says, looking down at her hands. "But they had a knife and all I did was cut myself."

"Who was it?" I ask.

"I do not know," she says. "It was dark, there were two men. They came upon me from behind, and even when I fought them, I could not see their faces well enough." She is still trembling from the ordeal, wiping away tears as they continue to fall.

"I can give you something," I say.

"What sort of thing?" she asks.

"To stop a child from growing in your womb," I say.

She shakes her head. "I have cleaned myself," she says, under her breath.

"Are you certain?" I ask. "It might be better if you took something."

"No, thank you," she says.

I think she is foolish, but I can hardly force her. I give her bread and dried fruit and she eats both hungrily. I give her more to take away with her, along with a blanket. I think for a moment of offering her shelter in my house, but I am not sure that she would accept, nor whether it would be right for me to share a house with a Jewess. Besides, the law says she must not live within the city walls. I believe that she was taken by force, as she says, but I do not know enough of her not to be certain that she did not in some way encourage such an advance, if she is a woman of loose morals. If she were, I most certainly could not have her near me.

She leaves me, sobbing her thanks, clutching the blankets and food to her. I spend much of my night unable to sleep, wondering at the daily dangers she faces and what might come to me, too, as an unprotected woman in this city. Yes, I am Yusuf's slave, but few would know that by now, as I rarely see him.

Murakush swirls with rumours. Abu Bakr is returning,

having subdued the unrest in the South. He has sent messengers to announce his imminent arrival. In his absence, Yusuf has been commander of the army, has married Zaynab, and is beloved by both the army and the people of this new, growing, city. If Abu Bakr returns, is he to take back the leadership he left in Yusuf's hands? And if so, what is to become of Yusuf? Must he step down? The people are unsettled, they are afraid of a fight for leadership. I think of how Yusuf always spoke of Abu Bakr, with loyalty and family love, and I cannot imagine them fighting one another, yet neither can I imagine Yusuf stepping down. But if he were to challenge Abu Bakr for leadership and fail, he could face execution for treason.

The response to Abu Bakr's imminent arrival is twofold. The messengers bearing the news, high-ranking officials and soldiers, are greeted as old friends, at a vast feast over which Yusuf and Zaynab preside, held in the central square. They are fed and entertained, then taken into Zaynab's own tent and offered gifts of honour. After this, the more important men are kept within Murakush, by Yusuf's side, whilst the mid-ranked men and common soldiers return to Abu Bakr to report back and issue an invitation to meet. He will see from this that their numbers and loyalty have been diminished, that Yusuf has already issued a silent warning. And sure enough, Abu Bakr agrees to meet away from Murakush, at a place closer to the humbled Aghmat, as though echoing his own possible future status.

The party that rides out to meet Abu Bakr is vast. At its head are Yusuf and Zaynab, side-by-side, powerful consorts, surrounded by Yusuf's personal guards, including Imari. They wear identical armour, carry giant matching shields, their black skin forming a dark shadow around the two leaders. Behind them are carried vast chests, made in carved wood. Each is filled with treasures: silver, gold and jewellery, skins and fine cloths as well as robes of honour, and of course weapons, always treasured by warriors. Behind this offering, this all-but-bribe, ride several thousand soldiers of the army, men in full battle armour, a show of military strength and power, of leadership already held, which will not be released without a struggle.

I do not ride out with the party of course, I wait with the commoners of the city to know our fate, powerless to influence it. I try to return to my own home, to tend my plants and pray as I should, but I find it impossible. I find myself pacing the tiny courtyard, until I can bear it no longer and make my way to the central square, eager for news. Little children balance on the growing city walls, looking out across the plains for a sighting of our army returning, their keen eyes ready to spot who leads it. The midday sun burns down on us, yet none of us take shelter, nor eat. There is talk, rumours. The general consensus seems to be that Zaynab is behind this show of strength, not wishing her husband to be demoted. That it is she, rather than Yusuf, who has masterminded this meeting. I find a part of the city walls onto which I can climb, make my way up it and sit, on its broad top, looking out over the plain with the children. Aisha finds me there, and, unwillingly, I climb back down and join her, wishing that I could stay in still silence, my eyes desperately searching the horizon for a glimpse of Yusuf.

"Imari thinks that Abu Bakr will not fight," Aisha says,

stroking her belly, which is growing again. She is hopeful for a daughter. She must be fearful for Imari's safety, placed as he is close to Yusuf, in the front line of any fighting that might occur. If anything goes wrong with this plan, this child may end up fatherless, before it is even born.

"I am sure everything will be peaceful," I say, trying to sound reassuring. I'm aware that my own hands tremble if they are not laid firmly in my lap, I clasp them together so as not to give away my nerves, not to make Aisha more worried than she already is.

"Kella is with child," says Aisha.

"I am glad," I say. I mean it. I am sorry for Yusuf's first wife, who has found herself usurped by a woman who has no qualms when it comes to getting what she wants. "Can you warn her against Hela?" I say. "She should not allow her to serve her, she should stay in her own home and only allow her own servants to care for her."

"I think she has realised that for herself," says Aisha. "She has barely been seen out of her house, and her belly already has a curve to it, perhaps she is far enough along that it would be hard to harm the child."

I say nothing, but I think that if Zaynab and Hela were prepared to take a child from Kella's womb, there is no knowing what they would do once a child is already born. I hope that Kella shows a stronger mettle than she has done so far, now that she knows what may be done to her.

"Still no sign?" asks Aisha, anxiously peering upwards to the top of the wall where the small children sit, shading their eyes from the sun, peering into the distance.

They shake their heads.

We wait. And wait. The sun is low in the sky when a shout alerts us that the army has been spotted, and it is not long before it is confirmed that Yusuf and Zaynab are still riding at the head of it. There are screams of excitement and celebration, cheering and applauding as they make their way back into the city, where a raised platform has been built and a feast is ready to be eaten. Zaynab, who recently appeared pale and tired, now seems to glow, her cheeks pink, her eyes dark ringed with kohl, something she has not worn for some time. Both of Yusuf's wives are present for the festivities, although Kella seats herself quietly to one side of the platform, while Zaynab reclines magnificently in the centre of the stage and lowers a hand to her belly, deliberately stroking the black silk enrobing her, showing off a tiny curve. Beside me, I hear Aisha gasp before the whole square erupts with celebration, cheering Zaynab's unexpected fertility at this most auspicious moment. I chastise myself silently for the sudden bitter thoughts that perhaps she is only faking a pregnancy. Deliberately, I bow my head and praise God for Yusuf's triumph and bless his future children. I watch as Yusuf speaks to the crowd, presents both his wives with magnificent pendant necklaces, offers gifts of honour to his generals. I see his happiness and pride, and am certain he does not think of me once, does not even search for my face in the crowd, unlike Imari, who, as soon as he is released from service, rushes to Aisha's side and greets her with great tenderness, the two of them beaming at each other with love and relief. I see their bond and have to acknowledge to myself that Yusuf shares just such a bond with Zaynab, that she is the right mate for him, a consort queen to an ambitious warlord, matching his power and ambition with her own. It would be best if I recalled who I really am: a discarded slave, property of a master who has forgotten me.

I increase my efforts to live as I once did. I have enough money to last me some time, so I cease trading in herbs. The market of Murakush has grown large enough by now that there are plenty of traders who can offer fresh fruits, vegetables and herbs. There is no need for my work to continue. I give over the little field to a family in need and retreat ever more into my own little world, seeking to know nothing of Yusuf's family life. I try to follow the timing of daily prayers as I would have done in the convent, I stop eating the food that they prepare here and instead eat as much as possible as I would have done at home in Galicia. I stay within the four walls of my tiny home, except when I must go to buy food. I wrap my hair tightly with a plain white cloth and seek out only dull colours for my robes.

I see Rebecca in the street, begging for alms. I look at her body and see that it has changed, she catches my eye and looks away, ashamed perhaps or sorry that she did not take my advice. She is with child and I cannot imagine how she will face life on the streets with a baby in her arms. I tell myself that I must keep away from those I have known, they only distract me from the life I should be leading. I have strayed too far already from the path I should have followed.

A month passes and Aisha is brought to bed with a child, a baby girl whom she and Imari welcome into the world with joy. I visit her, exclaim over the baby, stroke her little face and hold her hand in mine, but Aisha's new arrival means that I see her even less as she has two little ones now and she does not realise how much I have retreated from life here. I miss her, but I think it is as well that she does not see me as I am now, for she would only try to change my mind, and I can think of no other way in which to continue my life here, except to mimic that which came before. Let the months pass, I think, let time pass as quickly as possible. Let the seasons change from one into another, let this new life become the only life I can imagine.

I am at prayer when a dark-skinned slave woman finds me.

"Healer," she says, indicating me.

I nod and wait.

"Need help," she says. "My mistress."

"What is wrong with her?" I ask.

"Baby," says the woman.

"She is in labour?" I ask.

She nods.

"What is your name?" I ask.

"Adeola," she says.

I gather a few things and follow her. When I see the shuttered house she has brought me to I step back, shaking my head. It is Kella's house.

"Please," says the slave.

I shake my head again. "I cannot serve this woman." I say. "You must tell your master, her husband."

But Adeola looks alarmed at this idea. "No!" she says quickly. "Secret."

I think that it is no secret that Kella is with child, it is common knowledge. But she is in labour too soon, and she is Yusuf's wife, this is a woman who should have the very best physicians attending her. But then I think of Kella's visits to my stall, the green parsley she let fall into the dust when I told her the damage it could do, had already done, to her. I swallow and gesture to the slave woman to lead me into the house.

Inside it is very dark, for all the windows are shuttered, and there seems to be only one other servant, a male slave, dark-skinned like Adeola. She tells me he is named Ekon. By the way she greets him and touches his arm they are, perhaps, a couple. They hurry me to a bedroom, where I find Kella on her knees, panting and clutching at her covers as a wave of pain overwhelms her. I stare at her, shocked. Yusuf's wife, left alone to bear a child come too early? How is this possible?

"Why do you not have a midwife with you?" I ask.

"There is no-one I trust," she says, gasping at the pain. "Zaynab…" she does not finish the sentence, but I nod. Her words confirm my thoughts, I do not need to hear more. I kneel beside her, pull open my little bag of remedies.

"What is your name?" she asks.

I hesitate. "Isabella," I say at last. She will have heard my hesitation, will know that I am in some way lying, but it is the only name I feel able to give her. And anyway, for now I have more important things to worry about. "Your child comes too soon." I say, without even examining her. Everyone in the camp knows that Zaynab's child will be born first and Zaynab is not yet at her full term.

But Kella shakes her head, awash in another wave of pain.

I give her my hands to hold, which she grips tightly. As the pain dies away, she sighs in relief.

"Not early?"

She shakes her head again.

"Zaynab…" I begin.

She continues shaking her head.

I nod to myself. "So." Zaynab has lied, then, I think, perhaps saw that Kella was with child and claimed the same. I wonder whether she is truly with child now, or only pretending, still. Or whether her handmaiden Hela has done something, used her skills and whatever powers she has to bring about a child for her mistress.

I do not question Kella further. I examine her carefully. Certainly her belly is very large and she seems well enough in herself.

She looks up at me hopefully. "I think it will be born very soon," she says. "I have been in pain for a long time."

I try not to smile. I have attended births over the years, both for noblewomen who wanted to be attended by the sisters of the convent to feel adequately protected at a difficult birth and occasionally for the local peasant women, although most of them gave birth with little fuss and ceremony. First babies are always the hardest and come the slowest. Kella does not know this, of course. But it is best to be honest. "You have not yet felt pain," I say simply. "And your baby will not be born for a long time yet."

She stares at me in horror.

I try to make Kella comfortable as the hours pass. She is healthy, the baby is well placed. There is little I can do but allow her to grip my hands when the pain comes, to offer her sips of tea that will help her body to open up, made from the dried leaves of the raspberry plant. Adeola fans her as the heat of the day grows and Ekon brings cool water and food, though she is not hungry. I force her to walk about the room, for this will help the baby to come.

At last I examine her and see that she is ready, that the baby will come soon. I dismiss Ekon and help Kella onto her knees, Adeola helping to hold her up. I place my hands ready and feel a hard skull pressed against my fingertips, urge her to push again and feel the sudden movement of the child's head as it emerges, followed by the whole body, a slippery rush and a small cry. I look at Kella's exhausted face as she falls back on her bed.

"A son," I tell her, cutting the cord that lies between them with a sharp knife and tying it tightly. I give the child to her, her fingers slipping on his wet skin, her face lit up with awe at him.

Adeola and I busy ourselves with cleaning the bed and the room. I massage Kella's belly to release the afterbirth, which comes away whole, filling me with relief.

Kella is laughing out loud, full of joy at her son and I cannot help but smile. I take him from her briefly, to wrap him warmly while Adeola washes Kella and covers her. The baby nuzzles at me and I touch his silken skin, look down on him. His face is all Yusuf's, it is like seeing him as a babe and a great tenderness rises up in me. I give the boy back to Kella. A baby is a sweet thing, I think to myself, a gift of God, though I know that it is the dark eyes and wide eyebrows that have touched my heart, the rounded earlobes of his father that I should not even have noticed. I will pray later, I think, to give thanks for this child's safe arrival but also to ask forgiveness for the desire I felt to hold him a little longer.

I call for Ekon to bring food and water and to make a strong golden broth that the local women drink after their births, to which I have added garlic, thyme and mint to warm Kella. Adeola insists on bringing two raw eggs, a common food for new mothers here, although I warn her that these are too cold in nature and harmful to the intestine, but she is stubborn and places them on a dish anyway. I sigh and think that I will tell Kella not to eat them. I show her how to feed the child and he learns quickly, impatient to be fed.

"You shall be called Ali," I hear Kella say in a half-whisper, touching his dark tufts of hair. "As your father wished. You are his first son, and you will be much loved."

I wonder what Zaynab will say when she sees this child, but Adeola suddenly pushes past me, gives Kella the broth and takes the child from her. He lets out a grumbling snort, but she is already indicating that Kella must drink the broth.

"The eggs," I begin but Adeola pulls me hard by the hand to another room. I follow her, wondering at her behaviour but even as we reach the room, I see a figure at the end of the corridor, entering Kella's bedchamber. Zaynab. I would know her walk anywhere.

"Leave now," says Adeola in a hissed whisper.

"The baby?" I ask.

She nods, clutching him to her, pushes me towards the door.

I look up and down the corridor but Zaynab must still

be with Kella. I wonder what she will say, what she will do when she realises that Kella has birthed a child but cannot see it anywhere. I think for a moment that I could take the baby with me but then I think it is better if I simply slip away. I must not meddle between Yusuf's wives. I find a way to leave the house without passing Kella's room and hurry through the darkening streets. I am certain that no-one has seen me, and I know that both Kella and the baby are well. I have done my duty. Even so, when I reach my own home, I find myself praying for the child's safety.

I am already in bed when I hear a soft knocking at the gate. I ignore it, thinking it may be meant for my neighbours, it is such a quiet sound. But the sound comes again. I throw a robe over my head and make my way to the gate

"Who is there?" I ask. There is no answer. I pull the gate open a little and see Kella standing in the dark street, alone, clutching what can only be her baby to her. I stare at her. "Is the baby ill?" I ask and then, stupidly, "Do you bleed?" although if she were bleeding, she would never have made it to my home.

She shakes her head. "May I enter?" she asks, not answering me.

I step back so that she can move past me into the courtyard. I look behind her, almost expecting armed guards, but there is no one there. I close the gate and follow her into my tiny home. She is standing in the centre of the room, looking about her. I am aware of how bare, how plain, the room must seem to her, how strange, with its cross on the wall and my stack of paper, the calligraphy of another land.

"Kella?"

She turns to face me, frowning.

"Why are you here?" I ask.

She takes a deep breath, swallows, as though she cannot say something that must be said. "I want you to take my son."

I stare at her, unable to believe what she has just said. "Why?"

"Zaynab… threatened him."

"You could go to your husband."

She only shakes her head as though what I have suggested is not even worth considering.

I think of Zaynab and think that perhaps she is right, although I am also angry with Yusuf for not protecting this girl from the power of Zaynab, for not seeing the imbalance and seeking to redress it, as he should.

"Will you take him?" she asks. Her voice shakes, I can see tears welling up in her eyes.

I look at the tiny shock of dark hair emerging from the bundle in her arms, am about to reach out. But I am unsure. "For how long?"

"Forever," she says.

I step back. "Forever? Where will you be?"

She shakes her head. "I do not know," she says. "I may have to leave this place to ensure Ali is safe. But I cannot visit him, cannot see him again, or Zaynab will know I am his mother."

"She came to your house."

"She did not see him," she says. "I will say he is dead."

Even the thought of it makes her arms tighten round the baby and he stirs in her arms, lets out a tiny cry but then settles again.

"And his father?" I think of telling Yusuf his son has died, what pain that would cause.

She swallows again. "He will know him when he is old enough."

"How?"

She fumbles one-handed in her robes and pulls out a string of silver beads. They are shaped like slender tubes half a finger long, marked with tiny designs. "Yusuf gave me these for our child. He will recognise them when he sees them again. You must keep them safe for Ali when he is old enough to make himself known, when he is a man."

I stand silently.

"Will you take him?" she asks again.

"I must pray," I say abruptly.

I turn away from Kella and kneel below the cross. I know she is watching me, but my hands are shaking, my stomach is roiling. Perhaps she thinks that I am unwilling to take the baby, that I want no part of this falsehood, that I will not allow lies to be told over his birth, his ancestry.

She is wrong.

I want this baby desperately.

I am lonely here and yet bound by my vows. The person to whom I gave my heart I cannot have, yet here is his son, alike to him in every way, his tiny face a copy of his father, of Yusuf. I want this child more than anything I have ever desired. I want to have him for my own, to feel close to his father, to pretend, in my sinful soul, that there is something between us, that his child might have been my child, our child.

I try to pray but the words do not come, not even of prayers I know by rote. I should be asking for the strength to refuse this child, and yet I cannot form the prayer to ask for His guidance. Rather I find myself imagining holding the baby again, as I did when he was born into my hands, of clasping his tiny warm body close to mine, of looking into his dark eyes and knowing that I am holding Yusuf's son.

At last I give up. I know exactly what I am doing and why, I know that I am sinning because of my desire for a man, because of my loneliness here. I cross myself even as I commit this sin and rise, turn back to Kella. Even now I might refuse, might do what is right.

"I will take him," I say and now it is too late. "I will keep him safe until he is grown to be a man and I will bear witness to your husband that he is your child and his." My voice is shaking, my arms tremble as I hold them out to receive the child, every part of me aching with desire.

She tries to move, tries to hold him out to me but her whole body convulses in sobs. She rocks him in her arms, her face buried against his skin and I see a desire that matches mine, a pain like nothing I can imagine. I wait, but I can see that she will not, cannot, let him go. That if I do not take him from her, she will be unable to give him to me. I reach out and take him from her very gently, my hands cradling him, trying to show Kella with my every tiny movement how much I will love him. She lets out a low moan of pain, tears falling so fast down her face that the floor is covered with tiny drops of her grief. Ali begins to cry and at once her hands reach out for him, but I shake my head.

"You must go now," I say. "Or you will be found out."

She backs away from me and then turns. I hear her footsteps in the darkness of the tiny courtyard and the heavy thud of the gate.

Ali begins to cry, and I realise suddenly that he will need feeding, milk. How could I not have thought of this before? For a moment I think I will take him back, run after Kella and return him, to deal with Zaynab as she sees fit, without involving me in her rivalries and struggles. But I have given my word, and I do not know what may become of this baby, Ali, if I do not care for him. If I return him, will I hear that he has died, and know that I am to blame? No, I have given my word, and now I must face the consequences. I try to rock him, but he is displeased with my awkward efforts. He cries more loudly.

I think of the beggar woman Rebecca, her belly swelling day by day and wonder whether her time has come and if she could be persuaded, for a little money, to feed another mouth. I rock Ali in my arms, his warm body struggling against mine, dissatisfied with his treatment. Already, I have failed him. I grab a cloak, one-handed, marvelling at the difficulty of holding a baby and doing anything else at the same time. Clutching him to me, still wailing, I make my way through the night, out to the city walls. I slip through a gate and then follow the edge of the walls, nervous at being outside the safety of the city. But I do not walk far before I see a shape huddled against the wall. I crouch down beside her, noting as I do so that her shape has changed, the broad belly she held before her has gone, and now there is only an empty pouch.

"Rebecca," I say, shaking her shoulder. "Rebecca, wake up."

She stirs, mutters something and returns to her sleep, pulling the worn cover I once gave her over her head. But I cannot let her escape me so easily.

"Rebecca, I have need of you."

It is not my voice but Ali's whimpering that she responds to. Slowly, she pulls away the cover over her head and stares up at him, eyes narrowed.

"Jacob?" she says, in a whisper. "Jacob, is that you?"

I squat down next to her. "His name is Ali," I say. "What happened to your baby?"

She keeps her gaze on Ali. "Jacob?" she asks, one more time.

"Ali," I repeat.

She looks away then, unhappy, disappointed.

"Did your baby die?" I ask. "Or was he taken?"

She shakes her head. "Died," she says dully, without emotion, as though all her feeling has already been drained from her.

"When?" I ask.

"Don't know," she says. She shakes her head, as though trying to remember, although her life has little need of dates. "Three days?"

I do not know if what I am about to suggest is cruelty in its highest form or a kindness. Perhaps it is both. "Can you feed this child?" I ask. "He has no mother," I add.

"Where is she?"

I shake my head. I have to know what lie to tell,

from now until forever. "She died in childbirth," I say. "I promised to care for him. Can you feed him? I have no one else to ask. I can pay you."

"I – I don't know," she says, but her eyes are fixed on him again.

"I will pay you," I say again. "You can live with me, there is food and a warm bed, I have a little money."

"What if my milk does not come?"

"It will come," I say with certainty, although I am not as sure as I sound.

She does not look at me. She looks at Ali. "Yes," she says at last, and reaches out to touch the little tuft of black hair he has on his head. "Yes."

We make our way back through the streets, back to my home. By the time we reach the gate, Ali is screaming, his lungs belying his size. As soon as we are inside, I find her a seat and thrust him into Rebecca's arms. "Feed him," I say.

They fumble together, the two of them, she uncertain of what to do and he certain of what he wants, frustrated at the inability to get it immediately. I try to help, but only get in the way. Suddenly she gasps and he is silent, and I realise that he has found what he sought.

"He is sucking," she says.

"God be praised," I say, my voice weak with relief. "I will make you a tea, it will help your milk."

I make her fenugreek tea, preparing a large pot of it and giving it to her every hour that night, waking her from where she sleeps on my bed. I do not sleep. I hold Ali in my arms and rock him throughout the night, while thinking of all I must do when the morning comes. I watch her sleep huddled in my blankets, watch Ali sleep in my arms, and give him to her two or three times that night when he wishes to feed again. When he sleeps, near dawn, I make bread and more tea, prepare nuts and stewed fruit and a broth to strengthen Rebecca. When she wakes, I feed her until she can eat no more, give her a basin of warm water with which to wash herself, and my spare robe to dress in, so that she is clean. When she is clothed and fed, I give her Ali again and tell her I am going out.

I walk through the marketplace and buy things I have never bought before, spending much of the money I have. I buy more food, cloth to sew new robes for Rebecca and myself and to use for swaddling bands. I buy plates and cups, more fenugreek seeds than Rebecca will ever be able to drink, another blanket. I ask for a carpenter to come and build a second bed, a second chair. My household has tripled in one strange night. By the time I reach home, I find Rebecca asleep, with Ali contented by her side.

I take a blanket from the bed, wrap myself in it and sleep on the floor, so tired I cannot even think, nor feel the hard tiles beneath my body.

When I awake Rebecca is feeding Ali and we sit together, for a little while, not speaking, only looking at him, the two of us wondering how our life has changed so fast and so unexpectedly.

"What will your master say?" Rebecca asks me.

"I do not know," I say. "He is a kind man. I will tell him the baby is yours but that I have agreed to help you care for him." I do not say what I am thinking, which is, what will Kella say to Yusuf? Will she claim the child died in childbirth? Will she even stay strong enough to tell such a lie, to not break down in his arms and tell him everything that happened, leading him back to me and my part in all of this. I shake my head. What lies will I have to tell him? What will he say when he sees this child? And what if – what if he recognises his own son?

I take Ali, now half asleep, from Rebecca and stare into his face. He is the very image of Yusuf. I cannot imagine how anyone could look at him and not see the resemblance. But perhaps, I think, it is only I who sees this, because I have gazed at Yusuf's face once too often, have let my eyes linger on every part of him that I can see, and thought of him daily. Perhaps it is only my eyes that wish to see his countenance in this baby.

The sun is sinking when I hear the gate open and look out to see Yusuf standing in the courtyard. His eyes are rimmed red. He comes to the doorway, and looks at Rebecca, frowning.

"She's a beggar girl," I say, too quickly. "She had a baby and nowhere to live. I have taken her in, for now."

He looks at Rebecca, and the tiny dark head of Ali. I freeze, waiting for him to ask to see the baby, to look into his face. But he only nods and makes a gesture of dismissal. Rebecca quickly stands and leaves the room with Ali, murmuring something about a walk. I look into Yusuf's face, to see if I am about to be unmasked, called a liar and worse. Yusuf takes a few steps forwards, so that he is standing in front of me, closer than he has ever been. I swallow and look up into his face, seeing again the red rims of his eyes, realising that he has been crying.

"My son Ali is dead," he says, and suddenly he sinks to his knees before me, puts his face against my belly and weeps.

I do not speak. I find my hands on his head, pushing back the veil that has always hidden his face from me, letting its folds of cloth slip down onto his shoulders as he sobs against me, his shoulders shaking so hard that I think I may fall over. I brace my legs against his grief and run my hands through his dark hair, that I have never seen before, let alone touched.

He looks up at me, and I see his face in its entirety for the first time since I have known him. The skin below his eyes is very pale, protected from sunlight and drained by grief, his dark eyes, the only part of him I know, now flooded with tears. I stare back at him, my own eyes filled with tears as I think of the pain he is being unnecessarily caused.

I open my mouth to tell him it is not true, that his child lives and is safe in Rebecca's arms as she paces the narrow street outside, that he is a strong baby and will outlive us both. But I cannot. I have sworn otherwise, and I am afraid for this child, for the lies surrounding him and the power of Zaynab's jealousy. I am afraid of what Hela might do to serve her mistress, I am afraid that she has powers greater than mine, that she is no common healer and that she serves the darkness in Zaynab's heart without question. I have to look into Yusuf's eyes, raw with grief, and lie to him.

"I am so sorry," I say, and my voice shakes. "I am so sorry."

"He was my first son," says Yusuf, the words gulped and choked in his mouth.

I cannot bear to meet his gaze and so I pull his head towards me, pull him tight against my belly and my thighs, against my most secret parts and feel his warmth and strength against me. I am swept all over with a desire so strong it frightens me more than the lies I have told. I know now that I have told myself greater lies than I would have thought possible, that those lies and these new ones I am telling will have to live together, side-by-side, for the rest of my life. I wonder what I have become, what kind of a nun I could possibly claim to be, who lusts for this man, this heathen man, who holds a baby in her arms and tells lies about his birth to his own father's face. I am committing sins such as I never dreamed of, teetering on the edge of the abyss, the devil himself calling my name in ever more seductive tones. And I know that it would take so little, so very, very little, to take one more step and fall.

"What is the woman's name?" asks Yusuf at last, sitting back on his heels, his head bowed low. His voice is still hoarse.

"A beggar girl," I repeat. "Her name is Rebecca."

"The Jewess?" he asks.

I stare at him in surprise. "Is there nothing you do not know?" I ask.

He stands, face still unveiled, looks down at me and shakes his head. "I look about me. I listen."

I nod in silence. I wonder if he will insist that Rebecca

must leave Murakush, that she may not live within the city walls, as is the law.

"You must keep her here," he says. "There has been enough sadness for one day. I am glad at least one person has been made happy today, has been cared for. I will send you money, enough for both of you to live well."

"Thank you," I say. "I will ask her to name the baby Ali, in honour of your son," I say, knowing that I am casting myself ever deeper into dishonesty.

He bows his head as though acknowledging this offer. "I will find you a bigger house," he says. "I must go now, Kella has need of me." His hands are swift. Suddenly the dark veil is wrapped around his face again and once again I can see only his eyes. I try to think of something to say, but he has already gone.

It is a long time before I see Yusuf again, although he sends me money, as he promised, far more than Rebecca and I have need of. He also sends a tiny ivory rattle for Ali, a grand gift for the supposed child of a beggar. I wonder sadly whether he bought it in anticipation of Ali's birth and am comforted that if so, at least it has reached its intended recipient.

Murakush celebrates, for Zaynab gives birth to another son for Yusuf, this child named Abu Tahir al-Mu'izz. Zaynab's legend grows greater, her prophecy seems more accurate than ever. For she was barren for three marriages and now, at an age when many women might have stopped bearing children, she has given Yusuf a son and heir. His younger first wife has lost her son at birth, so it has been given out, but Zaynab has succeeded where her younger rival has failed. Zaynab's son is surrounded by servants and slaves, as though a tiny baby has need of much. When I catch glimpses of Zaynab I see that she is recovering well from her pregnancy, filling back out again after the nausea rumoured to plague her, standing tall and powerful once again.

It is she who will prepare everything that is needed to support Yusuf's army as it marches against Fes, a twin city, whose two amirs have been given due warning to surrender, which they have ignored and for which they will pay a heavy price. The troops march north, and I can only pray for Yusuf's safety, hoping that Ali will not lose the father he does not even know is his.

At first, I care for Ali's needs with brisk efficiency. He is kept clean and well fed, I keep a note of when he feeds and when he sleeps. Rebecca, I see, pours the love intended for her lost child into Ali, sometimes she weeps when she is rocking him, but she also smiles and murmurs to him, sings to him, strokes his hair. But I begin to find my own care of him growing softer, caught up in his wide-eyed gaze and the scent of him. He holds my finger in his whole fist one day and I sit with him for more than an hour in the warm sunshine, unwilling to move lest he let go again.

I do not see much of Kella, catch sight of her briefly sometimes in the market crowds, but it is a rare thing. I wonder whether she sometimes sees Ali with Rebecca or me and hope that she knows he is cared for. I wish that she could see him at night, curled by either my own or Rebecca's side, his chubby little hands held in ours, the loving embraces he wakes to each day. I knew that I desired this baby, and so it proves. He is showered with love, both by Rebecca who has lost her own child and by me, attempting to fill the emptiness in my heart made by his father. Our days revolve around him and I already know that if Kella were ever to demand him back, I would struggle to give him away, even to his own mother.

I wake to shouts in the streets, hurry to the windows, afraid of what such commotion means, but see smiles on people's faces, hear chants of celebration. Fes has fallen. Yusuf now holds an important city in the north. Any amirs across the breadth of the Maghreb whom he has not yet conquered must tremble in their shoes today, knowing their time will come soon. A few, lying close to Fes, surrender immediately, bowing to the inevitable moment when Yusuf will claim their territories. Better to be his tributes and allies and keep their lands than suffer the consequences of defying him. Rebecca and I are grateful for his success, for our continued safety and prosperity.

"Yusuf's first wife seems happy for a woman who has so recently lost her child," says Aisha. She has taken to visiting me each day, her own baby girl and Ali lying side by side on a mat beside us, gurgling, beginning to wave their arms and legs about, occasionally succeeding in rolling over for a different view of the world. Her older son toddles about the courtyard, poking at my plants and attempting to befriend the neighbour's cat, who has until now considered my tiny courtyard a good place to rest peacefully in the sun.

Rebecca sits with us, sewing. There is a peaceful feeling to these days, a comfort in seeing these small children explore the world around them, their desires so simple, so easy to grant.

"In what way?" I ask, my ears pricking up at the mention of Kella. I have never confided in Aisha about Ali's parentage, although when she first saw him, she cast me a look which suggested that she did not quite believe my story of him being Rebecca's child.

"I saw her in the marketplace," says Aisha. "Shopping for more goods than she can possibly have need of, laughing and bartering with the traders as though she had no cares in the world."

I ponder this. I wonder if Kella intends to leave, and shudder at the idea that she might return for Ali, take him with her somewhere else.

That night I wrap myself in a heavy cloak and leave Ali with Rebecca, making my way through the streets until I reach Kella's house. I stand outside it in the darkness, wondering whether to make myself known to her, to ask her how she does. But I am not brave enough, I fear she will ask for Ali's return. I return several nights in a row. Each night I turn away, always uncertain whether my own questions will prove our joint undoing.

On the fifth night, I am about to turn away when I see a side gate open. A cloaked figure leaves the house. It is Kella, I am sure of it. I step forward to speak with her, but there is something about the way she moves, hurried and secretive, that makes me stand back in the dark and let her go her own way, wherever that is. I hear a tiny *chink*, as of something metal striking the ground and see her head turn, but she does not stop, only walks swiftly away in the direction of the stables where Yusuf's personal steeds are kept. When she has gone, I retrace her steps and see something on the ground, the tiny glint of metal I heard fall. I pick up the object and retreat to a street corner where a lantern bobs. In the flickering light I see a tiny necklace, the shape of which, I know, is a betrothal necklace amongst Kella's people, a simple thing for such a weighty promise, made up of tiny black beads interspersed with silver, and dangling triangles. It must be the betrothal necklace Yusuf gave her when he took her as his bride. It lies in my hand, tiny, insignificant, yet loaded with the past. I am certain from her behaviour that Kella is leaving Murakush, but I do not raise the alarm, nor chase after her. She knows better than I what risks Ali may face in his life and she is taking steps to mitigate them. I trust her judgement and besides, I am relieved that she is not taking Ali away. My oath to her still stands, indeed it is strengthened by her absence.

I place the tiny necklace in a little casket in my own room, which already contains the string of silver beads she gave me with which to prove Ali's parentage. Perhaps, should the day ever come when such proof is needed, this necklace will only strengthen his claim on Yusuf.

News spreads fast that Yusuf's first wife has disappeared. Scouts are sent everywhere, but there is no word of her, it is as though the desert has swallowed her up without a trace. There are rumours and gossip everywhere. It seems she left with a man from her own tribe, perhaps a childhood sweetheart. That she left with slaves whom she had already set free. That her favourite camel from when she was a child has also disappeared from Yusuf's stables. Ludicrously, there are rumours that Zaynab spoke with the djinns of the desert, who magicked Kella away.

I await a visit from Yusuf, dreading the lies that I must tell, but he does not seek me out. This news has come at a time when he must plan for military success, it is too easy for Zaynab to claim to have searched for her everywhere and failed. Myself, I doubt she looked very hard. Zaynab never wanted Kella here, it is surprising enough that she did not kill her off in person. There are rumours of that as well of course, spoken more quietly in darker corners, for everyone knew that Zaynab was jealous of Kella being Yusuf's first wife. I choose to believe that Kella, adventurous as Yusuf described her, ever seeking a life of freedom, thought it best to seek out the life she longed to lead and in so doing lend protection to her son. I pray that she is safe and happy, but I also allow myself to look at Ali sleeping and pray that I may keep him with me and bring him safely to manhood, that I may know the joys of motherhood through him, however selfish that may be.

Aisha comes to me, her face doubtful at the message she is bringing. "The Queen's handmaid Hela is ill. She has asked to see you," she says. "Do you wish me to make your excuses?" she adds, as though to protect me.

"I will see her if she has asked for me," I say. I follow Aisha back to the palace where Yusuf and Zaynab live, noting the shuttered empty house nearby that used to be Kella's, still sitting empty without her. It would seem Yusuf has not yet given up hope of seeing her again.

Aisha knows her way through the palace, so that I do not need to risk meeting Zaynab. She leaves me outside a room with a pattern of flowers painted over it. I nod to her, then slip inside.

The room is very dark, I stand for a moment blinking, trying to adjust my eyes to the gloom.

"You came," says a voice. I barely recognise her, her already deep voice now rasps, wheezes with the effort of speaking.

I think of Sister Rosa, of her last days and swallow.

"You do not need to be afraid," she says. "I will not harm you." She pauses for a moment. "Nor die in your presence, if that is what you are afraid of."

"How did you know?" I ask.

"I felt it," she sighs. "Do you not know what I can do by now, Isabella?"

"I do not know all you can do," I say, unnerved by the sound of my childhood name in her mouth. "Nor would I wish to."

"So certain of yourself," she says, almost sounding amused. "After all this time, after all you have been through, still so certain of yourself, of your religion, your vows, your holiness."

"I can only pray for holiness," I say. "I have never felt so far from God."

"Surely that depends on how you define being close to God?"

I do not wish to speak with her of such matters. "You sent for me," I say. "What do you want?"

"Learn from me," she says. "Open up your life, do not close it down to nothing. You help no one that way. Your skills as a healer are valuable, use them for a greater good, learn more."

"I have been an apprentice and a healer for more than twenty years," I say. "I doubt I have much more to learn."

Her laugh turns into a coughing fit. When she has finished, she breathes heavily for a few moments. "You know almost nothing," she says. "Have you studied the medicine that we practice here? That is practised across the Muslim world?"

"No," I say. "It can hardly be that different."

She closes her eyes, as though what I am saying is exhausting. "You have no idea," she says. "I have seen your herbals. They are laughable. There is so much more medical knowledge of which you are unaware."

"Such as?"

"So much," she repeats, but she begins to cough again.

I stand waiting. When she has recovered herself, she looks me over again, her breath still coming with difficulty.

"I know how you feel for Yusuf," she says. "How you still burn for him."

I say nothing.

"He is drawn to you," she says, as though it were an insignificant thing to say.

I feel my heart beat harder, swallow at the rush of heat in my cheeks.

"Oh, did you not know that?" she says. "Of course he is. I was surprised when he did not bed you before the marriage with Zaynab. The drink I gave him… It was intended to increase his desire for Zaynab. Which it did, of course, she is a hard woman to resist. But it almost went the other way. I could see him watching you. I could see his desire growing for you, I had not realised before, that he already cared for you, that it would take so little to turn that into love."

I think of the night when Yusuf knelt by my bed, how his hand brushed my cheek. "I must go," I say.

"Take my advice before you do that," she says.

"Why should I trust you?"

"I have nothing to lose now," she says. "I am dying."

"You serve Zaynab," I say. "And that makes me distrust you."

"A fair enough assumption," she says. "But you know nothing of my own story. And I do not have the time to tell you. Only that my choices have not always been right. Neither in the past, nor more recently. I will only tell you this. That there is more to healing than you know, and that a woman like you, gifted with such skills, should know of it. And as for Yusuf…" She sighs. "Try to put him aside in your mind. He is as drawn to you as you are to him, but Zaynab is a dangerous enemy. And besides, he needs her by his side, she is everything a leader needs to create a kingdom."

"You serve her," I say. "It is you who makes her dangerous."

"I serve her for my own reasons," she says. "Do not cross her, with or without me when I am gone. She has a past of her own and it has made her ruthless."

"Is that all your advice?" I ask.

She is silent, as though thinking. "Love can be found in many ways," she says at last. "And hidden in many guises."

"I doubt you know what love is," I say.

"Do you?" she asks.

"I am a Christian," I say. "I seek to follow God's teachings on love."

"And what have you learned so far?" she asks.

I do not answer.

"Sometimes we have to learn for ourselves," she says. "Not everything can be taught." She struggles with her breathing for a few moments, I stand and watch her, uncertain of whether to help her, although when I step forwards, she waves me away. "You may go now," she says.

The brightness outside her darkroom makes me blink, I stand, pondering her words. I wonder what Zaynab will do without Hela by her side, whether she will grow more or less ruthless. Is it Zaynab, who gives dark orders to Hela, or Hela who carries out Zaynab's wishes no matter what it takes? If Hela dies, no doubt we will all find out soon enough.

Aisha is waiting at the foot of the stairs.

"What did she say?" she asks.

"She was confused," I say. "I believe she is dying."

Within two days I am proved right, word spreads that Hela has died. Zaynab has lost her handmaid even as she has gained Fes.

We begin to shape our days a little more, to know what and when we should eat, when Ali will want to suckle and when he will want to sleep. He is an easy child, content, and I marvel at this, after such an entrance to the world.

We prepare a little food for him, so that he may taste fruits and grains, he explores them, wide-eyed. He chuckles at the smallest things, from a bird landing nearby to the sound of a spoon banging on a cup and Rebecca and I end up giggling at his antics.

It is not Yusuf who comes to tell me that I have a new house, but one of his men.

"Follow me," he says, briskly.

I look back at Rebecca, nod to her and hurry after him, wondering what is going on.

"The Commander says you're to have a new house," says the man as we walk. "He says you're his healer."

I can hear doubt in his voice but do not correct him. The man does not care, anyway, if his commander has a slave woman as a mistress, as he no doubt thinks of me. Plenty of men of importance have slave girls here and there, hidden away in houses or even kept in their homes, whether their wives like it or not. Yusuf has already had two wives, a slave woman added to the list is hardly a surprise.

We walk down a narrow street a few moments' walk from where I now live, then come to a stop outside a poorly painted orange door, set into a high wall, newly built. The shabby door is an odd contrast to the newness of the wall. I think that this house may be bigger than where I am now but that it will be as simple. But I am mistaken. The creaking gate hides a secret. Inside is a courtyard, tiled in glorious colours, a fountain at its centre. The house is two storeys high, and there are ten rooms in all, including a spacious kitchen and its own bathing room, a ludicrous extravagance of a house. It is fit not just for a mistress, but for a wife.

I walk from room to room when the man has left,

wondering what Yusuf means by giving me this house. I am a slave, not even his mistress, and yet he has given me a house worthy of a wife. I think again of the creaking gate and the way it conceals what this house truly is. I know that Yusuf, for all his love of Zaynab, is aware that I need protection from her, that she must not know of my existence. I know this without being told, without him saying a word. The peeling paint of the orange gate tells me this even as I walk from room to room and look down into the beautiful courtyard.

When Rebecca sees the house, her mouth stays open and I catch her looking more than once at me, her eyes full of questions that she does not speak aloud. I do not try to answer them, for I do not know what the answers are.

The man who brought me here left me with a leather pouch that contains more money than Yusuf has ever given me before.

I fill the courtyard with my plants and with a tree. I give Rebecca a bedchamber of her own and set aside a room for when Ali is older. Besides my own bedchamber, I now have a room in which I may write and pray, a room sparse and simple enough to make me believe I am back in the convent. Rebecca ignores this monastic impulse and hangs bright covers and drapes in all the other rooms. Water splashes in the fountain, we fill the house with Ali's contented gurgles and our shared laughter at his antics, with the good smells of cooking and my drying herbs.

I set aside a bedchamber for Yusuf, should he ever wish to stay here, and even as I do so I know, as Hela said, that I would rather this room did not exist, that he should come to my bedchamber instead. But that is a step too far into the darkness that calls to me, louder every day.

The Chest of Books

Blow upon my garden, that the spices thereof may flow out.

Song of Solomon 4:16

ALI IS GROWING. HE LEARNS to walk. Rebecca and I clap our hands and rejoice, although now nothing is sacred. Not my plants, from which he rips leaves and flowers, threatening to stuff them into his ever-eager mouth. I have to remove those which are poisonous if misused and keep them on a high wooden shelf in the courtyard, specially built to withstand his interest. He splashes water from the courtyard fountain everywhere and slips and slides as a result, wailing when he hurts himself and rushing to one or the other of us for comfort. He enjoys walking through the market, pointing to everything he sees to hear its sound, to taste or smell whatever it has to offer. I tell him the names of my plants and he repeats them back to me, stumbling over the longer names.

He calls both Rebecca and me 'Mother' and we accept his naming, although officially we always say that he is Rebecca's son to anyone that asks, we brush away further questions by saying only that she was in difficulties and that I offered to help her raise him.

I sometimes see Zaynab's son, Ali's brother, in the markets with his nursemaids. I marvel at how similar the two boys look. I wonder that Yusuf cannot see it, but perhaps men do not look so closely.

The first time Yusuf visits us in the new house he walks round the rooms, nodding at Rebecca's bright and inviting decoration of each room, at the domestic warmth she has brought. His mouth twists a little when he sees his own bedchamber. "I will only end up sleeping in the courtyard, as you well know," he says. "Where is your room?"

I feel heat in my cheeks. I show him my own bedchamber, strewn with little signs of Ali's presence, such as the ivory rattle Yusuf sent for him.

"Do you not have a prayer room?" he asks. "I thought you would."

I lead him next door to the bare room I work in. A table and chair set under my wooden cross. A pile of paper, ink, pens, the pages of the herbal I am trying to complete.

He lets out a snort of laughter. "Exactly as I pictured it," he says, as though satisfied.

"I cannot tell you how grateful I am," I begin, but he cuts me off.

"It is nothing," he says. "How is the child?"

I lead him back to the courtyard where Rebecca is waiting with cakes and fruits, tea and Ali, who is eager to taste the unexpected treats.

"A fine boy," says Yusuf, patting Ali on the head as he waddles unsteadily towards him.

"He grows well," I say.

"Suckled by a Jewess and cared for by a Christian," he says, chuckling.

Fathered by a Muslim, I want to say, but I do not. I watch Yusuf lift Ali and dip his toes in the fountain's clear bubbling water, hear Ali's shrieks of glee, and Yusuf's deep chuckle. I wonder what it would be like, to be Ali's mother, to sit by Yusuf in the sunshine and feel such love.

A man comes to me with a carved chest. It is plain, unscented. When I lift the lid, it is full of books. I stare at it in amazement.

"Who is this from?" I ask.

"The Queen's handmaid," he says. "Hela."

"She is dead," I say.

"Yes," he says. "She sent the chest to a scholar before she died. There was a note to say that it should be sent to you, once she had gone."

"To me? What did it say?"

The man shrugs. "Send these books to the healer who used to be a nun," he says.

I can hardly argue that there must be many such women. Clearly, Hela intended me to have these books. I look down at them. They are huge tomes, very many of them. "There was nothing else in the message?" I ask.

The man shakes his head and leaves.

I look through the books. I cannot read any of them, but the illustrations are exquisite, in many colours, like the holy books in our convent. Some concern medical matters, for I can see illustrations of herbs, of people's bodies. Some seem to be about astronomy, mathematics, and other scholarly subjects. I wish that I could read them.

But Hela has even thought of this. The next day, an elderly man presents himself at my home. "I am here to teach you to read and write," he says.

"I can read and write," I say. "And who are you?"

"You cannot read and write in Arabic," he says. "I was paid to teach you."

"By whom?"

"A woman named Hela," he says. "She paid me a goodly sum, she said that I was not to leave you until you could read and write in Arabic."

I hesitate. I am not sure that I want gifts like these from Hela, from beyond the grave. I wonder why she thought of me so much, when our paths crossed so little. I wonder if somehow, with her strange powers, she knew something of what happened with Kella. Is this gift a curse? A blessing? A trick? But I think of the tomes of learning held in the chest which has been placed in my work room, of the knowledge held within them to which I would dearly like access. I nod and step back to let the man enter.

So begins a period of learning for me, such as I have not undertaken since I was a girl with my father and then under Sister Rosa's care in the stillroom and sickroom of the convent. I am as an ignorant child, learning once again the letters and sounds of a language, turning meaningless symbols into knowledge, shaping clumsy letters and sighing over my lessons. The letters I have known until now are useless to me, these new shapes bear no resemblance to them. I must even learn to write in a different direction, to read right to left rather than left to right. I no longer possess the flowing script of an educated woman, instead I know, by comparing my efforts with my tutor's hand, that my script is awkward, inelegant. My fingers grow ink stained and I spend money on more and more new paper so that I may practice longer and harder. Rebecca watches me in surprise but shakes her head when I offer to teach her in turn. And slowly, slowly, the books that Hela left me begin to open their pages to me, begin to share what they contain.

And such knowledge as I prided myself in having, such knowledge as I thought the Christian scholars held, is swept away by what I find. These books are the works of Muslim scholars, who themselves have drawn on past scholars from across the world and far back in time. Their knowledge surpasses all that I have ever read. I find myself staring in amazement at the books on medicine, on their depth and detail, on the knowledge that has been kept from me, a Christian woman who believed herself educated. And for what? Only because of my faith. I find myself thinking on my father, and his words, which my mother dismissed but which I now recognise as the truth, as containing wisdom. I think of the times he talked of in Cordoba, long ago, when scholars of all faiths came together and shared knowledge, wisdom, such books as these. They did not allow their faith to create a barrier, they looked beyond it and waded into a pool of shared knowledge, adding to it through their time together, their shared discussions. The more I read, the more I wish my father was still alive, so that I could return to him and ask for more.

In particular I study medicine, finding volumes from *The Complete Book of the Medical Art* and more from a scholar and physician named Bin Sina, whose work is called *A Canon of Medicine*. I stare, fascinated, at illustrations of anatomy. I learn of the importance of the six 'non-naturals,' which are the surrounding air, food and drink, sleeping and waking, exercise and rest, retention and evacuation and the mental state of the patient. I learn that to maintain good health all of these must be balanced. There is mention of being able to inoculate a person against illness such as smallpox, through introducing a tiny amount of the disease into them, which leaves me stupefied. My education in healing, of which I was so proud, feels childish, like the work of a new apprentice when I set it against this vast collection of knowledge.

I grow hungry for what has been denied to me all this time. I seek out the booksellers, the scholars' libraries, and I purchase or borrow whatever they can give me, adding book after book to those already in my possession. I read of geology and chemistry, of mathematics and philosophy. My tutor holds up his hands and says that he has nothing more to teach me, that my script has grown smooth and my reading fluent. He invites me to join him, at the school where he teaches, that I may learn more. But I am always wary of being too visible, and so I refuse. But I pay him myself, now that he has fulfilled his work for Hela. I ask him to come and read to me, to discuss with me the ideas that I have found in these works. I feel that I have been set free from my bonds as a slave, now that my mind may wander wherever it wishes.

I wonder if Hela read all these books, I assume she must have done. Was she so knowledgeable then, so gifted in medical work? And what of her other powers, which I still believe she held? Were they there from birth or did she find them in these books? Perhaps she sought answers for what she could do in these tomes and did not find it. I wonder if she was afraid of her own abilities, if she found them too much to bear. I wish she could have exercised them for the common good rather than in service of Zaynab. And I think that perhaps I could use what she has given me to help others more than I have done so far.

I look about me when I walk through the city and when I see a girl, sitting begging for alms, instead of passing by or giving her a small coin, I bring her back to the house, and offer her work as my servant, which she gladly accepts. She is an ill-favoured girl, being hunched in one shoulder, her back bent forwards and to one side, as well as having a twisted mouth from birth. I use ointments on her and teach her exercises to stretch and relieve the aches she feels from her twisted back. There is nothing I can do for her looks, but now that she is fed and dressed well, has a safe warm bed to sleep in at night and a household to be part of, her face seems prettier, for she smiles more often, and her gaze brightens. She was born to a slave woman who died, and her master, seeing no possibility of selling her and disliking her looks, cast her out into the street. Her name is Fatima, name of the daughter of the Prophet Muhammad and considered here a virtuous woman to be emulated, as women of my own faith might emulate a saint. She proves to be a hard worker and of a cheerful disposition, once she comes to trust me and to believe that she will stay with us, that she will not be cast out again. She watches me when I work with plants and begins to ask their names and uses, which I gladly share with her. I think that in this way she might learn a useful skill which she may use throughout her life and perhaps even have as a source of income, should she ever leave us. I tell her that she may have been born of a slave, but if her master abandoned her, she should consider herself a free woman. And as such, that she may create her own life and make it a happy one, despite her base origins.

A servant bangs on the gate and Rebecca comes to me, her face anxious, to tell me that I am summoned to Zaynab.

"Why?" I ask, trying to ignore the drop in my stomach. Why should Zaynab summon me? How does she even know I exist? Does she know, has she found out about, Ali?

The servant shrugs. "The order was to bring you to her. At once," he says.

"I will come in a moment," I say, trying not to let my voice shake. I pull Rebecca to a corner with me. "You know what to do if anyone comes here, if I do not return?" I ask her.

She nods. "Hide Ali, take him elsewhere if needs be. If anything happens to you, seek Yusuf's protection."

I look beyond her to where Ali plays in the sunlight, dipping water from the fountain into a little pail and back again, immersed in the games small children play. I want to embrace him, in case this is the last time I see him, but I do not want to startle him or frighten him, nor do I want to draw attention to him if the servant has not seen him. I raise my hand a little, make the sign of the cross over him and slip through the gate.

I follow the man through the streets to Zaynab's rooms, the grandest within the palace that has been built for Yusuf. Servants are everywhere, the courtyard and rooms are large, although I can see Yusuf's restraining hand on the decorations that have been used. The plasterwork contains only calligraphy praising Allah, the courtyard relies on plants rather than overly-elaborate tilework, even the many guards and servants we pass are plainly dressed, considering they serve an amir and his queen.

Guards stand at the entrance to Zaynab's rooms. At a nod from the servant they spring apart and allow us entry.

The room into which I am shown is very large. A rich powerful perfume fills the air, the perfume of a queen. Most of the room is taken up with a bed, on which Zaynab is sitting, looking down at maps spread out across her lap. Zaynab's bed. I recognise the carvings. Now it is draped with every kind of silken coverlet, with blankets of such fine wool they are more like gauze, all in reds and golds, yellows and oranges, as though it were aflame. The lustful carvings are polished so well that they seem to glow with life. This is the bed in which Zaynab lies with Yusuf. I swallow. It should not bother me, and yet it does.

Zaynab has looked up from her maps and is watching me. My heart is beating fast, but I stand in silence. Whatever accusations she makes, whatever she knows, I will only refuse to speak until the end, will deny all knowledge of Ali's birth and even of his very existence. It is all I can do.

"I suffer with great sickness from this pregnancy," Zaynab says. "I have need of your healing powers."

I wonder if this is a trick, if she intends to somehow catch me out, but I am not sure how, I am not sure what trap she is laying. "I do not have powers," I say at last, as it becomes clear that she is waiting for an answer. "I only have knowledge of herbs and I pray to my God for His guidance." It comes out more sharply than I intended, I sound as though I am defying her.

She stares at me in silence and I wonder whether in fact I have misjudged this meeting, whether she is indeed asking only for my help. I know that Zaynab suffers greatly from nausea with her pregnancies, everyone knows this and now that Hela is dead perhaps she is truly only asking for herbs that will help her. Certainly, she is very thin and pale, her beauty watered-down.

"What have you tried?" I ask cautiously.

She lists various remedies: eating acrid things such as capers, *not* eating such things, avoiding rue and all legumes especially chickpeas, the use of fresh air, gentle walks, wool placed over her stomach. Various wines, either diluted or added to. A range of amulets.

The relief I feel at her listing such commonplace remedies makes me light-headed. I shake my head a little to try and dispel the feeling. "I will make you a syrup," I say, hoping that by promising this I can quickly leave her presence. "Take it when you feel the sickness and at least twice a day even if you do not. Eat small meals and often."

"I can barely eat anything but unleavened bread," she

says pitifully. Her voice sounds as thin as she is. "Everything else I vomit."

I shake my head again. I do not want to feel pity for this woman. "I will send the syrup," I say, already beginning to move towards the door, eager to leave.

"You must tell me what is in it," she says sharply, as though she is suddenly distrustful of me, having sought my help.

"Pomegranate syrup with yarrow, stinging nettle, comfrey root, cinnamon, turmeric and bentonite clay," I say. The list comes quickly, I have made the remedy so many times, for one woman or another who had called on the convent for our help, even for ladies of the local nobility. It is an effective remedy; I have never not known it work.

She nods slowly, as though my quick recital has comforted her. "Send it to me," she says.

Rebecca nearly cries when I return. "I was afraid you would not come back," she says, embracing me.

Ali has barely noticed my absence, he has moved on to water the plants, using a battered old ladle I gave him, dripping most of the water all over the tiles of the courtyard. He beams at me when he sees me and continues his task, earnestly over-soaking each plant.

I gather the ingredients I need and mix a syrup for Zaynab, take it to the palace gates and give it to one of her servants.

A few days pass and I am summoned again. I wonder whether this is the moment when a trap will spring but now the guards bow when they see me and Zaynab looks up as soon as I enter the room.

"Did the drink work?" I ask.

"Yes," she says. There is a little more colour to her cheeks. She nods to a servant, who hands me a large leather pouch. It is weighty with coins. I grasp it, dumbfounded.

"You will continue to send the drink throughout my pregnancy," she says. "You will be well paid for your service."

The leather pouch sits heavy in my hands. I should bow, perhaps, should thank her, but I am too shocked at what has happened, at finding myself somehow serving a woman whom I despise, a woman I believe to be a handmaiden of the devil. Am I, too, serving the devil, through my healing skills? "I can tell your servants how to prepare it," I say, trying to sever the bond she is creating between us.

"No," she says. "I want you to prepare it."

I nod and step away, hoping to leave as quickly as possible. I dare not refuse to make the syrup, nor her payment, but I wish to leave her presence.

"Wait," she says.

I stop and wait. Is this the moment when she reveals all of this has been a pretence, that she knows everything?

"You could work for me," she says. "My own handmaiden Hela has passed away and I have need of a healer in my service. Will you be my handmaiden?"

"No," I say instantly.

She frowns. "Why not?"

The words spill from my mouth, as though they have

been waiting to be said, as though a higher power has taken over my body. "I do not wish to serve you," I say. "I cannot serve a woman who has such darkness inside her."

Without asking her permission, I turn and leave the room, walk through her palace and back to my own home, all the way fearing a hand on my shoulder, all the while burning as though an invisible light is inside of me. This, I think, this is how Our Lord felt when he refused the devil's temptations, when He looked out over all the kingdoms that he might command and refused such earthly wiles, holding true to His given purpose. I cannot even speak with Rebecca when I return home, only tell her that I must pray. I spend all night on my knees and when dawn comes, I wake to find I have fallen asleep at prayer, that Rebecca has draped me with a woollen blanket while Fatima makes breakfast for Ali. My knees cramp when I try to stand but for now, it seems, we are safe.

Ali is a scholar in the making. He finds my paper and a pen and spills ink everywhere but manages to form a clumsy letter and I, enchanted, begin to teach him his letters and numbers. He loves them. He draws the shapes in water in the summer, in sand, in the mud of winter. He sits himself by my side, like a little scholar and attends to his studies.

Rebecca finds him a little kitten and he is careful and soft with it, a gentle soul. I think of his mother's adventurous spirit and Yusuf's leadership, but I do not see it in him. I see a scholar and a kind heart, a child who loves lullabies and stories, embraces and soft words. I think perhaps, as he is Yusuf's son, that he should be taught the skills of war, that he should have a dagger and a shield and think himself a soldier. But I cannot bring myself to do this, to harden his little heart against the outside world. Instead, I read to him the legends of his own world and recite the stories from mine. I take him to the market square, where we sit in rapturous silence and listen to the storyteller peddle his wares. Ali likes to imagine that he is a great king, with a queen who tells him such stories as Scheherazade once told her lord, although I cannot imagine him being so unkind as to behead any previous wives. His eyes grow round with the tales of Sinbad, of the forty thieves, of adventures and heroes, monsters and good-for-nothings populating a city like his own. He examines large oil jars in case he should find thieves hiding there, waves his hand to command doors to open and reveal their hidden treasure. I hold him to me when he will keep still long enough to let me and smell his hair, the perfume of innocence and happiness.

The scholar who taught me suggests that I might like to work alongside physicians, in the first hospital that is being built in Marrakech. But I am afraid of drawing too much attention to myself, as I surely would working alongside physicians, a woman from another country. Instead I look about me, at the over-large house Yusuf has given me. I see Rebecca's smiling face and listen to Fatima's cheerful singing as she goes about her chores. I look at my plants and remedies and make up my mind.

"I wish to care for the sick," I tell Rebecca. "Here, in this house. We could work to heal the sick, and to help those who have nothing, as Fatima had nothing."

"Nor did I," Rebecca reminds me, "I would do anything to repay my debt to you."

"You did that long ago," I say. "You saved Ali's life; he would have died without your milk. There is no debt to repay to me, but we could do much good here, this house is too big, even for the four of us."

And so we make changes to our household. I set aside a room to be an infirmary, and another to be my stillroom. I find a beggar boy to fetch and carry and find a young girl to join our household as a servant, while Fatima becomes my assistant. I let it be known that I will use my healing skills for anyone who needs them. My days grow busy, preparing and using remedies, looking to use my newfound knowledge as well as my existing skills on those who come to us for help. Since I have already engaged the services of a tutor for Ali, I offer the opportunity to learn to read and write to any who wish to attend, and so there is always a little group of slaves, children and women who cannot attend a formal school but can spare a little time to learn alongside Ali.

"You are privileged," I tell him, "and so it is meet that you should share that privilege with those whose lives are harder than yours." He straightens with pride at the thought, offering, even though he is a little child, to help others in their quest for knowledge. He will show them how to form a letter, tongue between his lips as he shapes them, frowning in concentration. His little finger traces across the Qu'ran while he speaks its words aloud for the benefit of those still learning. He is a born scholar, with a scholar's desire to share what he knows.

Rebecca, meanwhile, is absent for much of several days

and when I ask her where she went she whispers that a Jewish trader invited her to his home, outside of Murakush, to celebrate Passover, knowing her to be of his faith.

"I told him I had been disowned by my family," she says. "I did not want to lie to him, but he said we are far from Al-Andalus here and there are so few of our faith, we must stick together."

There is something lighter about her, a brightness in her eyes and I am not surprised when a few months later a man presents himself at our house and asks to speak with me. He is named Daniel and he asks if he may marry Rebecca.

"Gladly, if you will love and protect her," I tell him. "But she is so much a part of my life. Can she still work with me?"

He is happy with this arrangement and so Rebecca marries back into her faith, a homecoming for her after all these years being cast out. I see a new confidence grow in her, a sense of belonging rather than the pitiful gratitude of the early years together. She seems an equal with me now and although she leaves our house each afternoon to travel home with her husband, she spends most of each day with us. Ali, of course, latches on to Daniel and asks him all manner of questions about the Jewish faith, even attends one or two prayer meetings to observe their rituals. He is insatiable in his desire for knowledge, with an open-mindedness that continues to amaze and humble me.

I do not often see Yusuf but having work to keep me busy each and every day, having a household that is full of need and noise fills the silence and emptiness within me, lessens a little the longing for what I cannot have. I think sometimes of Hela, of her gift to me of knowledge, and whether she meant for it so that I might use my healing skills, or whether she thought it might help to lessen my desire for Yusuf, I do not know. I know nothing of her past. I know only that she saw something in me that needed help and gave it in the only way she knew how. When I make my daily devotions, I pray for her soul, wherever she may be.

City of Light

Until the day break, and the shadows flee away...

Song of Solomon 4:6

WHEN I LOOK AT ALI now, standing taller than Rebecca and me, I wonder where these past years have gone. He is not yet a man, but I can no longer call him a child. He has grown up with no father, with two mothers, in a household full of the sick and impoverished and he is wiser than I was at his age.

"Your son is an excellent scholar," says his tutor proudly. "He has a great feeling for the Qur'an, for its nuances. He has a great understanding both of religion and the law."

"I am glad to hear it," I say, although I feel again the familiar uncertainty. Am I doing the right thing, raising him as a Muslim when it is quite possible that Yusuf will never know he is his son, when perhaps he will only have me for a mother? It draws attention to us, for I am known as a Christian, and people will wonder why I am raising a child in my care as a Muslim. But I know that if the day comes when I may return him safely to Yusuf as his son, I cannot have raised him against his father's wishes.

I do not tell him much about my own life before I came

here, only that I was a religious woman, in a religious house in my own country, but I was brought here and became Yusuf's slave. I tell him that I have been well treated, that I owe Yusuf a great deal, and he, hero-worshipping Yusuf as he already does, adds this to his list of glories and behaves ever more as a son to him. He waits for him to return from campaigns, hangs upon his every word, and takes every opportunity to show, his face a little flushed with pride, how his studies have progressed. He writes a beautiful script in Arabic, my own, by comparison, having come later to it in life, is not as fine. I teach him to read and write my own letters and he attends to them with great care, begs for the use of all my books in both languages and spends many hours a day reading them. His Latin is good, although his accent betrays our location, but still he would not disgrace any gathering of scholars. I think sometimes of my father, and how he would have been proud to have a scholar in his family, how he would have showered him with books, introduced him to the scholars who visited his shop. He would have praised his fine hand and his turn of phrase when he writes or speaks. I miss my father. My mother, of course, would be utterly appalled at what I have done. She would turn away in horror at the very idea of me being a slave to a Muslim master. That I would choose for a child I was raising to become a Muslim and not a Christian, would be beyond her understanding.

"Tell me again how you pray," Ali says. He is eager to learn, it does not matter what. He has been taught to pray as a Muslim, but he continues to ask all manner of questions of Rebecca and Daniel about the Jewish faith, listening wide-eyed to stories from her childhood, of the rituals of their family life. He follows me when I go to my room to pray and watches me earnestly, confused by the silence of my prayers.

"But what are you saying inside your head?" he asks.

I repeat my prayers for him out loud, they sound strange in this place, for I have not spoken them aloud for many years now. He learns them quickly, learns the Hail Mary and Our Father. When I mention in passing that we used to sing, he asks me to sing again and I do so, my voice faltering without my sisters all around me. He tries to copy me, although he is not a gifted singer. I think of our choir mistress, that she would wince at the way he sings, as she used to when I was a child before she improved my performance with endless repetition and practice. It feels strange to have another person to pray with, for Ali will willingly pray with me as well as with the other scholars and people of the city in the mosque.

"I have never met someone like you," I tell him, honestly. "You remind me of the people of Cordoba, about whom my father used to speak."

"Tell me again about Cordoba," he begs.

And so I tell him about Cordoba, trying to remember everything my father told me, while I refused to pay proper attention. I wish I had listened more closely now, for Ali's face lights up at what I describe.

"Yes!" he says, enthused. "It does not matter what name we give to God. In matters only that we share his wisdom and the blessing of knowledge he has given us, whatever name we in our mortal ignorance have given him."

I have such pride in him that I sometimes wonder if it is sinful, but I cannot help it. I show him all the books Hela gave me and he reads them avidly, sits up at night to discuss what he has read with me.

Rebecca and Daniel have been blessed with two children, both of whom I brought into the world. Her son is named Samuel, her daughter she asked me to name and I called her Rachel, for another Jewess long ago who tried to befriend me. Now that she has little children to care for again and Ali is older, she comes less frequently to the house, but I still see her every few days and she, Aisha and I are often together, working and talking together as we help those who come for healing and learning. Aisha has learnt to read and write and now she passes on what she has learnt to the little children who come, sitting patiently by their side as they gain in confidence.

Yusuf visits us often. His eyebrows have grown grey. He has secured the Maghreb now, he need no longer go to war, he may rest and reap the rewards of his courage and faith, as befits an older man. Usually of an evening, between training with the army and returning to his palace, he will slip in through the gate to our courtyard, as twilight falls and most of my patients have left for the day. Those who are truly sick, who must stay in our infirmary for a night or more, are by now asleep, cared for by earnest Fatima, who has become an accomplished healer in her own right. Yusuf squats amongst my potted plants. Always disdaining of luxury, he will wave away chairs and even soft rugs. He accepts cold water to wash his face and hands, plain bread, which I have baked for him late in the day, so that it will be fresh when he needs it. A handful of dates, a few scraps of roast meat if there are leftovers, this is all he wants. I bring him cold water and sit with him. Sometimes we will spend all of his visit in silence, listening to the fountain play, watching as the first stars come out. Then he will rise and leave, with a smile for me and a wave and nothing more. On other days, he will talk to me of something he has seen that day, of a bird, a plant, a child in the street. He does not talk of military strategy, of plans for conquest, of amirs surrendering to his growing power. The whole of the Maghreb is now under his control. It is divided up into four great provinces, two in the north and two in the south, each under the control of a governor appointed by Yusuf, every tribal commander pledging loyalty to the kingdom. His generals have little left to do, although he still commands a vast army. I know of his conquests from others, never from himself. Long gone are the days when Murakush was a city of tents. The city walls rise high, surrounded by palm trees. There is water in the public fountains and the houses of the well-to-do, the whole city fully built at last, including a great mosque at its centre. Yusuf owns Fes and the northern port of Tangier, he controls the trade routes, including all trade in salt, slaves and gold.

On some evenings, Ali finds and joins us, his face all alight with hero worship. Yusuf is always kind to him, always welcoming. He will question him on his studies, and then listen as Ali recites from the Qu'ran. Ali asks him about matters of law and taxation regarding how the kingdom is run. Yusuf answers him honestly, explaining even minor details in great depth. Illiterate himself, he seems to relish Ali's learning. The better his tutors say he does, the higher quality tuition Yusuf purchases for him, calling on great scholars of the city to spend time with Ali, sharing their knowledge and their debates with him.

"He has a learned mind," he repeats often. "There will be a place in my Council for him when he is grown to manhood. A leader must have wise counsel from those about him, and young eyes see what old minds have forgotten."

Ali glows at such praise, bends ever more earnestly to his studies. The warmth of their relationship pleases me, although always, there is something in me that worries when they are together, that the moment of discovery will come when I least expect it.

I see Zaynab's children at a distance, over the years. For each pregnancy, I must make and send to her the syrup, each time I am amply rewarded, the gold I receive then used to heal or teach, while I try not to think of Yusuf lying in her arms. One after another they are born, six sons and three daughters, and all of them are prepared for a future in her footsteps or those of Yusuf. The boys are warlike, they follow the army out to the plain and copy their every movement, they carry miniature swords and drums, they are trained to become warriors of the future. Her daughters are dressed as befits princesses, they are shown maps of their parents' empire and sit in Council from when they can barely speak, future consorts to great lords and rulers, every one of them. Zaynab herself grows older but never less than beautiful, her eyes dark with power and the knowledge that she has achieved great things. If Yusuf were to die, she could rule this kingdom alone, for she has done as much as he to create it.

Twice in those years, I hear from Aisha that Yusuf has also fathered a child with a slave, a boy and a girl born to one woman, one boy born to the other. I see that he acknowledges these children, that they take their place alongside their legitimate siblings, as though there were no difference between them. But I see also that their mothers are not accorded the status of a wife, they are kept secret and hidden away, as I am. At first, their existence wounds me, makes me feel that I am one of many, perhaps dozens of slave girls and their offspring hidden all over Murakush and beyond. But I see no more children born to such women, and so it seems that they were little more than dalliances, the children acknowledged, the women left behind, though no doubt Yusuf, being a generous man, will have provided for them. I do not speak to him of them, ask no questions, just as I rarely mention Zaynab. Instead I speak of new knowledge found in my books, of what I have tried and whether it has worked, whether it is time to pick this or that petal or leaf, of the birds who have made a nest on the corner of our rooftop and wash in our fountain at dawn.

From the way Yusuf talks to Ali, I make the mistake of thinking that he is content, that now that his kingdom is complete and peaceful under him, he seeks no further conquest, no further adventure. But I am wrong. It is hard to tame a warlord, a warrior-made-king.

It seems that there is trouble in Al-Andalus. Divided into princeling *taifa* states, each a tiny region, ruled over by Muslim kings, it seems they have forgotten the shining days of Cordoba and instead squabble amongst themselves, grown lazy while living lives of luxury. They might have worked together, to create a kingdom, an army strong enough to defeat Alphonso the Sixth, the Christian king of the North, but they prefer to continue in their comfortable lives and pay him tribute. But now the Amir of Seville, Al-Mu'tamid, having been late in paying the annual tribute demanded by Alphonso, has tried the king's patience too far. Alphonso demands not only tribute but recompense for the delay, insisting on the delivery of many strong castles in Seville's region. Rather than negotiate, the Amir of Seville kills Alphonso's messenger and then, worried by what he has done, writes to Yusuf, as one Muslim king to another, asking for his support against the Christian king. He claims that the scholars of Al-Andalus agree that this is righteous.

"But Yusuf has no seagoing ships," I point out to Aisha, when she tells me this.

"He has demanded a ship from the Amir," says Aisha. "The Amir of Ceuta, on our northern coast, has yet to be conquered, but with a ship Yusuf will defeat him in no time. If he can do so, he has promised his aid to Al-Andalus."

I had thought my years of praying for Yusuf's safety were over. It seems they are to begin again. I think that I should perhaps be praying for Alphonso, but that thought comes and goes in an instant. Galicia was too long ago, I cannot summon the desire to support a Christian king I know nothing of, against a man who sits amongst my plants in the twilight, eats food prepared by my hands and talks to me of nesting birds. I hope that Yusuf will support the taifa states only as long as is necessary for them to form a stronger alliance of their own, to fight their own battles against Alphonso and let Yusuf return safely home to Murakush. To me.

Shadows in the Alleys

The watchmen that go about the city found me…

Song of Solomon 3:3

*I*F I THOUGHT THAT YUSUF's time in Al-Andalus would
be brief, now I learn my mistake. The taifa kings cannot
be relied upon, Yusuf leads them to one victory after
another, and yet still they squabble amongst themselves,
turn traitor on each other and on him, showing loyalty to
Alphonso when they think to gain from him, returning
to Yusuf when they need his help. Yusuf is not a man
to accept disloyalty. The scholars of the Council are in
agreement: the amirs of Al-Andalus have been shown to
be impious libertines who care only for their own comforts
and luxuries, corrupting their own people with their poor
example and commanding illegal taxes, expressly forbidden
by the Qu'ran.

After some debate, Yusuf agrees on a new strategy. He
will embark once again for Al-Andalus, but this time he
will ignore the lying ways of the taifa kings. He will fight
his own war against Alphonso, and he is determined to win.
If he does, he will be able to claim the whole of Al-Andalus
for himself and his kingdom will become an empire.

I am making my way home from the market when I realise I am being followed. I take first one street and then another, circling my house, unwilling to lead the man, whoever he may be, into my world. At last, in a narrow alleyway one street away from my home, I turn to face him. He is dressed like a local, but his skin is fairer than most and when he speaks, I swallow. His accent is like mine; I hear in it the notes of my childhood.

"May I speak with you?" he says.

"You are already speaking with me," I say, wanting to hear him speak again, so that I can be certain of what I heard, so that I can hear again a voice from my past.

"I would like to speak with you in private," says the man. He does not move forwards; he does not sound threatening.

"How do I know I can trust you?" I ask.

"I have not harmed you," he says. "I have known who you are for some time and have brought no harm to you or your household."

"My household?"

"A child, I believe," he says. "And a handmaiden for many years, or companion, whatever she is. A Jewess."

"Why would you need to know about me?" I ask.

"I am from Galicia, like yourself."

"And what is that to me?" I ask.

"I could return you to your home," he says. "The Convent of the Sacred Way, was it not?"

I have not heard its name for so long and yet in his mouth, I am suddenly there, in the silent cloisters, in the peace of my stillroom, tending to the sick along the pilgrims' route, surrounded by my sisters in God, my fellow brides of Christ. The scent of my plants rises up before me in the garden that I tended for so many years.

"How do you know its name?"

"That hardly matters," he says. "But it is your home, and I have the means to return you there."

"How?"

"In return for something," he says.

Of course. There is always a price to be paid. "What do you want from me?" I ask.

"Not much," he says. "May I enter your house?"

I take him away from curious gazes. I take him to an empty room, unwilling even to show him my study, wanting to share as little as possible with this man, this stranger, this person who knows so much about me. I do not offer him a seat; I do not offer him refreshment. I only take him to the room and turn to face him.

"What do you want from me?" I repeat.

"I believe you could do my master a great service," he says.

"And who is your master?" I ask.

"Rodrigo del Diaz," he says.

"I do not know this man," I say.

"He is a great warrior in our homeland," says the man. "But now he must face a vast and powerful army from a foreign land. He has need of knowledge."

"What army?" I ask, knowing the answer already.

"The Almoravids," he says. "Yusuf bin Tashfin intends to come against my master. And I believe you are in a position to find out when, and how, and other such knowledge as may benefit my master."

"Yusuf bin Tashfin is my master," I point out. "It would seem our masters are set against one another."

"Perhaps we could share a master," says the man.

"Meaning?"

"My master would gladly become your master," says the man. "And would set you free in return for your service, would return you to your home at the convent, with a goodly sum of money to benefit your holy community."

"You cannot promise such a thing," I say.

"I can," says the man. "It would not be impossible to take you away from here, to the sea, to have you set sail on a ship and be returned to our homeland. It can be arranged. For a price."

"And what do you want to know?" I ask.

"Timings. Numbers of men. Locations."

"I know nothing of these things. These are not things my master discusses with me."

"But you could ask."

"Then he would be suspicious."

"I am sure a woman of your learning could find a way."

"What makes you think I am disloyal to my master?"

"You are a slave," he reminds me, "and a slave has little loyalty to a master who has not set them free."

"He has given me a great deal," I say. "He has treated me well."

"But you are still a slave," he says. "Or are you more to him than that?"

"That is not your business," I say.

"Is the child yours?" he asks.

"He belongs to the Jewess," I say.

"Does he?" says the man.

"Yes," I say.

"I wonder," says the man. "I wonder if I should look into his parentage."

I stand in silence before him.

He waits, then nods his head. "You are not as eager to return to the convent as I expected," he says. "I thought your vows were sacred."

"I think you should leave now," I say.

"Of course," he says, and bows to me in the style of our country, which looks odd in the local robes he affects. "But think on what I have said. If you need to find me, you may tell the storyteller in the marketplace and he will know where to seek me out."

"Leave," I say.

"Think on it carefully," he says, walking down the stairs, his voice drifting back to me. "Think on where your loyalties lie, Sister Juliana."

I spend the rest of the day at prayer, shaken by the man's visit, by his knowledge of my life before here, by the offer he has made, even the use of my old name. I could leave here. I know that Yusuf would tell me enough that I could please the man's master, that I could ask questions carefully, without arousing his suspicion. I know that I could gather what has been asked for, and be stolen away from here in the night, travel far away before Yusuf finds out, sail across the sea and return to the convent, return to the life I once led. I believe what the man offers, I know that such knowledge as he has asked for would be of sufficient value that it would be worth his while to honour his promise to me in return. And have I not longed for the convent, all these years? I could leave here, with Ali in Rebecca's loving hands. I am sure he would be safe enough. I could leave here, and sail away from the past years, from all my sins and failings, from all the temptations this world has offered me and have my slate wiped clean. Begin again, anew, ask for forgiveness and receive absolution, for was I not sinned against? Was I not taken by force and kept without my will by heathens? I would be welcomed back with open arms; of this I am certain. Years have passed, but my sisters will have remembered me, prayed for me, hoped that I might one day return, whilst grieving for my loss. They will have thought me dead. If I returned, I would be a holy miracle, proof of God's will and blessing.

It would be so easy. But I cannot.

Ali hugs me goodnight and I bid Rebecca farewell for the day as she returns to Daniel, before retreating to my prayer room.

And I lie to myself, as always. I know full well what keeps me here, and it is neither Aisha nor Rebecca, who now have their own families, nor Fatima, now a healer and grown woman. In part it is Ali of course, although I know that he would be cared for in my absence. But it is my own heart that I think of, not the hearts of others. It is my own treacherous desire for Yusuf, and the knowledge that he is not just my master but my beloved, that means I cannot leave this place while he still lives, nor can I ever choose what I long for.

And now that I know this, why do I not give in? Why

do I not choose the life I long for, choose Yusuf? Perhaps I cannot let go of the vows I once made, perhaps I am too much of a coward to knowingly pit myself against Zaynab, knowing what she is capable of, what I might have to face. Or perhaps I am too afraid to open my heart more than a crack, that I cannot face what emotions I might feel, if I were to love Yusuf as I long to.

The next day I go to the market square and watch the storyteller. I wonder if I could touch his arm and ask him under my breath where the man from Galicia is, to send him a message that the woman he spoke with wishes to speak with him again. But I do not. So now I know where my loyalties lie. I am going against my own homeland, my own king and his chosen warrior. The man they call El Cid will not be my hero, will not be the man whose armies and banners I cheer on. Instead I send against my own countryman another man, a veiled warrior who carries my heart by his side. I have forsworn my own people and cast in my lot with the heathen army that seeks to vanquish them, an army whose God is not my God.

Who am I then, who am I if I have forsworn my vows and the God to whom I made them? I kneel to pray but cannot find the answer.

Yusuf does not hold back. The King of Granada is taken and bound in chains, then sent across the sea to Zaynab, who decrees that he will henceforth live in Aghmat, now only a humble outpost. He is followed in less than a month by the King of Malaga, then the King of Seville. Zaynab must be enjoying her power over these foreign rulers, who must kneel to a woman and show gratitude for having their life spared. Valencia holds out the longest, but Rodrigo Del Diaz, known as El Cid, does not last long once his own son falls in battle. He dies shortly afterwards, broken by his son's demise and Yusuf's strength. And with this hero gone, the Christian armies lose their spirit. They huddle in the North, Al-Andalus is now wholly in Yusuf's hands. His kingdom has become an empire.

I hear from Aisha that Yusuf is due to return from Al-Andalus and my heart leaps. I try to pretend that I want the house cleaned from top to bottom out of the desire for cleanliness and order, but I know it is not true. I make Ali recite to me from his studies, I stand over him to see how smooth his handwriting is. I find myself stitching new robes for all of our household, in fine new wools and bright colours. I look down at what I'm stitching for myself, a golden yellow, so much unlike how I used to dress that I wonder for a moment if I should wear my customary grey or brown. But the colour mirrors what is in my heart, a lightening, a gladdening. I keep stitching.

The day that Yusuf returns to Murakush I feel giddy, I can settle to nothing. At last Rebecca says that she will take Ali out, that she needs to buy fruits in the marketplace. I agree that they may go, reminding myself that Yusuf will not visit us today, he has barely returned and will have much to do. He will not think of us for many days, I am certain of it.

It is a quiet day, Fatima tends to one or two patients upstairs, but most of the house is silent. I sit by the fountain in the empty courtyard and look into the water below, see my rippled reflection. Slowly I untie my hair wrap and look at how long and dark my hair has grown in these years. I should shave it of course, should return to the pale scalp that earned me the cruel name of moon, but I have not done so and I know, running my hands through its thickness, that I will not do so in the future. I see many strands of grey, and wonder whether, if I were to wash it with rosemary and walnut shells, whether I might reverse the greying, return my hair to the darkness of my youth. I reach out to rub a nearby sprig of rosemary between my fingertips, pluck it and hold it close to my nose, the smell overwhelming. Such vanity.

"There you are. With your plants, of course, as always."

I leap to my feet and take several steps towards Yusuf before I come to a sudden halt, holding myself back from throwing myself into his arms. I cannot do such a thing, but for one moment it was all I thought of.

"Have you changed your mind about greeting me?" he asks, closing the gap between us and coming to a halt so close in front of me that I take a step backwards.

I breathe in to answer and smell his scent, the rough smell of camel and sweat, but beneath that the smell of his own body, which I know too well. I breathe out again, unable to answer.

"You need not step away from me," he says, and his voice has grown deeper and quieter. He lifts his arm and to my astonishment runs his fingers through my hair. "I have never seen your hair unbound," he says.

"It is supposed to be veiled, like your face," I say, my voice shaking.

He takes his hand away from my head and instead pulls at his face veil, dropping it to the floor beside him, so that we stand face to face, the paleness of the skin beneath his eyes still startling to me. He has aged, these past years of fighting have been hard on a man already advanced in years. I feel myself trembling, think to kneel and collect my own head wrap, to pin it fiercely about myself and turn away from this intimacy. But I do not. I stand and gaze into his eyes in silence, until his hand reaches out again and this time touches my cheek.

"I have found a name for you," he says.

I jerk out a laugh. "After all these years without one that pleased you?"

"It is a name that suits you," he says.

I can think of nothing but his fingers on my skin. I have to blink, have to focus on what he has said. "And what is this name?"

"Fadl al-Hasan," he says.

I frown, then give a forced laugh. "Perfection of Beauty? I am hardly perfect."

He does not smile. His finger slips over the skin of my cheek, over my scars at the side of my face, usually hidden under my headwrap. "I think a better meaning is 'More than Perfection,'" he says softly, and I feel my skin turn to goose flesh, my cheeks grow flushed beneath his touch. "You are more than perfect."

I do not know how to respond to this intimacy from Yusuf. "You have changed," I say, my voice still shaking. "You have not spoken like this to me before."

"I missed you," he says simply.

"How did you have time to miss me?"

"I told you before. I miss speaking to someone of the small things."

"You have achieved great things while you were away," I say.

"Perhaps it is time to achieve something else," he says.

I should step away. I should make some light-hearted jest, to break the moment.

"It seems I must rule two lands now," he says. "But I have only one queen. Perhaps I should have another."

I say nothing.

"If each queen had her own land to rule over," he continues, his voice very low, "there could surely be no rivalry."

"Jealousy does not arise over lands," I say, my own voice barely above a whisper. "It arises when it is a heart that must be shared."

"You could rule as my queen over Al-Andalus," he says. "I will divide my time between there and here."

"I have no desire to rule over a kingdom," I say.

"Do you desire anything else that is in my power to give?" he asks.

I breathe in. The scent of him, standing so close to me, is almost too much to bear. "Do not ask that question," I say finally. "I cannot bring myself to answer it."

"And if I continue to ask?"

"I beg you not to," I say, and the effort it is costing me, to stand so close to him yet not touch him, to speak without accepting what he is offering, grows too much.

I turn and run away from him, make my way up the

staircase and into my own bedchamber. I kneel by the window and look up at the bright sky above me, breathe deeply, wipe tears from my eyes.

Near to my hand is the small carved box in which I keep my most precious items, such few things as I have. I take it and turn around so that I am sitting on the floor, knees pulled up, the casket in my hands.

Falling Silver Beads

Let him kiss me with the kisses of his mouth.

Song of Solomon, 1:2

I TRY TO BREATHE SLOWLY, OPEN the casket to soothe myself with its familiar contents. I pull out the ivory rattle that Yusuf gave to Ali when he was a baby. I shake it and smile, replace it in the casket. There is a tiny cross that Rebecca gave to me when she married Daniel. My fingers touch the betrothal necklace I picked up from the ground when Kella left Murakush. I pull it out and look at it more closely, it has been years since I held it. It is a simple thing, little black beads interspersed with silver triangles, marked with symbols from her people, which mean nothing to me.

"Where did you get that from?" Yusuf has followed me, he is standing in the doorway, frowning. He has replaced his veil, I can only see his eyes and brows.

"It is nothing," I say quickly, replacing the necklace in the casket. My fingers are on the lid, ready to close it. My breath, which had begun to slow, comes faster again.

"Show me it."

His tone tells me I cannot disobey. Slowly, I reach back into the casket and hold up the little necklace.

He crosses the room and takes it. His fingers are shaking. He turns the necklace over in his hands, looks for something I cannot see and then stares down at me. "Where did you get this?"

"I – I found it." I feel vulnerable, sitting so low down, but I do not have the courage to stand and face him. I try to look away, but it is not a good enough answer. When I look up again his gaze is still on me, the hand that holds the necklace still shaking.

He is waiting.

"I found it after Kella left," I say. It is clear to me that he knows to whom it belongs, although I have seen other such necklaces. There is something about it that has identified it to him as Kella's and there is no use denying where it comes from.

"Where is she?"

"I do not know," I say honestly. "Truly, I would tell you if I knew."

"You found it where?"

"Outside her home."

"What were you doing there?"

"I – I saw her leave."

He stares at me in disbelief. "You knew she was leaving, and you did not call for me? You did not tell me afterwards where she had gone?"

"I did not know where she was going," I say.

"You did not try to stop her?"

I hesitate. "She was afraid of Zaynab," I say at last. "She had to leave."

"No harm would have come to her," says Yusuf, and

his eyes have grown angry. "She was under my protection. Zaynab would not have harmed her."

"If you say so," I say.

"What is your meaning?" he asks, his voice tight.

"She set Hela to serve her and Hela saw to it that she lost a child." I say, standing up. He comes very close to me, looks into my face as though to seek the truth in my eyes. I meet his gaze without flinching, without looking away.

"Why did she leave?" he asks. "She could have come to me for protection."

I shake my head. "I do not know," I say. "I do not know all that was in her mind."

"What else do you keep in that casket?" he asks.

I feel the blood drain from my face, then rush back, my neck and cheeks hot. "Nothing," I say.

"You will forgive me, but I do not believe you," he says. "Give it to me."

"It is mine," I say.

He holds up the little necklace, the tiny silver triangles dangling. "But this was mine," he says. "It was mine and I gave it to Kella. It was not yours to keep, all these years. Show me the casket."

This is the moment then, the moment as I have thought of all the years that I have raised Ali. This is the moment when all I have done will come to light. I hold out the casket, my hands shaking so hard that the lid rattles, my knees suddenly weak. I try to steady my breathing. Yusuf takes it, his eyes never leaving my face.

"What is it?" he asks. He looks concerned now, he does not even look at the casket that he holds, he looks only into my eyes.

I shake my head. "Open it," I say.

He looks down at the tiny casket, lifts the lid and pulls out the tiny rattle he once gave Ali, looks at me.

"The beads," I say, my voice almost a whisper.

He looks down again, frowns, then returns the rattle to the casket and instead lifts out the long string of silver beads. He holds them closer, looks at the engravings on each and suddenly the casket drops from his other hand, hits the floor with a shattered thud, lies broken on the tiles beneath our feet. Neither of us look at it.

"What is the meaning of this?" he asks. "Why do you have the beads I gave to Kella for our son? He died at birth."

I try to speak, but my mouth is so dry it will not even open. I try to wet my lips, finally manage to open them and whisper. "He… did not die."

He stares at me. "What?"

I try again, speak a little louder. "He did not die," I say. "He lives."

"She took him away with her?"

I shake my head.

"How would you know whether he is alive or dead?"

"She gave him to me," I say.

He says nothing, only gazes at me for a long moment. "*Gave* him to you?"

"To protect him," I say. "From Zaynab. Kella was afraid of her. She gave Ali to me and left, so that Zaynab would leave him alone."

"She gave Ali, my son, to you?"

"Yes," I say.

"And he lives?"

"Yes," I say.

He is silent. "The child you have raised all these years," he says at last, "and whom you have called Ali, he is…"

"He is your son," I say, and the relief of saying it, after all this time, brings tears pouring down my cheeks so suddenly that they surprise me. I put a hand up to wipe them away and Yusuf takes me by the wrist, pulls me close to him, so close that our bodies touch.

"Swear," he says, and I am almost afraid of him for a moment, his voice is so hard, his grip on my wrist so tight that it is painful.

"I swear," I say.

We stare at each other. His grip on my wrist does not lessen.

"I swear," I say, my voice stronger now. "Your wife Kella gave me her son, your son Ali, to raise, to protect from Zaynab. She left this place and you to protect Ali. She gave me those beads to prove his lineage. I watched her leave and saw the necklace fall. I have kept them all these years. And I have raised Ali, as I promised Kella I would do."

"You have raised my son?"

"Yes," I say.

"He is the child I have seen all these years? Now a man?"

"Yes," I say. He is repeating himself but I can see belief beginning to dawn in his face.

He lets go of my wrist. Slowly, he kneels before me. I look down on him, uncertain of what he is doing. He takes the hem of my robe in his hands and kisses it. When he looks up at me, his eyes are overflowing with tears. "You have performed a greater service than I could ever have asked of you," he says.

"I swore I would care for him," I say, my tears falling

down onto his veil. "I brought him into this world and now I deliver him back into your hands."

He makes me tell him everything, every time that my path crossed with Kella, everything she said, however small. It should be difficult, after all this time, but such were the events of that time that they are emblazoned on my mind. I tell him of Ali's birth and of Kella's visit to my home, of her desperate request and my promise to her. I explain how Rebecca came into our lives, and he blesses her name, laughing through his tears.

"I must see him," he says suddenly, as though the idea has only just occurred to him. "I must tell him everything."

"He knows nothing," I say. "Tell him gently, it will be a shock to him. He thinks of Rebecca and me as his mothers. He knows nothing of Kella. But he will be proud to be your son," I add.

Yusuf is beside himself. He cannot wait to speak with Ali, he paces impatiently about the house until he returns from his studies. I find myself growing nervous. The son I had is about to be lost to me, he will no longer call me mother. I find the tears welling up in me and force them back down. I am not his mother, I remind myself, he has a mother of his own and a father, whose identity he is about to learn. My promise is fulfilled, I have protected him all these years and I am about to deliver him safely to his father.

When Ali does come home, Yusuf's face is flushed with joy. I watch from the upper storey as he takes Ali's arm and pulls him towards the fountain, the two of them sat side-by-side on the tiled edge, Yusuf's voice is low, his words rapid. I keep my eyes on Ali's face and watch it turn from puzzlement to wonder. He looks up at me, searching for my confirmation of what he's being told and when I nod, his shoulders shake, and Yusuf takes him in his arms.

"I must go," says Yusuf to me, after some time has passed. "I will return tomorrow," he adds, looking at Ali, whose face is both lit up with the wonderment of what has happened and blotched with his tears.

When he has gone, I stand awkwardly, waiting to hear what Ali has to say to me, but when he comes to me, he kneels at my feet and looks up into my face. "You are still my mother," he says. "For you and Rebecca are the only mothers I have ever known."

"I can tell you about your mother if you wish," I say.

"I would like to hear about the woman who gave me life," he says. "But I cannot call her mother. You are my mother."

I sit with him and tell him all I can about Kella, about her life before she met Yusuf, about the moment when she threw in her lot with him, and how she came to leave this place. I try not to accuse Zaynab, for I cannot risk Ali taking offence against her. A young man might foolishly swear vengeance on such a woman, should he know the true story between her and his mother. Instead I say only that Zaynab was fiercely jealous, that Kella did not wish for Ali to grow up with such rivalry around him and that she was unhappy herself, unable to live alongside Yusuf as she would have wished. That she made her way to a different life, that I know a good man went with her, along with loyal servants. Throughout, I tell him how much she loved him, how distraught she was on the black night when she brought him to me and begged for my help. I show him the string of silver beads, I show him the engagement necklace Yusuf gave her, and he holds them as though they were holy relics. Some of his questions I do not have the answers to but again and again he embraces me and thanks me, calls me mother. Our tears mingle and that night I retire to bed, exhausted from the emotions of two decades released in one afternoon.

The days that follow are filled with even more emotion. Rebecca hears what has happened and spends time with Ali, telling him her own story. Yusuf returns daily, speaking with Ali and embracing him constantly. He kneels to me every time he sees me, thanking me over and over again for what I have done, offering me anything, anything I desire, to which I shake my head and insist he stands. But then the arguments begin.

"Council will be held," Yusuf tells me while Ali is absent. "I will name Ali as my son. Once he has been accepted, I will name him my heir."

I feel myself grow cold. "You cannot," I say, too quickly. "Why?"

I want to say Zaynab's name, but I dare not, even here, alone with him. "Ali has not been raised to be your heir," I say. "He has been raised to be a man of peace, not a man of war. Your empire is still so new, it will need a warrior to hold it."

But Yusuf only beams. "I have created an empire," he

says. "Now it needs a man of peace to rule it, to create a land of plenty, a land filled with knowledge and goodwill amongst my people."

"He – " I begin.

"I have known him all his life," says Yusuf, interrupting me, still delighted. "He has been taught by the finest scholars, he is a man of knowledge, a man of the law. There is not one scholar who could argue with his knowledge of our religion and the law."

"He knows nothing of military strategy," I say.

"He has an army at his disposal," says Yusuf, unperturbed. "He has experienced generals at his command. His brothers, my other sons, will guide him in these matters."

"One of his brothers will expect to inherit your throne," I say. "They will be angry at being passed over. Why should they help him?"

"The choice of heir lies in my hands," says Yusuf. "Ali is my first son and the son of my first wife. And he has been raised by you," he adds softly.

I cannot help myself. "Zaynab – " I begin.

"The decision is mine to take," says Yusuf and from his tone I know it is useless to argue any further. I am greatly fearful for Ali's safety once Zaynab knows of his existence, but there is nothing I can do to change Yusuf's mind and Ali himself glows when he is told what is to come. He looks into the future and sees himself following in the footsteps of Yusuf, leading the empire into an era of peace and tranquillity, of stability.

"It will be like Cordoba," he says to me, his eyes alight with joy. "It will be everything you said Cordoba once was, but greater. Muslims, Christians, and Jews sharing knowledge, an empire the like of which has never been seen before."

I want to believe it is possible, that the vision he has for the future can come true, but at the same time I curse myself for having told Ali stories of the past that may be impossible to emulate. Cordoba's glory did not last long. I wish that I could consult with my own father, to ask him how Cordoba came to be and whether it is possible for this boy, this man, whom I think of as my son, to make such a time come alive again. I think that if anyone can manage it, this child, son of a Muslim, raised by a Christian, suckled by a Jewess, could be the one to do it, but I am afraid for him.

"I will pray that you are successful," I say. "I will pray every day of my life that your empire shines greater than Cordoba.

"We will go there together, you and I," he says enthusiastically. "We will pray together in Cordoba that its light may shine out across this new empire again."

I can only embrace him and nod, can only pray for his success and that he escapes Zaynab's wrath.

"Council has been summoned," Yusuf tells me. He has come to my house early; the dawn prayer was less than an hour ago. "You will attend with Ali," he tells me.

"There is no need for me to attend," I say quickly. "Ali is your son, I am not even his mother," I add, forswearing my child in an instant, for the chance to avoid being in the same room as Zaynab when she hears this news.

"Zaynab was calm enough," says Yusuf, knowing full well why I refuse to go.

"I do not believe that," I say. "Does she know that you are about to name him your heir?"

"No," he says. His tone is set, stubborn.

"Then I will not be there when you tell her," I say. "How do you think she will react? She surely expects her own son to succeed you."

"It is my choice," repeats Yusuf. I give a tiny sigh and he frowns. "Surely you want Ali, the child you have raised, to succeed me?"

"It will be as you wish," I say.

"Yes, it will," he says, and sweeps from the room. "You will attend with Ali," he calls over his shoulder as he leaves.

I have no choice. Guards are sent to accompany us. Ali, dressed in his best robes, is glowing, although his demeanour changes a little as we come close to the Council chambers set within the palace. I can see him growing nervous and reach out a hand to touch his shoulder as Yusuf comes to greet him with open arms, gesturing to me to follow them into the chambers. I stand in the doorway, half hidden from the room, watching as Ali steps into the space. I look beyond him, to Yusuf's other sons, most born to Zaynab, two to slave women I do not know the names of. They are so very different from Ali. All of them have broad shoulders, their forearms ripple with muscles. These are men of war; they have been trained by the best warriors in Yusuf's army. They may have completed some studies, but they have not been held to their books day after day. Instead they have learned to fight, to command, to face the enemy in battle and ride out with courage in their hearts. They carry swords on their hips, daggers in their belts. Zaynab's eldest son, Abu Tahir, sits next to her and he looks every inch a future amir, the man everyone expects to succeed Yusuf. I swallow. Will he step aside and let Ali rule? Or will he seek him out in some deserted backstreet and end my son's life with a single stroke of the sword his hand is resting on?

Ali has joined the scholars, who are seated at the far end of the room, speaking with them, his back turned to the generals and governors that make up the rest of the room.

Yusuf stands and I brace myself.

"I ask the council to welcome my son, Ali. Child to my first wife Kella, now no longer with us."

There is a murmur, a ripple of interest. The council members turn their heads, stare at Ali with curiosity. He stands, a little pale, but with his head held high, looking to Yusuf for his confidence.

"The woman who raised him will vouch for his birth," says Yusuf. He gestures to me. "Isabella, join us."

I step forwards, my stomach churning, vomit rising in my throat. One of the scholars is rising, no doubt to question me. I look towards Zaynab and see her face has grown white, her hands are clenched into fists at her side.

The scholar is old, one of Yusuf's most important advisers. He begins to question me. I try to give my answers in a clear voice, without trembling.

"I swear that this man is Ali, son to Yusuf bin Tashfin and his wife Kella."

"Do you know where Kella is now?"

"I do not."

"Is she alive?"

"I do not know."

"How did you come to have this child in your care?"

Zaynab leans forwards, her dark eyes darker still in her white face.

"His mother summoned me as a midwife when she birthed him. He was born into my hands."

"Did she give him to you at once?"

"No. She came to me in great secrecy later that night. She claimed that the boy's life was in danger, that he must be raised by another. She begged me to take him. I did so." I swallow, trying to stop the tears that are welling in my eyes at the thought of that night, that request, that choice.

"From whom was he in danger?"

I do not let my eyes flicker towards her. I know that she is watching me. I know that she is waiting to hear her own name, preparing herself to fight. I shake my head.

"Give me a name," the old man insists. I can feel the tightness in the chamber, can hear the Council members waiting.

"I cannot."

There is a pause, while the scholar and the rest of the Council wait to see if I will relent, if there is any value to be had in continuing to press me for a name that I appear unwilling to give. Certainly, they know there is a name, but for now they have more pressing matters.

"Can you prove this story?"

I pull the string of silver beads from my robes and explain that Kella gave them to me to prove Ali's lineage. I look to Yusuf and ask if they are the same beads that he gave to his first wife and he agrees that they are. He adds that he confirms my story, that he believes the truth of what I say, that he himself accepts Ali as his son, his firstborn son.

The council cannot gainsay a father's word, nor the evidence I have provided. Besides, they do not need this proof. Ali may look like a scholar rather than a warrior, but no one could doubt him for Yusuf's son, the eyes are the same, even the way he turns his head from one side to another is the same. There is no argument. Only the elderly scholar wonders worriedly whether Ali, under my influence, has been raised a Christian, but I shake my head and tell them that he has been raised a Muslim, in deference to his lineage. There is a murmur of approval and the scholar himself presses my hand and declares me a blessed woman for having protected Ali all these years and having delivered him back to his father. The rest of the Council welcomes Ali as Yusuf's son and I feel my shoulders drop with relief. Even Zaynab gives a long slow nod, her face stony, but the nod has been given.

"There will be a banquet of welcome for my son," declares Yusuf. "You will all accompany us to give thanks and celebrate on this joyful day."

I try to steady myself at the thought of sitting at the same table as Zaynab. She is already approaching me.

Ali turns to her and bows deeply. "Lady Zaynab," he says, "I believe you knew my mother."

She looks him over and her eyes do not flicker, her mouth does not curve into a smile. "I did not know her well before she left," she says. Her smile comes as she watches Ali's face flush at the deliberate reminder that his mother abandoned him. I want to step forward, but I remind myself that if all she is going to do is make pointed barbs about his mother, then he is still safe.

"Come," says Yusuf, gesturing to Ali to precede him out of the door. As Ali does so, Yusuf turns to me, ignoring Zaynab, who is waiting for his hand. Instead, he extends his hand to me. "Join us," he says, his voice soft, pulling me towards him with his fingertips, my body brushing against his as we move forwards together. I should look behind me. I should be wary, but I cannot help it. I look up at Yusuf and he looks down at me with infinite tenderness. For one moment I am his queen and we are celebrating our son. Zaynab is far away and we can be happy. Behind me, I hear her voice say something, very low, but then she brushes past us and moves away, followed by her son Abu Tahir, whom she waves away as though he were unimportant. She is not headed towards the palace, rather back into some other part of the city. But I am swept away in this moment of happiness and I do not watch to see where she goes. She does not attend the banquet, and because I have Ali with me, I do not wonder where she has gone, I am only grateful that I do not have to sit near her, that I can celebrate with a full heart. No doubt, she cannot bear to attend such a celebration, and for this I do not blame her. She will hide away in her rooms and emerge later, when I have gone, and Ali is no longer being toasted.

We are sent a messenger the very next day. Yusuf does not wish to wait. He will announce his heir today, in the Council chambers. Again, we set out, again I am overcome with nerves but have to smile for Ali, have to nod at his happy talk of what is to come. When we arrive, Ali is seated amongst Yusuf's sons and daughters, as is now his right. He takes his place happily and his half siblings nod graciously, well versed enough in court etiquette to know that it would be unseemly to scowl and turn their faces away, especially when Yusuf's eyes are upon them.

Abu Tahir has not yet joined his siblings. Instead he stands with Zaynab while the council members arrive, and I feel myself grow cold as I see all of them, scholars, warriors, governors, major and minor officials, bowing deeply to the pair of them. It is clear that the Council expects Abu Tahir to be named as Yusuf's heir today. I take a seat far at the back of the chamber, afraid of what is to come. I wonder if fighting will break out, or whether Yusuf's authority will keep them all in check.

Yusuf himself looks excited, rejuvenated. When he stands, the Council falls silent and everyone leans forward, their faces beaming, expectant, their eyes half on Yusuf, half on Abu Tahir. Zaynab, sat by her son, lifts her chin high, waiting for the moment that will acknowledge everything she has done for this empire.

Yusuf stands. "Today I will declare my heir," he says, loudly and clearly. "Now that I command an empire, it must have a named heir, so that there can be no doubt over its future, nor any disruption nor disputation when my time to leave this world comes."

Zaynab is openly smiling. Her beauty is still exquisite despite her advancing years, she is every inch a queen.

"Ali will be my heir," says Yusuf.

There is utter silence. Mouths open, eyes widen. Abu

Tahir's face drains white, his hand tightens on the hilt of his sword.

Quickly, the Council members gather themselves. They nod and smile, they make comments to indicate that they knew this all along, that they accept Yusuf's word. There is movement and chatter, there are loud voices.

Zaynab stays absolutely still. She is frozen, made of stone. She does not speak to her son; she does not look at Yusuf. She stares only ahead, as Ali kneels for his father's blessing, makes a speech about loyalty and peace, turns to greet the most senior Council members who offer him their fealty. His half siblings reluctantly swear the same, even Abu Tahir, unable to do otherwise under his father's watchful eyes, although he then strides from the council chambers, hand still on his sword, people hastily making way for him. Through all of this, Zaynab sits still, her face empty of emotion.

"There will be a ceremony of allegiance," says Yusuf. "Here and in Cordoba. Each governor will make a pledge of loyalty to Ali."

I know that this location has already been agreed upon with Ali, who thinks of Cordoba as a sort of holy land, a city that encompasses a past that he wishes to resurrect. Yusuf and Ali embrace, then leave the room, as do all the Council members. I join them, trying to hide in the crowd, aware that all of us are filing past Zaynab as though she were not there, pretending not to see her upright body, her set face, waiting for us to leave so that she can release the rage and grief inside of her. I hardly dare look at her, but when I do, I see that her eyes do not even follow any of us, she looks only straight ahead, as though seeing something we do not, perhaps her empire crumbling.

Aisha comes to my house, her face white.

"What is it?" I ask. "Has something happened to Ali? To Yusuf?"

"Let me in," she says in a half whisper.

I stand aside, and she pushes past me, pulling her hood back from her face as she does so. She refuses to speak until we are fully inside the house, sitting at my table.

"Well?"

"Zaynab is dead."

"That is not possible," I say. "I saw her yesterday. She was well. I saw her at the naming ceremony for Ali." I stop speaking, aware of what I have just said, of where I saw her, of what had happened. I meet Aisha's gaze. "Did she – " I cannot complete the sentence, do not want to complete the thought.

"They think so," whispers Aisha, as though we were surrounded by listeners. "They found her with a cup in her hand."

I think at once of Hela's cup, but that broke long ago, this would have been another cup, nothing magic about it, but containing something that ended Zaynab's life. She would have known what to make, she would have known what to put together, which ingredients to mix. The mixture would have smelt strong and unpleasant, even fetid, but she would have drunk it anyway, she would have set the cup to her lips and swallowed, knowing full well what she did. I shiver, knowing that she did this, took this action, because of Ali, because of Yusuf's choice to make him his heir, and

I know that he did this in part because he loves me. It is a choice of emotion and love, not the choice he should have made. I know full well that Zaynab's son would have been a better choice, he has been raised as a warrior, has been raised as a future ruler. I think of Zaynab's face as Yusuf spoke the words that crowned Ali as his successor. I was too grateful for her absence to wonder where she had gone, to think of how she felt, having her empire given to a child she had long thought dead, son of the mother she managed to get rid of, raised by a woman whose relationship with Yusuf she never knew existed. But she knew before she died, I would swear to it. She knew in the very moment that Yusuf touched my arm, in the deepness and softness of his voice when he spoke to me. She was a clever woman; she could not fail to see. I sit in silence while Aisha stares at me.

"I must pray," I say.

She sits beside me. I do not know if she, too, prays, or whether she only thinks on what has happened. I try to pray, but the words do not come. I try to empty my heart and have God's word fill it, but nothing comes. There is only an emptiness and below that, so deep below, so far down that I should not acknowledge it even to myself, there is relief and gladness. I am free. I am safe. The woman I have feared all these years is gone. The boy I think of as my son is Yusuf's heir. And Yusuf... Yusuf is now mine alone, should I wish to claim him. I rise from my knees. Aisha follows me back to the table, and we sit again in silence.

"What will you do now?" she asks.

I shake my head. "I do not know," I say.

In the days that follow, my prayers for Zaynab come

unbidden. I try to forgive her sins, though I am not sure that I do so fully, but I pray for her soul and I pray that what she and Yusuf created together, this great empire, may endure without her. I cannot but acknowledge that she was a great ruler, for all her savage jealousy and the cruelties she inflicted on others. I know that if I had been by Yusuf's side, his empire would have failed. I think of the three of us: of Kella, who gave Yusuf a son but could not withstand Zaynab, of Zaynab herself, a great and terrifying queen who created an empire. And myself? I have not been a mother, yet I have mothered Ali. I am nothing to Yusuf and yet I know he is everything to me and that I am held in his heart. I have played no part in creating this empire, yet I have raised the man who will rule it one day. I wonder at the strangeness of my life here. I have saved one abandoned woman and raised a desperate woman's child, I have loved a man and know I am loved in return, I have made a Jewess and a Muslim my closest friends. And yet, I am still a virgin untouched, a bride of Christ, my vows are still upheld. I wonder at God's ways, at his intentions for me. I wonder if the whole of my life since touching that red fruit so long ago has been one long punishment or an endless gift. Was I cast out of the Garden of Eden or sent out on a holy pilgrimage? I do not know, even after all these years I still cannot tell.

I do not see Zaynab's body before she is buried. She had grown old, but her beauty was legendary, it remained undimmed by time. Servants and slaves cowered away from her, thinking her powerful beyond this world. They claimed she spoke with djinns and other such nonsense, though I did not believe that. I believe, instead, that she was a woman who knew how to make others talk, divulging secrets they would not entrust to anyone else.

I think back to the first time I saw her, riding past in the streets of Aghmat, queen to a powerful amir, more beautiful than any woman I had ever seen, loaded down with gemstones and rich silks. She had everything, and yet her face was that of a truly unhappy woman. I believe she found a better match in Yusuf, although it burns my heart to think of it. She was his equal, the right woman to have led his empire with him side-by-side. However she ensnared him, I have to admit that she was a peerless queen for him. My own feelings for Yusuf are my own sin, my own temptation. She was free to marry, and she saw in him everything I did and more. She was right to claim him for her own, even though I have hated her for it all these years and tried to deny what I felt for her: jealousy, pure and simple. I am honest enough to admit it, now.

"I will send you home, should you wish it," says Yusuf.

I stare at him.

"I have had the documents drawn up," he says. He pushes paper towards me, and I look down at it, words appearing out of a blur: my own name, the word freedom, his name at the bottom.

I look up at him. Do not speak. My belly feels as though it is weighed down, I sense a rising nausea.

"You are a free woman," he says. "I have granted you a sum of money, to do with as you please."

I look back down at the document, see what has been

granted to me. It is a vast quantity of gold, a sum for a princess, a queen. I raise my eyes to meet his.

"If you wish to return to the convent," he says, "I have appointed Imari to take you. He has been paid a goodly sum to carry out this task whenever you should wish to go, be it now or after my death. I have made enquiries; he has maps and all the needed directions to return you to the place you came from. You have only to call on him and it will be done."

"You are sending me away?" It comes out of my mouth so fast I blink.

For the first time in this conversation, he looks amused. "I would never do that," he says. "As you know full well. I would rather ask you to be my queen, but I believe the answer would be no."

I stare at him.

"Well? Will you be my queen?"

Slowly, I shake my head.

"Why?"

"For the same reason as always," I say, and a tear trickles down my cheek.

He nods. "As I thought. So, given that you will not accept what I would like to offer, I thought I would offer something else. What you long for."

"I long for you," I say.

"But what you long for, you will not accept."

I nod. I no longer deny it.

"So, will you accept my other offer?"

"I cannot leave," I say. "I cannot."

"What holds you here?"

"You know what holds me here."

"I would like to hear it from you."

"Ali."

He waits.

"And you."

"If I were to die?"

"I would go."

"And Ali?"

"A grown man does not need a mother following him about," I say.

He nods. "Will you move into the palace with me?"

I shake my head.

He snorts with laughter. "So stubborn."

"Too weak," I say, serious.

"Weak?"

"I am not stupid enough to bring temptation so close to me every day," I say.

"I wish you would," he says.

There is a short time of peace, of sunlit afternoons when Yusuf visits me and we do not have to be hidden from the world, when Ali sits by us, his face lit up with love for the both of us. We talk of the small things, as we always did, sometimes we even walk through Murakush's streets together in the bright dawns and shining twilights. The city of cloth is long gone now, replaced by the towering minarets and sturdy city walls of an empire's capital. Yusuf's pace is slow now but there is no hurry to be anywhere. We eat fresh oranges together and I open my mouth to Yusuf as he feeds me dates, their rich sweetness unable to match my happiness. A golden time.

The call I have so long dreaded comes at night. There is a beating on my gate, and I do not even enquire of the veiled guard why he has come. I throw a warm wrap over my robe and follow him through the narrow streets until we reach the palace gates, where guards spring apart to let me pass, my status here well known.

The room is lit with dozens of lanterns, their flames flickering around Yusuf's bed, his guards and senior officers lining the walls, his sons kneeling by him. Ali stands when he sees me, comes to me and kisses my hands. Yusuf's eyes are closed.

"Is he – " I begin, but already my eyes have seen the rise and fall of his chest and my question is answered.

"It will not be long now, my lady," says the attending physician. I notice his deference, his knowledge of who I am.

Yusuf's eyes open, slowly, as though the action costs him an effort. He must already have heard my voice, for his gaze is already on me. "Clear the room," he says.

"My lord – " begins one of the generals.

"My heir is already named. You have no further need of me," he says, with a trace of humour. "Clear the room."

They do so, reluctantly, beginning with the lesser officials and guards, then his sons, even Ali at the end.

I stand at the foot of his bed, the two of us alone.

"Well, I have managed to make you enter my bedchamber," he says, half smiling. "It has only taken me two decades or so."

I smile, although the tears are already flowing.

"Oh, come now," he says. "A slave kept as a concubine

must make herself pleasant to her master. You must smile, at the very least."

I swallow. "You forget," I retort, trying to laugh. "I am no longer a slave. And I was never a concubine, not even to my last master."

"Indeed, how could I forget? I have never heard of any woman leaping from a window to avoid becoming a concubine."

"Then taking two decades to enter your bedchamber should hardly be surprising, by comparison."

He holds out his hand to me and I walk around the side of the bed and sit on a stool beside him. I take his hand in mine. It is surprisingly warm, dry, as wiry as ever.

"Everything is taken care of," he says. "You know where Imari is, you will be given an army escort if it is required, there will be a ship ready to take you at your command back across the seas. Unless you prefer to travel by land. Al-Andalus is under our command now; you may travel however you wish."

I say nothing.

"Will you go home?" he asks.

"I am not sure where home is," I say.

"For a rich woman, home can be wherever she chooses," he says, smiling.

I nod.

"A woman as rich as you will be made an Abbess," he says ruefully. "Perhaps those of faith should not be swayed by money, but they usually are."

"A woman who has lived among Muslims? A woman who has raised a child? Who is rumoured to be the concubine of the heathen warlord who killed El Cid?"

"Gold is a wonderful thing for creating memory loss," he says. "As a healer you should know that."

"As a healer I should cure memory loss, not create it," I say.

"Sometimes forgetting the past is a form of healing," he says. "You can forget everything that has happened and return to your life in the convent."

I laugh out loud. "There is not enough gold in the world to forget all that has happened to me," I tell him.

We sit in silence for a little while, then I kneel by his bedside and clasp my hands together.

"What are you doing?"

"Praying for your soul," I say.

"To which god?" he asks, his voice full of laughter.

"It does not matter," I say. "Be quiet and let me pray."

When I have finished, I stand and look down on him, at the dark eyes, thick brows, the sharp nose. I put my hand to his face and pull away his veil, so that I can see his lips.

"Are you afraid you will forget my face?" he asks. He is teasing but his eyes grow serious when he sees the look on my face, how I hold his gaze.

Slowly, I bend down, close my eyes and feel our faces touch, forehead to forehead, nose to nose. I breathe in his breath and he breathes in mine. Our lips meet, one moment of temptation given into, all the past years of longing and desire distilled into this one touch, this one moment. When I straighten up, I keep my eyes on him a moment longer and then I turn and leave the room. The corridor is full of men, who part before me as I leave Yusuf's palace for the last time and make my way home, where I kneel by the fountain and weep until a messenger comes to tell me that

Yusuf is gone. When he does, I send a message of my own to Imari.

I spend the days before my departure comforting Ali, who mourns his father but thrills with the thought of ruling an empire.

"Don't go," he begs me.

"I have to return home, to fulfil my vows," I tell him. "And you are a grown man, you have no need of me. You will be a great ruler."

"I am – afraid," he admits.

"There is no shame in fear," I tell him. "Rule by your heart. Be good to your people. They deserve peace after all these years of war."

He is excited by this thought, nodding keenly.

"And Rebecca is still here," I say. "She is your mother as much as I."

"I have had three mothers," he says earnestly. "And I will honour each of you."

"You have been a blessing in all our lives," I say and embrace him again and again, thinking of Kella and how she found it impossible to let go of him, how she clung just a little longer to the feel and scent of him.

Rebecca weeps and begs me not to go, but I hold her tightly.

"Ali is close by, you have your children, your husband," I say.

"My life has changed beyond recognition, thanks to you," she says.

"Thanks to your good heart," I remind her.

"I never thought the pain of life's path would bring me to call a Christian my sister," she says, wiping her tears and mine with a corner of her robe.

I have to laugh. "Nor I a Jewess," I say. "But you are indeed my sister."

"And I?" says Aisha.

"Both my sisters, God be praised," I say.

"I will not ask which god," says Aisha. "That much at least I have learnt from you."

We laugh through our tears, the three of us embracing while Imari waits with our camels.

"Send him home safe to me," says Aisha.

"You know I will," I say.

"Do not forget us," calls Rebecca, watching me mount an irate camel who will be my steed until we reach the sea.

"I cannot forget my sisters," I call back, steadying myself in the saddle and pulling my robe about me against the morning chill.

I look back only once, see their hands raised in farewell. I raise my own hand so that they can see it, hold it aloft until I know I am no longer in their sight, then use it to wipe my eyes of the tears that will not stop falling.

The journey I make now, retracing the steps of long ago, is entirely different. Escorts of soldiers follow us from encampment to encampment, in every city I am treated as a guest of honour, lavishly fed and bedded, bowed and scraped to by the nobles and warriors that make up each city's rulers. I am almost grateful for the quiet days, when Imari and I travel mostly alone, when our food is something simple, bread and dates eaten under the shade of a tree. I watch the landscape change, watch the mountains fade away and the coast approach.

When we reach the docks, I stand for some time in the market square, watching a slave auction being prepared. I allow the merchant, a different one now, to make his opening speech, to display all his wares, before I step out of the crowd and speak with him, my lips close to his ear, his eyes wide and startled. He stands by as every slave sees their names written out in my own hand, the gold passed over to buy their freedom and the coins in heavy leather pouches they each receive so that they may make their way in the world as free men and women, their children safe by their sides. I know more slaves will come tomorrow and tomorrow and tomorrow, but at least today's slaves are free. I hope that amongst them is a girl like Catalina, now destined for something better than a rich man's plaything.

Imari watches me with a strange half smile. "If someone had bought your freedom when you were sold," he says, curious, "would you have been grateful not to have lived the life that came after you were bought?"

I smile back. "There are not many slaves whose lives beyond today would have brought them what my life here has brought me," I say.

He nods at the truth of what I say and goes about finding a ship we can board, an easy task. There is no shortage of captains willing to be paid in gold for a simple voyage with a small cargo.

I do not know where in the dark waters Sister Maria died. I do not know which part of the sea received her body, nor where her spirit went. But when the stars are bright above us on our last night of sailing, I throw dried rose petals onto the waves beneath us and hope that my too-late tribute reaches her in some form. I think of her ready smile and her love for the world in all its forms, her kindness to others and her fear of what might happen to her when we were taken, how the darkness of our future must have been too much to bear. I think of what it must have taken for her to look into a different kind of darkness below and how cold the water must have been around her as she died. We took such different paths, she and I, each of which might be condemned, and by each of which we might have been blessed.

It is dawn when we land, still half-dark. I am not bound. I am not pushed, or pulled, lifted without my permission. Strong hands hold mine with courtesy, I am lifted gently and with all due care and respect for both my age and status, into a little boat which will take us to the shore. Again, I am lifted and now my feet touch the soil of Galicia. I bend down to touch it, lift the sand and let it run through my fingertips. I am home.

We brought two horses with us and they are helped to swim to shore. Imari sees me comfortable in the saddle, I am given the reins to my steed. We look out to sea to see the ship already setting sail.

We ride the short distance along the coast to A Lanzada. I think of Catalina's family still living close by but there is no news I could give them that would bring them happiness.

Instead I make my way to the hermitage while Imari waits on the beach with the horses.

The tiny chapel is very quiet. I have not been in a Christian church for two decades and it is both familiar and strange to me. I touch the pews, make my way to the altar and kneel.

I pray for Catalina, wherever she may be. She would be in her mid-thirties by now, as I was when we were taken. I hope that she has made some kind of life for herself in the Maghreb, that her destiny turned out better than I feared, as mine did.

I give thanks for my own safe return, the miracle I prayed for all those years ago now accomplished. I feel I have been sent on a pilgrimage of sorts and now I give thanks for the wisdom received, for the kindness I have been shown along the way.

When I return to the beach, I stand for a moment looking out to sea, watching the waves rippling against the sand. I wonder if the barren women of the area still make their way here once a year and stand in the moonlight while nine waves wash over them. I say a small prayer that those who do will be blessed with the children they so long for.

"Are you ready, my lady?"

I hesitate. Am I ready? Am I ready, to return to a world I had thought lost to me forever? But this is the moment I have thought about for years, it is a sign of God's blessing on me that he has brought me home. "Yes," I say, my voice so quiet that Imari has to tilt his head to look at my face, for he has not heard me. I nod and he nods in return. He helps me back into the saddle and then mounts his own horse. I take the reins in my hands, take a deep breath, and dig in my heels. The convent is only a few days' ride away, even at a leisurely pace.

Day of Judgement, Galicia, 1106

Set me as a seal upon thine heart.

Song of Solomon 8:6

I HEAR FOOTSTEPS COMING TO THE *heavy wooden door, and fastenings being undone. I know that I will be welcomed here, that the fortune which Yusuf left to me will elevate me to a place of honour in a short space of time. I may even end my days as a Mother Superior, for memories are short and money speaks, even within holy walls.*

I will miss my son. For he will always be my son, no matter that I pray in a convent and he in a mosque. For me, Ali will always be the baby whose hand took my finger and whose smile changed my heart.

This is a place where I can end my days in peace. I will not be stolen nor bought; I will fear neither man nor war. Here I will be able to rest, to speak with my God in the last years left to me, live without looking over my shoulder for watching eyes.

I could have wished for a different path of course, for a simple life, to have remained all my years in this protected place. I would have been spared fear and humiliation, pain and persecution. Had I lived here I would not have had to raise a son in another's faith, nor have loved and been loved by a man who could never be my husband. But I know now that I would have been a lesser woman.

I look back over my shoulder for the last time. Imari waits, patient as always, to make certain that I have entered the great door, returned to a place of safety.

"You will care for my sister," I call to him, my voice breaking a little.

"And love her," he replies, placing one hand over his heart.

I nod and turn back to the door as it opens.

When I stand before my God on the great Day of Judgement there are those who will charge me with having abandoned my calling, indeed my faith. They will accuse me of lusting after a heathen Moor and forgetting my holy vows, with raising a child to rule an empire whose people are set against my own, with consorting with both a Jewess and a Muslim as though they were my sisters in Christ. They will ask what I did with my life, to atone for such sins.

I will look my God full in His terrible face and I will say, "Lord, I learned to love."

And He will understand.

Your Free Book

The city of Kairouan in Tunisia, 1020. Hela has powers too strong
for a child – both to feel the pain of those around her and to heal
them. But when she is given a mysterious cup by a slave woman,
its powers overtake her life, forcing her into a vow she cannot hope
to keep. So begins a quartet of historical novels set in Morocco
as the Almoravid Dynasty sweeps across Northern Africa and
Spain, creating a Muslim Empire that endured for generations.

Download your free copy at
www.melissaaddey.com

I hope you have enjoyed Isabella's story. If you have a moment to spare, I would be so grateful if you could write even a very brief review for the novel so that her story can find new readers. Thank you!

Have you read all four of the novels in The Moroccan Empire series? They can all be read as standalone stories, but each one gives you more insight into the characters. Hela's story is told in *The Cup*, Kella's in *A String of Silver Beads*, Zaynab's in *None Such as She*.

Author's Note on History

In 11th century Morocco Abu Bakr bin 'Umar and Yusuf bin Tashfin headed up a holy army, the al-Mourabitoun, known later as the Almoravids (I have used this name for simplicity), intent on bringing the country under Islamic rule. Up to this time Morocco, along with Tunisia and Algeria (collectively known as the Maghreb) was primarily a set of tribal Berber states with more or less strict adherence to Islam.

They were successful, taking the important city of Aghmat early on. Abu Bakr married the queen of the city, Zaynab, said to have been a very beautiful and clever woman known as 'the Magician'. When southern tribes rebelled, Abu Bakr left both the foundling garrison city of Murakush (modern Marrakesh) and Zaynab to Yusuf (who married her) and went to deal with the tribes. When he returned, Zaynab advised Yusuf on how to negotiate keeping his power. They came to an amicable agreement and Abu Bakr went back to the south, leaving Yusuf as commander of the whole army in all but name and Zaynab as his queen consort.

Yusuf went on to conquer the whole of Morocco, plus parts of Tunisia and Algeria. When Muslim rulers in

Al-Andalus (Andalusia) asked for his aid, he went to help them, but they could not maintain loyalty to each other or him, so he ended up taking all of their small kingdoms for himself (this included fighting against and defeating El Cid). He died when he was very old. He had been a very religious man who disdained the riches of the world such as fine clothes or elaborate food and was said to be quite a kindly person.

From the very beginning of my research into Yusuf bin Tashfin and the Almoravids, one fact surprised and confused me. Yusuf was married to Zaynab, who apparently was very much a co-leader and a trusted right-hand woman, creating an empire alongside him. She also, it seems, bore him quite a few children. Considering Zaynab's undisputed beauty and intelligence, her status as Yusuf's right hand and that she had given him several children, as well as his own devout Muslim faith, it seemed very strange to me that Yusuf would choose as his heir a child named Ali, "the son of a Christian slave girl." It certainly made me wonder how Zaynab would have taken such a choice when she might reasonably have expected one of her own sons (the Almoravids did not use primogeniture) to inherit the empire. My series of books set around the Almoravids takes this strange choice and creates a possible narrative around it.

This era has a lot of missing information, so while Zaynab's historical record has a few paragraphs of information (some of it rather vague), the woman on whom I have based Isabella has even less information. It seemed to be important to historians of the time that she was a slave and that she was Christian, for this is almost all that has been recorded about her apart from a possible name, Kamra (moon) and nickname, Perfection of Beauty.

Ali seems to have been very ill suited in temperament for ruling a newly created empire, being described as studious, pious, peace-loving and not a warrior, which effectively led to him rapidly losing the empire his father had created to the Almohad dynasty. Given that primogeniture was not being used (so that, one presumes, a ruler could choose the most appropriate child to inherit) this choice seems very odd and suggests perhaps more of an emotional choice than a logical one. He treated both Jews and Christians better than previous rulers, with the number of Christians present in the Maghreb hugely increasing under his rule.

I thought that the "Christian slave girl" could well have been Spanish, given the Viking raids of the era. Her original name is Isabella because I like the name (this book is dedicated to my daughter Isabelle) and I then gave her the religious name Sister Juliana because I needed an early saint and chose the name from a list. It made me laugh to then realise that Saint Juliana was actually a martyr because she refused to marry a pagan husband and was scarred as punishment, thus beautifully echoing the plot I had already written... one of those strange coincidences that happens when you write historical fiction.

I chose to create a character who began with a very strong Christian faith which could come into conflict with people of other faiths she would encounter. I had read about the golden age of Al-Andalus, some time before the era of this novel, where Muslim, Christian and Jewish scholars had achieved a peaceful, fantastically knowledgeable and creative society with the city of Cordoba at its centre (there is a lovely documentary on this era called *Cities of Light*). I really wanted Isabella's character to move from a perhaps overly prescriptive understanding of faith into experiencing people of other faiths as friends and loved ones and receiving a lesson in 'love' (in both the romantic and wider sense) through those experiences. Isabella moves from a rather rigid and small world (emotionally, mentally and physically) into a bigger space and understanding. Although Isabella chooses to return to her convent at the end, she does so with a deeper understanding of the world and a greater ability to love people for who they are. The last few sentences of the book, where Isabella thinks about what people may accuse her of on the Day of Judgement (and God's wiser and kinder understanding of what she has experienced) were with me from the very beginning of planning this novel. They sum up my desire for Isabella's experiences to be both life – and faith – changing and I hope I have done the concept justice.

Isabella's fictional Benedictine 'Convent of the Sacred Way' is set in Galicia (North-West Spain) along the pilgrimage route to Santiago de Compostela, which was already a major pilgrimage destination by the eleventh century. The place where she is kidnapped, A Lanzada, is right on the coast, where there was both a watchtower against the Vikings and a hermitage at the time. The Vikings were known to use the Arousa Estuary to bring their ships close to Santiago de Compostela, hence the watchtower.

The Vikings conducted a lot of raids across Spain including Northern Spain/Galicia. They were referred to as Norsemen by the Galicians. They kidnapped people and mostly sold them as slaves to North Africa. Although there were far less raids at this time than in the previous two centuries, they still continued. If you'd like to see *Draken Harald Hafagre*, the world's largest replica Viking ship, just look it up on www.drakenhh.com, it's an amazing sight and was very useful to me in my research, although the footage of it sailing on the open sea made me feel pretty seasick!

Yusuf's first wife, Kella, is fictional, although it seems odd Yusuf would have had no wife at all until he was nearly fifty. Her story is told in *A String of Silver Beads*.

Zaynab was Yusuf bin Tashfin's queen and right hand, acknowledged as a superb military tactician. She was highly important in negotiating the transfer of power from Abu Bakr to Yusuf. She is described as follows: *In her time there was none such as she – none more beautiful or intelligent or witty ... she was married to Yusuf, who built Marrakech for her*. There is no clarity on when or how Zaynab died. Her story, including her extraordinary total of four marriages, is told in *None Such as She* and her fictional handmaid Hela's story is told in *The Cup,* a free novella which you can download from my website www.MelissaAddey.com.

Bin Sina would be Ibn Sina or Avicenna (I use bin rather than ibn in my books to help with pronunciation), the father of modern medicine, a Persian scholar and physician. The Islamic world was far ahead of the Western world in medicine at this time, having drawn on multiple sources including Graeco-Roman, Indian and Chinese medical knowledge and traditions, in a way that Western medicine had not. His book was not used in the West until the 13th century, when it set the medical standard for centuries.

A note on names: the names of some of the men (especially Yusuf's sons) were tricky to choose, especially where they are called Abu-something. This ought to mean 'father of' and would be a name they used as an adult, referencing their own son, but as there is no mention of their childhood names, it is all I can go on and I did not wish to make up names entirely. Therefore, I have simply stuck to their adult names.

It is not clear who were the mothers of Yusuf's children, so I have proceeded on the basis that most but not all were Zaynab's, since Yusuf had at least one son by a slave.

I have used Murakush (land of God), the original name for Marrakech.

Thanks

I remain grateful throughout this series to three scholars: first Aisha Bewley, for having translated *Les Almoravides* (The Almoravids) by Vincent Lagardère from the original French and making it publicly available on her website which covers many things Islamic (http://bewley.virtualave.net). It was an extremely useful source of information on the Almoravids' complex movements and battles. Also to the School of Oriental and African Studies. First of all for access to their wonderful library and then for the initial help and encouragement of both Dr Michael Brett for discussing my timeline right at the start and Professor Harry Norris for taking the time to read the first draft in this series and for sending me a lovely letter of encouragement, which I still treasure.

In addition, for this specific book, I was lucky enough to come across Santiago Muñiz: I initially contacted him about fruit varieties in Galicia at the time of this novel, in which he has expertise. My request was met with an outpouring of information on the era, from locations such as A Lanzada, to currency, medieval food (in Galician monasteries, no less!) and more, both from his own knowledge and from a wide range of his contacts and their research, including Jose Miguel Andrade Cernandes, Andrés Teira Brión, Antonio

Ceniza, Enriqueta Lopez Morán and José Luis López Sangil: I was thrilled and very grateful for their collective knowledge and Santiago's kindness in collecting it for me.

All errors and fictional choices are of course mine.

Thank you to my brother Ben both for his own medical knowledge and for finding a medieval reconstruction of how to set a broken leg bone, carried out by Wiel van der Mark at Archeon in the Netherlands. Thank you to Melitta Weiss-Amer of the University of Western Ontario for her very interesting article, Medieval Women's Guides to Food during Pregnancy: Origins, Texts, and Traditions (1993 Vol 10 of the Canadian Bulletin of Medical History) and the DIY Natural website which lists styptic herbs (to stop bleeding). I used these two references to invent Isabella's syrup to cure Zaynab's ongoing pregnancy nausea: I don't recommend nor take any responsibility for anyone trying to copy my made-up recipe, nor any of the other remedies I mention along the way! I drew on the combined herbal knowledge of Hildegard von Bingen, an 11th century German Abbess, healer and mystic, as well as *Health from God's Garden* by Maria Treben, for Isabella's healing work.

Thank you to Streetlight Graphics, you give me so much more time to write and always keep the stress levels down!

Thank you to David, who spotted where the title of this book came from and sent me a lovely audio version of the *Song of Solomon* which made all the speakers clear in the story. You can find the link on this book's page on my website.

Thank you to my beta readers for this book: Etain,

Helen and Martin. It is always so useful to see a book with new eyes.

Most of all and always to Ryan, for all our adventures shared together, especially in Morocco and his steadfast love and encouragement. In Morocco we fed eggs to eels, rode camels, got horribly sick (don't mention *pastilla*...), saw one of the last real storytellers, ate fantastic food and saw a different world that kicked off this series and indeed my whole writing career. Thank you for taking the luggage off and on the bus so many times. I love you.

Have you read The Forbidden City series?

18th century China. All girls aged thirteen to sixteen had to attend the Imperial Daughters' Draft, so that the Emperor could have the first choice of every woman in his empire as a possible concubine. This award-winning series follows the interlinked lives of four real women who entered the Forbidden City and whose lives were changed forever.

Your Free Book

China, 1700s. Lady Qing has spent the past seven years languishing inside the high red walls of the Forbidden City. Classed as an Honoured Lady, a lowly-ranked concubine, Qing is neglected by the Emperor, passed over for more ambitious women. But when a new concubine, Lady Ying, arrives, Qing's world is turned upside down. As the highest position at court becomes available and every woman fights for status, Qing finds love for the first time in her life… if Lady Ula Nara, the most ambitious woman at court, will allow her a taste of happiness.

Download your free copy
on your local Amazon

Current and forthcoming books include:

Historical Fiction

China
The Consorts (free on Amazon)
The Fragrant Concubine
The Garden of Perfect Brightness
The Cold Palace

Morocco
The Cup (free on my website)
A String of Silver Beads
None Such as She
Do Not Awaken Love

Ancient Rome
From the Ashes
Beneath the Waves
On Bloodied Ground
The Flight of Birds

Picture Books for Children
Kameko and the Monkey-King

Non-Fiction
The Storytelling Entrepreneur
Merchandise for Authors
The Happy Commuter
100 Things to Do while Breastfeeding

Biography

I mainly write historical fiction and have completed two series: The Moroccan Empire, set in 11th century Morocco and Spain and The Forbidden City, set in 18th century China. My next series will focus on the 'backstage team' of the Colosseum (Flavian Amphitheatre) set in 80AD in ancient Rome. For more information, visit my website www.melissaaddey.com

I was the 2016 Leverhulme Trust Writer in Residence at the British Library and winner of the 2019 Novel London award. I have a PhD in Creative Writing from the University of Surrey. I enjoy teaching and run regular writing workshops at the British Library and at writing festivals.

I live in London with my husband and two children.

Printed in Great Britain
by Amazon

55896450R00177